The Field

The Field

BY

DOLA DE JONG

TRANSLATED FROM THE DUTCH BY

A. v.A. van DUYM

The field is the world; the good seed are the
children of the kingdom; but the tares are the
children of the wicked one.

ST. MATTHEW 13:38

1979

Second Chance Press

Sagaponack, NY

First published in 1945 by Charles Scribner's Sons
under the title: *And the Field Is the World.*

Copyright © 1945 by DOLA DEJONG

Library of Congress Catalogue Card Number 79-84437
International Standard Book Numbers:
Clothbound 0-933256-02-7
Paperbound 0-933256-05-1

Manufactured in the United States of America

SECOND CHANCE PRESS, INC.
Sagaponack, NY 11962

In Memory of My
FATHER, STEPMOTHER & BROTHER

The Field

Dola de Jong

*Certainly all the characters
in this book are fictitious*

I

IT WAS SO HOT in the forenoon that the children had to keep moving, taking little, light steps so they would not scorch their feet.

You could not make yourself lighter than you were, Luba said to Berthe, who was laughing at her, but you had to *feel* light. Take quick, short breaths and keep your head up. *Comme ça* . . . She was swaying slightly on account of the heavy water tins which pulled her down, especially now that she turned her face to the sky.

The other children, Hans and Maria, who followed, said nothing as they carried even heavier tins and were so much older.

Since eight o'clock that morning they had gone back and forth between the well and the field.

The soil was as dry as the hand of an old man. It had not rained for weeks. Everywhere in the fields the Arabs went back and forth, back and forth, to draw water from the wells, fill the watering cans and sprinkle the fields, from sunrise until nightfall, which here in Africa came suddenly.

Dry as an old man's hand and the work was endless. Over the fields sounded the song of the Arabs, full and loud, back and forth in a slow cadence. Like the labor back and forth between the well and the field. All those summer weeks.

Aart and Lies, husband and wife, watered the field. Rainer, the eldest boy, emptied the tins into the watering cans as the children brought them and put them down in a row within his reach. Rainer could give an account of himself like a man, and he sweated like a man, grown-ups' sweat. It streamed from beneath his straw hat and along his strong neck, and showed in grubby spots upon his naked back.

In this field nobody sang. Silently and pent up, Aart and Lies watched how the soil absorbed the water. When they reached the end of a strip, the beginning was dry again. Now and then Lies would burst out cursing. "Jesus Christ, what a job. . . ."

At the beginning Aart had answered. "This is the topsoil, which dries out immediately. Of course, it helps. Don't you see the seed sprouting? Do you think that the Arabs are crazy?" He did not say any more. And Lies did not expect him to, but continued cursing. Towards evening she had given up swearing, but burst out occasionally with short, sardonic laughter.

The children had accepted it. When they had reached the limit of their tiredness it got better. They were too numb to feel anything. They did their work automatically, as if they were dreaming. Later in the evening, after they had eaten, they went to look by the moonlight. Then the earth seemed moist and fresh. Green shoots became higher every day. Salad, cabbage, beans. . . . There was a great deal of money in it, said Aart. They would not have to work that winter.

"Now I am going to rest for awhile," Luba announced, "I've got spots in front of my eyes."

"That's what you get from looking into the sun," said Lies. She put down the watering can and wiped her hands along the sides of her dress, making spots on the brightly colored material. It was still a garment from Holland. It had been a good dress, but now it was in tatters with a tear at the neck, and when Lies bent down the weight of her body made it tear more.

Luba, who sat on her haunches next to her, pointed at it with her finger. "Lies, your dress, do you want a safety pin? *J'en ai une.*"

"It's too hot, let it go," Lies pushed her breasts back into her dress. "Maria, you go and lie down. Take it easy today." She winked at her.

Weird, thought Maria, thick, blue veins, dark brown spots around the nipples, nobody wanted to look at them. The boys turned their heads away. But Lies didn't care. She also knew that Maria was embarrassed about her own situation, ashamed. Why then did she want Aart and Rainer to understand what was the matter with her? Since Maria had told her that morning what strange things were happening to her, Lies had been unusually gay. She often looked at her searchingly, asked her how she felt and winked at her, until Aart and Rainer had begun to notice. Aart had measured her from top to toe and Rainer had looked away deliberately.

From afar one could hear little Dolf crying. Next to the house of corrugated iron stood the trailer, a gay red spot in the white heat. There little Dolf was housed while the others were working. It was a safe place for him, on the floor between the settees, surrounded by his playthings. It was also cooler than in the house under its iron roof.

As Maria was walking towards him, she was again thinking of Lies. How was it possible to have a face that did not belong to one's body? White teeth, large blue eyes, a lean brown face, often laughing, animated; but a shapeless bulging body, ponderous in movement.

It was on account of the face that Maria had come along. That face looking out of the window of the trailer, that crazy trailer, so gaily red in the grey stream of refugees. That smiling, kindly face and its heavy accent, "Où vas-tu? Are you alone, do you want to come along?" That face, the only tangible definite object in an endless world. Long, dust-covered roads, endless walking. Keep going until the end. Again a new road. Walking along without an end. And holding Luba's hand, the little girl stumbling over her own feet, no longer even questioning, "Do we still have to go a long way? Where are we going?" Luba with lips pressed hard together; something that walked, moved along, but no longer had a life of its own.

When little Dolf heard anybody approaching, he would suddenly grow quiet. He stretched his arms out to her to be taken up.

"Are you all alone again? Are you hot, you poor worm? Is it so hot? Are you wet? And so many, many flies? Come then."

Carefully she went down the steps of the car, laid the baby boy on the table in the house and unfastened his diaper.

That was it, she thought, the head was something apart, it did not belong to the rest. Like the illustration in the history book at school, the head of Lies on a pike. That was a dream, which always recurred. The head of Lies borne on a pike and the heavy body walking after it. No, that was not a dream, it was a thought. The words that Lies uttered came from the head, warm, friendly words. But sometimes they came from the body: sticky, heavy things that she said, which never stood out by themselves, but spread like batter in the pan, and lay there pale and flat. When you were tired, thought Maria, you got such thoughts. Everything took on form, became something, especially towards the end of the day, when there were heavy pails to carry and your eyes were riveted on the path, and the sand burned your feet, and the handles of the pails tore into the palms of your hands, and your armpits were soaking wet and chafed. Then you could not work out your thoughts to the end, they became confused, took on strange forms and you made strange comparisons.

The oil, that she rubbed into Dolf's skin, was soft on her hands. Dolf grabbed for the bottle, gurgled, and laughed again contentedly.

"A miracle of God," the Consul's wife had said about him. Maria understood what the Mevrouw van Balekom had meant; how it was possible for a baby to remain healthy under such conditions . . . that was what she had meant.

When the Consul's wife came on her tri-weekly call she never sat down. Stiffly upright on her thin, silk-clad legs, she would stand in the middle of the cabin, and would strike at the flies with her white gloves. During the last minutes of her visit, which lasted exactly half an hour, she would relax slightly and walk around. Then she was glad she would soon be able to get away.

"Why do you have the manure pile so near the house?" she would ask. "I'll bring a few diapers for little Dolf when I come next time, he is so chafed." And, "What a big girl you're getting to be, Luba; and such lovely hair. Can you comb it yourself already?"

Did Lies really not understand these words? Or didn't she want to? As the Consul's wife drove away, Lies would burst into uproarious laughter, and say "To hell with it," and then laugh again. Lies knew that little Dolf chafed and that Luba had lice, that the manure spread a sweet and sickening stench, that there were thousands of flies. But now they had become accustomed to it. Aart would dump the manure there and nobody would say anything about it. Aart had lice. "Get a haircut, tramp," Lies said. But Aart did not want to, he had beautiful, thick, pale blond hair. "Funny tramp," said Lies, "funny tramp, get a haircut."

Maria held the baby boy on her lap, close to her. The warmth against her stomach, which was hurting. Cramps. Would it always be that way, or only the first time? She pushed her face into Dolf's small neck, the silky skin between her lips. Now she would be able to have babies herself.

They walked along the border of the path with their water tins so as to catch some of the shade of the fig trees. They dawdled at the well, and held their hands in the water. Berthe and Luba sat on their haunches, while Hans filled the tins.

In the field, Aart, Lies and Rainer continued working. It was really a plot, a small patch of soil, which Aart had rented from a French woman in the city. She owned quite a bit of land and made a good income. The Arabs worked painstakingly, patiently, lived from a small profit and paid in proportion too much for their holdings. When Aart had arrived here the rental had seemed small to him. Now he understood that he could not compare himself to the Arabs, that he lacked their cheerful patience and their fatalistic outlook upon life. For him time was a clock, ticking off seconds, minutes and hours, for the Arabs it was sunrise and sunset towards the end, towards the deliverance from this life by Allah. But Aart kept on working stubbornly and did not give up. He called the rental blood money. Even with the help of the Dutch Consul there wasn't enough to eat. But soon, he consoled the children, soon when the figs would be ripe, the fruits and vegetables brought to market, there would be enough money.

The children took his word for it. He had brought them here in his trailer. At least a hundred times Rainer had told them that Aart alone had made the impossible possible. "Do you realize it, with a common Chevrolet . . .?" The children vaguely recalled the nightmare of the trip in the tinny car through the desert. The scorching heat, Lies pregnant, deathly sick, the birth of Little Dolf in Oran, camping out on the beach, Aart in prison. . . . All that they scarcely remembered. What had happened before was an open book that they told each other about . . . Fathers, mothers, roller skates, a dog, whose name was Heller. But about the mutual adventures after Marseilles they never spoke.

None of the children had ever asked himself why Aart and Lies had picked them up and taken them along on the way to Africa. None of the children ever questioned why they were part of the Aart-Lies household. They accepted it as children will. Existence, no matter what turn it may take, is self-evident to children.

Only Maria had lately come to believe that everything was enacted for her in particular. She believed that she was the center and that Aart and Lies and the children, the Arabs in the village over the hill, the refugees in the city, yes, even the war itself, were there to make a background for her life. Who was it? Perhaps God—perhaps there was no God—perhaps Something, as she called it, had planned it that way. Later on the world would realize it. In this manner everything would be justified that Lies and Aart did for her now.

This feeling had suddenly manifested itself within her at the same time as her fear of dying. Just imagine, some day she would no longer be there. The thought that life would continue even without her made her feel desperate. In the middle of the night she would sit up straight and stiffen with fear, beaten because she felt so powerless. She would have to die. Some time later, inevitably.

Hans, who was sixteen years old, would sometimes stare at Lies and Aart, submerged in thought. He did not understand Aart's fanatical persistence. In the beginning he had just worked along in a dull resignation, waiting for the day that the Hollander would give up in his almost demonical fury to wring a crop from the field. Now he saw that only a miracle, a shock from events beyond his control, would break Aart's pent-up tension. He had taken a detached attitude towards Aart because he felt himself mentally superior. Thus it was possible for him to continue in the hopeless work.

During Ramedan at the time of the Mohammedan fast days Hans had stayed away. He was wandering through the town with his friends from the village. He came back in a happy mood, somewhat tired and looking terribly dirty, but well fed and not telling anything. When on the principal holiday the other children went to the city to look at the parade with Lies, Hans had stayed home with Aart and had silently continued his work; and he took care of little Dolf.

After this day his friendship with Rainer, who was a year older than he, had suddenly come to an end. Hans had obtained a favored position and Rainer lacked the imagination to create another though not so important position for himself.

Rainer worked like a machine. He never asked questions, and did not expect any explanation of the things he did not understand. His parents had sent him away for his own safety. That was his starting point and, as long as no other goal had been set for him, he stuck to it and did daily what was expected of him.

Shortly before five Pierre, the five-year-old French boy, came through the gate, dragging a bag filled with supplies, followed by his little Arab friends. His small face was pale and sweaty, but satisfied. When Lies saw him come in she left her work and crossed the garden towards him.

Pierre set the bag down at her feet and dug his hand into his bulging pocket. A tin of sardines, a piece of chocolate, a roll, a handful of almonds, some parsley—he laid them all separately in Lies' outstretched hand. "*Voilà*, I haven't got any more," he said. "There was such a crowd in the bakal."

Lies burst out into laughter, did not say anything, and went inside with the bag of supplies in order to prepare the food. There was a tacit understanding between her and the small boy. Once in the beginning she had taken him along to town and he had seen how she had snatched things from the counters and out of the vegetable baskets at the market. Not a day went by now that Pierre did not do likewise. Lies did not encourage him, she just laughed.

Now that Lies was cooking, the tempo of work was slackening. All felt suddenly that they were hungry. Pierre went to the well and his little Arab friends scuttled off.

"There was a man on the Boulevard Pasteur and he didn't have any hands," said Pierre. He sat down with his back leaning against the well, made a little old man's face, and stuck out his clenched fists. "You had to put your money on his wrists and he took it away with his mouth." Every day Pierre had a new story, especially weird stories, and that way he felt as old as the others. When he had seen nothing extraordinary, he would invent something. But this time nobody doubted his story. A man without hands was something you couldn't invent. And the bit about picking up the money with his mouth was a guarantee of truth. Even Pierre could not have thought that up.

Luba and Berthe stuck out their fists, laid small pieces of stone on their wrists, and picked them up with their lips.

"What can you do when you have no hands?" Luba said dreamily. "You can't do a thing. You don't have to work, because you can't do anything."

"When you have no hands, you can't get married," said Berthe. That was what she kept thinking about all the time these days. Berthe's favorite game was playing house.

But Luba was not interested in that. "When you have got no

hands, then your mother must do everything for you. You are fed, just like little Dolf, and in the evening you're tucked in bed."

From the field Rainer shouted to them to hurry. They lifted the tins. Pierre walked along with them to bring Aart the money that the Consul had given him.

"How often did you have to go back for it?" Aart asked.

"Three times," said Pierre, satisfied.

The Consul maintained that no procedure had yet been established for the payments to the Dutch refugees. He referred continuously to the pronouncements coming from London. London still had made no decision. The Dutch government in London had not answered. The money from London had not arrived. Aart did not believe it. Once a week he went during the evening to the city, sat in cafés with other Hollanders and inveighed against "the bakal" as they called the Consul. The word "bakal" meant grocer and it embraced all the attributes they ascribed to the Consul and which as a matter of fact he displayed: scrupulousness, lack of vision and a parsimonious disposition.

"You have no right to it," the Consul said to Aart. "You are not refugees. You left Holland a long time before the war. The Netherlands government can't be responsible for all those children you picked up on the way. That was very irresponsible on your part...."

"Then I suppose we should have let them die," said Aart. And then in his slow way, he would tell the story of each child for the hundredth time. How he had found them, what had been the circumstances.... The tale got around. People came to the house afterwards to see for themselves. But almost never for a second time. No, they did not have many callers, though Lies jovially asked everybody to have dinner with them. Even those refugees who were in the neediest circumstances did not repeat their visits. But they sent others because they thought it was something that ought to be seen, how they lived in the house, which was a long narrow space, a box of heat under its corrugated iron roof.

Here Lies was cooking now on the primus stove. Outside, near the door, she had made a small charcoal fire for the second course. Maria, sitting on her haunches, with little Dolf beside her, was stirring the porridge. Flies buzzing in a circle above the pan settled on the boy, who was happily playing with a bottle, and crawled over his whole little body, into the corners of his eyes, but never seemed to bother him a bit. The flies were in the pan of soiled diapers outside the house. They flew around and around, and then made for the open door of the house. Thousands of them left black dots everywhere, on the walls, on the boxes and cases which served as furniture, on the thin blankets, the bedding against the back wall, on the clothes hung from nails, on the boards scattered with tools, on the food, and the scanty toilet articles in the kitchen corner, on arms, legs and faces. Flies in clusters, flies on spots made by spilled food. Every one was used to it and nobody knew that Maria would have sudden crying spells chiefly on account of the flies. When she was tired, and vague remembrances upset her, she would start to slap at the flies and then, giving up, would cry silently somewhere in a corner, although nobody paid any attention.

But tonight she was untroubled; she followed attentively what was happening inside herself, and absent-mindedly responded to Lies' talk.

"Only two months ago you got twice as much for your francs. The rich bastards pay a fortune for potatoes. When a new shipment comes from Portugal, they fight for them on the market. Haisha says that people bring big sacks and so two hours later they are sold out."

"Yes," said Maria.

"You ought to see the bread that Pierre brings." Lies came outside with the two halves of the half-baked loaf.

"Gosh," said Maria politely.

"If it keeps up this way, I'll have to go to town myself." Lies sat down on an upturned box and wiped her perspiring face with her dress. Dolf, suddenly exuberant, threw the bottle at her.

"Murderer!" Lies laughed. "Did you see that, he threw a bottle at my head!" With a flourish she lifted him up to her face and kissed his reddish curls. "Throwing a bottle at your mother's head, well, did you ever!"

"The porridge is ready," said Maria.

Lies picked up the bread that she had laid down beside her and went inside. She called out through the little window to the field that dinner was ready.

Hans entered first, set down a pail of fresh water on the upturned box, took off his tattered shirt, and started pouring the water over himself. Then came Berthe and Luba. They were pushing each other away from the pail, quarrelling because they were tired, until Aart lifted his hand in a threatening fashion. Aart did not wash himself. He pulled up a box, and sat down on it with Dolf on his lap.

Rainer came in last. He had washed himself at the well. His face shone, his hair was dripping wet, but beautifully parted.

"There was a cow's head on the counter," Pierre began, with his mouth full of bread. But nobody was listening to him. That was an old story. Everybody knew the manner in which Arab butchers cut up a cow, calf or sheep, and exhibited the pieces on the counter to show that they were authentic cuts. When the children had first heard of this, they made a special trip to the Souk and had been elaborately creepy about it. Pierre looked a bit abashed as they ignored his story, and stuffed even more food in his mouth.

From the road along the garden sounded the hooves of mules, the shuffling steps of women, throaty voices. The Arabs from the village over the hill were returning from the Souk. They had sold their wares there, and fetched their purchases home. A few came to the opening in the green along Aart's land and shouted a greeting, "Lila saaida . . ."

Lies shouted back that she would come over after sunset. That Maria was now a woman, she would tell her friends in the village over the hill. She looked forward to the conversation with pleasure. In such a case marriage plans were made for the Arabian girls.

Lies divided the porridge on the plates which were licked clean. "Now you must eat well, Maria," she said emphatically. Maria awkwardly spooned her porridge. I hate you, she thought, I hate you . . . No, I don't hate you . . . God, forgive me, no I don't hate her. . . . She felt Aart's glances. He was feeding Dolf the porridge with the help of a crust of bread, looking at Maria. He nodded understandingly.

2

THE CHILDREN did not have much time to themselves. In the evening after dark they were tired and hung around near the house. Often they fell asleep just where they were sitting or lying down. Regularly, Pierre, Luba or Berthe were awakened in the morning by the sun, somewhere near the house or on the field, soaked through by the dew, but completely unconcerned and happy. Sometimes their tiredness at the end of the day suddenly turned into an abnormal burst of energy, as with Luba, for instance, who became noisily excited; and then they would play hide and seek or a war game. At night Maria and Hans would go to the village over the hill, where they would get together with the Arabian children, each of them going his own way, and taking great care that they should not meet each other going home.

This evening Luba wanted to go to the beach and Pierre and Berthe followed her, as if this whim were the only one in the world. They did not give a thought to the fact that it was dark, nor that even in the light of a brilliant moon they would have great difficulty in finding their way through the dunes. Luba had indeed a great yearning for the "salty sea breeze." This she was quite conscious of, but Berthe and Pierre just followed her aimlessly.

Previously, before they had had to help with the sprinkling of the field, they had wandered around a lot. They had their path through the dunes to the beach. For hours they would watch the fishermen, gathering in the nets—Arabs and Spaniards in double rows from the water to the dunes—patiently pulling up the ropes, then walking backwards until their feet sank deep in the loose sand and ran ahead to their place again as the first in the row. It was an endless game. It was so inviting that the children filtered into the group, measured their weight against the slippery ropes, stumbling as they

13

walked backward, until it was their turn to run ahead. The fishermen would pretend good-naturedly that their help was of great value, and sometimes let the ropes slip just for the fun of it, and would laugh loudly at the children's excitement.

Breathless excitement; breathless admiration for the men, who would drag the net far into the sea, until they were up to their necks in the water. They would work all day long getting soaking wet.

When they were bored with watching the fishermen, they would admire the passing Arabs, who, seated high upon their horses, were counting their day's profit from the market and would look neither up nor around; or the women, who docilely followed their masters on foot and bore tremendous loads, heavier than those on the burros that they drove before them, as they scolded and laughed.

Probably Luba had unconsciously been looking for quietude and she was disappointed that at this hour the Arabs were turning homewards. She shoved her bare feet through the moist sand and stuck out her tongue at the shadows that ran in single file along the moonlit sea. Then she resolutely chose the opposite direction, towards the city. Berthe trudged along behind her holding Pierre by the hand, as if this walk were a self-imposed task. It took over half an hour to get to the city, and for twenty minutes the children walked with the same tired-out numbness that made their work in the field possible.

They had now come to the place where the last beach cabins of the summer guests stood, and Pierre, who apparently suddenly realized his necessity for shelter and sleep, pulled and jerked at Berthe's arm, and started to cry angrily when she did not want to go his way.

"Come on, *mon petit*," Luba quieted him down as she knelt at his side. "Shall we rest for awhile?" At the same time she looked at Berthe with a mixture of superiority and reproach.

"Are we almost there?" Berthe asked, too tired to remember whether or not they had made plans for a destination in this escapade in the dark.

"Let's rest for awhile at that cabin." Luba pulled the little boy towards her and dragged him over the sand as she stumbled along.

It was one of those little beach cabins summer guests rented for the season, where they could dress and undress and keep their things. It had been colored white, red, blue and green, so that here again the harmony of the beach, sky and sea had been disturbed by man's paintbrush.

This little cabin had a few steps leading to a sort of terrace, and it caused Luba some pain to hoist up Pierre, who hung against her like a dead weight. Berthe shuffled up behind her, too tired to utter the vague notion that the cabin might be locked.

"This is now our home," Luba said with emphasis. She pushed down the handle and what a miracle! the door was not locked.

It was broiling hot inside, but there was a pleasant smell of tar and tobacco smoke.

Luba let Pierre down to the floor, where he immediately fell asleep, and walked around touching the walls.

"This is now our home," she repeated.

"*Mais non*," Berthe protested feebly. But Luba found her way around in the dark holding on to the walls, quite sure now that the little house was not only open by chance, but would also have some surprises. Indeed, she found a stub of candle and some matches, and when the flame rose, she saw a mattress and a cover on the floor, a man's shirt on a nail and a few bottles and glasses on a small bench.

"This is my home," she said quickly, afraid that Berthe would be ahead of her in the assertion that it belonged to somebody else.

She took off her dress and hung it up in place of the man's shirt, which she folded up and hid in a corner under the bench. With this gesture she had taken over the place and Berthe was now also reassured.

"If we lie crosswise we can all three fit on the mattress," said Luba. Berthe stood sleepily in a corner while Luba straightened the mattress and dragged the little boy towards it, spread the cover over him and lay down next to him. Berthe came too, but Luba would not let her sleep.

"This is now our home," she said. "We are safe here." Safe from what she did not know. But Berthe was satisfied with it. "Shall we have something to drink?" said Berthe, looking contentedly around her in the cozy cabin, with yellow light from the candle dancing on the wall.

"Those are wine bottles," said Luba.

"One little swallow won't hurt us, Lies says," Berthe pointed out.

"Nasty girl," said Luba as Berthe now mentioned Lies and therewith threatened to break the spell of the intimate atmosphere.

"I'm not doing anything," said Berthe. "I'm thirsty."

"You stay where you are," Luba commanded. "I'll fetch it." She scrambled to her feet and shook each bottle.

"Just one swallow," said Luba severely, "there is hardly anything left in them." She brought the two bottles and giggled when Berthe made a face as she drank.

"Are you getting drunk already?" Luba asked.

"Oh, I am getting so drunk, so drunk," Berthe shouted. She had tipped the bottle straight up over her mouth and the deep-red liquid trickled into her neck and over her dress. "It tastes nasty," said Berthe, getting her breath. "Sour."

"That's real wine," said Luba, wiping her mouth with the palm of her hand. "Now let's go to sleep." She blew out the candle and crawled with the others onto the mattress.

"Fine, isn't it?" she sighed. When Berthe was already asleep Luba was still happily awake.

They were roused by a loud voice.

A man stood at the entrance.

"*Merde alors,*" and then in Arabic the loud command: "Out of here, and hurry up!"

Drunk with sleep and shivering, they stood at the foot of the steps looking up at the man.

They were not Arab children, that he could see. He suddenly burst out laughing at the little troop. Luba, stark mother naked, subconsciously ashamed, her hands pressed between her legs, Berthe

covered with wine spots, Pierre still asleep, with wobbly knees leaning against the girls.

"Come over here," said the man.

"My dress," said Luba, pointing at the cabin.

He made an affirmative gesture and she slipped in past him. With
her dress she had found her composure again. She sat down next to
him on the steps.

Berthe remained standing at a safe distance, her arms folded and
one foot brought forward, though this position was most uncomfortable. The small boy fell asleep again on the sand.

Luba stared at the man. Probably she was only half awake and
her imagination was strengthened and the power of observation had
left her. Next day she maintained to Berthe that the man had no
eyes, but nevertheless was watching them. At the second meeting,
she saw of course that his eyes, which were light-blue, appeared even
lighter because his skin was so deeply tanned. He was naked except
for his swimming trunks and very muscular. He held a pipe between
his sound white teeth, and every now and then he would take off his
beret to scratch his clipped blond hair. There was something animal-
like about him, Luba thought vaguely. You could feel safe with
him.

"What's your name?" she asked him, less to start a conversation
than to make clear that she wanted to make friends with him.

"Don't you have to go home?" the man asked.

"She is asking you for your name," Berthe helped from her safe
position.

"What's *your* name?" He now looked at Berthe. A plump little
girl with fuzzy hair and a stupid little face. He examined her severely
and minutely. Berthe clamped her lips firmly together and in her
embarrassment she kicked Pierre's foot. The little boy groaned and
turned in his sleep.

"Don't you have to go to bed?" the man asked.

"No," said Luba dreamily. "My mother is dead." She had never
mentioned this before. Aart and Lies were convinced that she was

not aware of it. Apparently she was, and this was the best excuse that she could find for her actions.

"What's your name?" the man asked emphatically.

"What's yours?" asked Luba.

"Oh Jesus," said the man. "My name is Manus."

"Mine's Luba."

"I'm Berthe."

"Another quarter heard from." He laughed out loud.

"His name is Pierre." Berthe unfolded her arms, pointed, folded them quickly again, and then, somewhat hesitating, she slumped down on her haunches.

"Are you French?" Luba asked now. They had spoken in French. The children used broken French, Spanish, and Arabic with equal facility. They spoke Lies' language. They had learned, as she had learned, by sound. Even among themselves Maria and Luba no longer spoke Polish, Hans and Rainer no German. And Berthe garbled French, her native tongue.

"I am a Hollander," said the man.

"Aart and Lies are Hollanders too," Luba told him. "I am **Polish.**"

"Who are Aart and Lies?" he asked, suddenly all attention.

"Aart has built a trailer, because he wanted to get away from civilization," said Luba seriously, "and Lies is married to him and their baby is called Dolf."

"I am a Belgian," Berthe interrupted, afraid that they would pass her by.

"My father is dead too," said Luba.

"Are you Jewish?" Berthe asked for information.

Manus sighed, knocked the ashes out of his pipe, and refilled it.

"Rainer says Hans is no Jew but Rainer is a Jew. That's what he says," Luba said confidently.

"Who are Hans and Rainer?"

Luba pointed behind her, where she thought the field might be. "We have two big boys," she said then.

"Do you know how to get home?" Manus asked.

"I'm staying with you," said Luba. She laid her hand on his arm and pushed her head against his knee.

"*Allons*," he said. He lifted the sleeping boy, locked the door of the beach cabin and drove Berthe and Luba in front of him. "I shall take you home. Otherwise you'll still be here tomorrow."

The moon hung within reach, orange and massive. The fields behind the dunes calmly stretched out, surrendering to the heavens. They were fragrant with the heavy and secret odor of all that they held beneath them. Here and there stood a tree, reaching its naked branches towards the sky.

Holding hands, Luba and Berthe found the way home, half asleep. Manus followed, the small boy slung across his shoulder, the child's body warm against his bare skin.

Refugees, he thought. He looked at the small brown feet on the path, trampling unconcernedly through the dung of the burros. Skinny legs, charity clothes, too small for the little one, too big for the blond one, apparel only fit to be thrown away, rags over naked bodies. How old could the blond one be? It was hard to guess with little girls. This one already had small breasts under her voluminous dress. He changed the little boy to his other shoulder.

Refugees, he thought again. Children of good families, these, too. There were swarms of them in the city, children with parents who were always well dressed, and who tried to create a well-ordered life for them that would bring back former days. Put to bed at the proper time and whenever possible sent to school. But no matter how hard they tried, they could not make normal children out of them. They remained children who had lost all initiative, now that their games had been upset.

But these three were different. He was curious as to what kind of compatriots he would find, and admonished the girls to hurry.

He had the feeling of having experienced something like this before. It had been a wish which in the past he had fostered every day. He had so much yearned for it that the dream of then now seemed like reality. On a country road at evening, a sleeping child in his arms, in the distance a light where somebody was waiting. The desire for responsibilities, the dream of every man. He had not kept that illusion for long. Still he had clung to the picture, because of tradition, education. It had driven him for confirmation back to his father, who behind the door opened at a crack has asked the question, what are you doing here? The next year he had left for Morocco, had drunk mint tea with the Arabs and wine with the French. Now and then he would go into the mountains riding his donkey on a job of prospecting for the Moroccan government. He knew no fear, did not even carry a rifle, spoke the language of the Berbers, and camped among them. He had been really happy, at least in so far as his nature allowed him to be, until he committed the stupidity of marrying a German woman, who needed Dutch papers and was willing to pay for them. When the war broke out she had returned to Germany and he had been sent up North. Such things had happened because of the hysteria of war. He, a Hollander, had been put out of French Morocco. He had not protested, it was not in his nature. Now he had a beach cabin here, a candle, and a nail in the wall for his clothes.

His thoughts went back to the children.

"Come here," he ordered Luba. He took her hand, a chilly little bit of life that hid away in his fist. Berthe, dozing, continued walking in front of them.

They found Rainer on the steps of the trailer with Dolf on his lap. The little fellow had cried all night long, the heat had been unbearable in the trailer. Rainer had tried not to pay any attention to it, he wanted to complete what he had started to make, a gauze-covered food cabinet from a box, but finally he had had to comfort the child. Now he had looked after Dolf for hours. Lies had gone to the village over the hill and Aart to the city. Of the others only Maria was home. She had rolled herself in a blanket in the house, where the oil lamp was lit, and lay on the mattress with her face to the wall. Rainer thought that she was crying, and he understood why.

"*Armes*," he mumbled to himself, "*Armes, Du,*" he said to the small boy.

He remembered how he had played with little friends in the courtyard, how they had built fortresses with ramparts of boxes and cans and used rags to fill up the holes. One day a woman neighbor had passed and scolded him as she took away from him the rag he had in his hands. Later on his mother had explained to him how it was with women. Since that day he had acquired a certain awe for girls. You could not call it so much as a revulsion, but he stayed out of their way.

When Manus came into the gate with the children, Rainer thought for a moment of making excuses because Aart and Lies were not home, but Manus asked right away how it was that the children went out alone at night, and Rainer evaded answering him with a haughty silence.

As Manus walked around, looking everywhere without the slightest embarrassment, he exclaimed, "God almighty, what a gang!" He seemed to be enjoying himself, grinned inwardly, and drew contentedly at his pipe. Rainer followed him with his eyes, sitting helplessly on the steps with the child on his lap. When Manus went into the house, he followed him with the child in his arms.

Yes, Manus was enjoying himself. He found here a marvellous mess of European sloppiness, which bears the mark of artistry, and the primitive hygiene of the Mohammedans. Everything indicated laziness, poverty, but also adaptability.

Berthe and Luba had gone to bed on the mattress with Maria, who started crying anew and pressed Luba closely against her. But Luba wriggled herself loose and shouted: "Come and tuck me in, Manus?"

Still hesitating a bit, because he did not know who was lying there with her, he went over to the corner. He stood there over them, looked, and smelled the somewhat sweet odor of sleeping children.

"Hello," said Luba roguishly, then playfully she dove under the covers.

Already a woman, he thought, not older than eight and already a woman. He looked at Berthe, who without any interest made preparations to go to sleep lying on her stomach, her blond, fuzzy hair spread over her arms.

"Do you want something to drink?" Rainer asked at the door in an attempt to get him away from Maria. "Shall I make tea?"

But Manus paid no attention to him, and spoke to Luba.

"Get to sleep fast, little scamp, it's time for children to be abed, and take care that I don't find you on the beach again at this time of the night."

"What is a scamp?" Luba's voice came from under the covers. And without waiting for an answer, "I am coming to see you again tomorrow."

It seemed a long time before the Hollanders, for whose return Manus was waiting with curiosity, came home.

Rainer did not utter a syllable, he kept his eyes open with great difficulty, though he did not want to hear about going to bed.

Manus, without any interest in the boy, made a few lazy remarks and then became completely silent. Often he had sat that way with the Arabs in the little cafés in the Kasbah and the villages in the mountains, every one of them huddled in his own cloak of silence. Hours, that stretched into days of contemplation, an art he had completely mastered.

Silence, for a moment interrupted by Maria, who timidly slid past them, disappeared around the corner of the house and came back, a slender figure that brought a breath of bed warmth.

Lies, pleased after an hour's conversation with the women of the village, came humming through the hedge, and then quickened her step when she saw the silhouette of a visitor next to Rainer.

At once she was the Dutch housewife, busy and hospitable. She made tea, and brought him a cup with much sugar and even milk. Manus would have preferred mint, but obedient to her unuttered wish, he played his part in the scene that Lies enacted—the Dutch teatime visit. The sentiments that she had pushed into the background served as a decor. Nostalgia for Holland, for the time when she could be herself, pleasantly bourgeois. Everything that she had accepted, so that she could adapt herself better to this existence, social indifference, wilful rudeness, was now forgotten. She babbled on and on, a chain of words, cozy: how long had he been in North Africa, from what Dutch city did he hail—and perhaps related to so-and-so?

Manus called himself an idiot. What had he really waited for? He cursed his curiosity, the ego, which had again proffered a hand to touch the past, like a child that has been warned about a burning stove.

The Hollander abroad, who is oh so happy to meet a compatriot, he thought mockingly.

He was surprised to realize how attractive she was, in spite of her sloppy clothes and unkempt hair. He imagined this woman in the dress of the Berbers, the ideal frame for this face with the large dark eyes. The open laughter when the cloth was taken from the mouth in the safe retreat of the home. For him alone.

If she had been able to adapt herself to this life, and indeed it seemed hard, she would be able to get used to the Arabs' way of life. A wish, a fugitive dream image, that made him stand up impatiently in order to awaken. He still felt guilty after all these years, that when a grown woman was meant for him, it could only be an Arabian. The torturings of his two elder sisters were the cause of it all. Thus at least he explained it. Hate for his sisters, disgust of all women in skirts and coats.

Towards midnight Aart came home, withdrawn into himself, distant toward Manus.

"I met a bunch of your kids on the beach, thought it was safer to bring them home," Manus explained.

"Oh, they find their way all right," Aart said indifferently.

"They are real tramps," Lies added.

"Then I could have saved myself the trouble," said Manus. He felt as if his attempts to protect the children were superfluous, ridiculous. On the other hand, he saw that Aart's indifference was a pose.

An excuse for the hardships, the split in the children's lives that he could not remedy.

Still Manus revenged himself by saying that one might expect self-reliance from children who did a man's work. Had he not seen the field, dark from moisture now, where the tins, large and small, stood in pairs, shining under the moon? He knew about the heavy labors of the Arabs in the spring. It began to penetrate to him what this work must mean to children. Pity, for Lies, too, who put into practice the formulas of the marriage ceremony. Not from an inner urge, but because there was no other way out.

The flippant declaration of Luba, "Aart wanted to get away from civilization," had originated in Lies' mouth. The clincher of all dis-appointments, excuses for all she did not understand in Aart, and for which she could not be held responsible.

For the moment the conversation did not flow so easily, but Lies had put her mind to the coziness of being with a Hollander. She chatted about this, that and the other until the men had regained their self-esteem.

"Sitting here this way," said Manus, "you can hardly believe that over there they are slaughtering each other by the thousands." He pointed towards the sea, on the other side of which lay Europe, Spain, and Gibraltar that was visible in clear weather. Puffs of smoke sometimes and the rumbling of the bombs on the fortress from Italian and German airplanes, the only sign of war that they noticed. They sat silent for a moment, looking into the night, the calm and the silence like a glass bell over the land.

Manus laughed bitterly. "We won't be able to say that for long any more. In a few months we will all be behind barbed wire. Tonight on the Souk—God, how squeezed they are, the Hungarians, the Poles, the Czechs, the whole bunch of them. Affidavits, tickets, visas, that is all you hear."

"Oh, those," said Aart indifferently.

"You probably have plans for going to America?" Manus asked.

Aart shrugged his shoulders. "What do you think? That I am

working myself to death to pass the time away? Next year I'll build a small house on the hill. You'll see what the garden will produce. Next year I'll have Arabs to do the work. In time I'll start an irrigation system. . . ." He continued to speak about his plans. Lies hung on his words as if she were hearing about it for the first time.

Manus did not say a word. He knew that there was nothing to be said. Aart continued like a horse with blinkers. He saw none of the world, nothing but himself. He had nothing to do with the war, he had voluntarily left Holland. Manus thinking about the children, quietly asleep in the corrugated iron house, in the trailer, hastily got up and took his leave.

On the way to his cabin at the beach, the noise, made by his shoes on the road, accompanied him like a comrade in the silence. He thought about Aart and Lies, the children in the field. "Stay away from them, Manus," he said half aloud, in warning. "You are such a softy. Before you know it you'll be in misery again up to your ears." The children's faces, Rainer, Berthe, the small boy, the nursling, Luba the last. Poor kids, he thought, from the fire into the frying pan. Helpless, he thought. Yes, children, so helpless. He saw his own youth, no definite memory, no image. Only the ego, when he was a child, possessed him, pushed a fist into his stomach, clutched him at his throat. "God, what a mess. Poor things."

His steps grew quicker on the road until his feet pushed through the sand of the dunes and silence deepened.

3

NEXT AFTERNOON, before the meal was ready, Luba, gay and excited, slipped away through a hole in the hedge.

She wanted to go by herself.

During the long, hot day she had thought about what she would tell Manus, just as if she were a grown-up person.

On the route between the field and the well she had thought out long conversations and the day had flown by. She paid no attention whatever to the others.

Berthe, who had suddenly been left to herself, deprived of all distraction, had gone through a series of moods; astonishment, indignation and jealousy, because of what she didn't know. But Berthe had the ability to shake off things that bothered her. She was like a small poodle after his bath.

At three o'clock the handle of one of Maria's tins had broken and had been repaired by Rainer, showing a complete lack of devotion as she thought, with a bit of string. Maria fled crying and locked herself in the trailer.

"Now we are in for something," said Lies, who had anxiously awaited the first time one of the children would throw up the job.

But Aart went on as if nothing had happened, and Maria was not fetched from her hiding place.

Embarrassed because of the figure she had cut and with nobody to help her regain her composure, she stayed in the broiling hot trailer.

Finally, after an hour she got everybody's attention by shrieking hysterically.

It was Berthe who went to her with one of her tins.

"Here, take mine, I'll take the one with the string." An utterly simple solution, which was accepted by Maria when she recovered from her surprise.

"Shut up, now," Lies warned the others, before Maria came back with Berthe's arm around her.

But this warning was superfluous. The boys, annoyed by the scene, but even more embarrassed by it, did not make any comments.

Aart also did not say a word. He kept back what he wanted to say, because if he said it he would let himself go into a rage that would have been utterly unreasonable, because Maria's conduct had nothing to do with his unhappiness.

Maria's yearning for attention was merely an echo of her becoming a woman, a desire for warmth and understanding. His anger was turned upon himself, his fanaticism, which he recognized, but could not change, and the cause of which he did not know.

The field was a hopeless undertaking. He saw it, but did not want to give up. He just couldn't. The shoots that appeared turned yellow in a few days' time. Only here and there were patches of green, where the soil was low and the rays of the sun were broken by trees.

He had gone to see other fields. He had asked the Mohammedans, of course by circumlocution, what was the secret of their labors. He had looked into the friendly, laughing faces, listened to the glib Arabic speech. He had felt their amusement, their fun over his undertaking. Certainly, they were fond of Aart and tried to help him. But how in the world could they? A foreigner, a Rummy. A man had come to them in his red house on wheels and had dug his spade into a poor field. He had taken possession of the soil, as he might have seated himself on a cushion in a stranger's house, uninvited, and without asking himself if perhaps it was the cushion of the oldest son. The Arabs laughed as one laughs at the first steps of a child. But without the respect they showed for a child's walking. At night they would tell their wives about it and the women came to look for themselves. They would find Lies and the children busy. They greeted them and giggled. They stood at a certain distance in their white haiks, with the formless shape on their backs where their nurslings were suspended.

They stood there at the edge of the field, spoke to one another, and did not respond to Lies' inviting gestures.

They saw the poverty, never before displayed by foreigners.

After consultations lasting for weeks, between themselves and their husbands, they brought gifts. A piece of material, an earthenware pot, a glass, and good counsel.

Lies walked towards them, speaking a few words of Arabic and making broad gestures with her arms.

A friendship sprang up with a few families in the village over the hill. They went visiting. Aart and Lies sat with crossed legs around the board and ate fish with their fingers, sardines cooked in oil and herbs. They were taken into the village community. But the field stayed by itself.

When Aart went to town and saw the refugees on the café terraces, he felt very superior to them, and the working and drudgery was an excuse. "Great God," he mumbled, "look at them sitting there." He clenched his fists, felt the callouses on his palms, looked down his trousers at his dirty feet in sandals, with crusts of earth on the material and on the leather. He was a country man, he earned his bread. He did not belong among this dingy humanity at their little tables behind their black coffee or absinthe. Pale yellow people, they exuded misery. He carried the smell of sweat, sun and earth. Jesus, look at them sitting there.

Yes, then Aart was satisfied. Well all right, the field was a failure, but he did not belong to that gang. That was the main thing.

As long as the children stuck it out, he could do likewise. That outburst of Maria did not mean a thing, he thought. Pay no attention to it. As soon as you started to make an issue out of it, and spend words on it, then it became an event. Then the children would start to think about it. No, Aart said nothing.

Later than afternoon Pierre had come home without having done his errands. A dog had bitten him, two small wounds, like a snake bite.

He had run home more from fright than because of the pain. An African dog, dirty yellow with its tail between its legs, chased, beaten, victim of the hatred for dogs of the populace. The dog had not understood the approach of the boy, his outstretched little hand and friendly call. He was accustomed to the pestering of Arab children. Yellow African dog, with a vicious head, and his hindquarters slung low in fear.

They stood all round Pierre.

"That dog may have had the rabies," said Hans.

"Oh Jesus Christ!" Lies held the little fellow in her arms, looked around wildly and laughed nervously. "What shall we do?"

"Calm yourself," said Aart. "Where was the dog?" he asked.

"Near the house where the women do their washing," said Pierre. He struggled to free himself from Lies' arms. Suddenly he wanted to be grown-up again.

"Don't you worry," said Hans, "I know that dog. There are two of them, aren't there, Pierre?"

"Yes," Pierre nodded, "two big mean ones."

"Must be cleaned thoroughly," said Aart.

Lies took the small boy into the house and rubbed salt into the wounds, scolding him, because she felt so sorry for him.

But afterwards she forgot his misery because there was nothing to eat.

"You can leave nothing to these children," she complained. "Playing on the way, pestering dogs and coming home with nothing to eat. Dope!" she scolded. Pierre, embarrassed because he had cried before, now stuck out his tongue at her, and went in hiding with little Dolf in the trailer.

Lies sent Berthe to the village over the hill to borrow some flour, oil and sugar.

"Pancakes," she promised the children, when she came back to the field.

But Luba did not wait for the meager results. In the program with Manus, which her imagination had devised for the evening, eating was an item. Dinner with Manus!

There were two kinds of meals for Luba. Eating in front of the corrugated iron cabin from a tin plate on her lap; a picnic, in which she had little interest but the quelling of her hunger. Her memory: an unpleasant feeling at a square damask-covered table. The white linen, spotless for Sunday night, after a few days lost its sheen of silken flower patterns and became crinkly and dull. She clearly remembered still the chewed meat that she would not swallow and put in the pockets of her apron. The fury of Fräulein when Maria would not eat. The slaps. Asparagus eaten with small tongs, which Fräulein did not but Luba did consider a game.

Luba ran breathlessly along the fields, over the dunes to the beach. It was so far to Manus' cabin, distances that seemed endless, you never seemed to get there, a heavy feeling in the pit of your stomach, despair. But still you got there.

When Luba arrived at Manus' she found him on the steps of his cabin, in conversation with an Arab. This was completely unexpected, nothing she had thought about in the afternoon.

She quietly sat down in the sand.

"Hello, monkey," said Manus. That was all. He did not pay her any further attention.

The conversation was about the war. They spoke seriously, the Arab with supple gestures of his hands, a stream of words, Manus softly, paying full attention to his pipe.

The bay, blue as in picture postcards, lay enclosed between the pier on one side and the green hills on the other.

Spanish fishing smacks struggled with their anchorage in the harbor, against the wind; stayed by skillful maneuvering outside of the sucking current. At the end of the pier stood the beacon like a warning finger.

The high putt-putt-putt of the motor accompanied the shrill

voices of the little Arab boys at play on the beach, the throaty
noises of the market women who drove the burros home, and the
plaintive braying of the heavily laden, emaciated animals.

Luba did not allow herself to go unnoticed any longer. She threw
herself resolutely into the conversation on the possibility of still
being able to make the visit come up to her expectations: "When
we were in the war the Germans passed us by on their motorcycles,
but they did nothing to us." That was the only thing that occurred
to her at the moment. The Arab, insulted that a child and a girl at
that, should intrude into the conversation, kissed the tips of his fingers
in salute and went away.

Manus chewed at his pipe and looked at her pensively. He tried
to conceal from himself that he could not define his attitude.

But later they walked, her hand hidden in his, up the steeply
inclined streets going to the Kasbah. Luba had simply declared that
she was hungry. He took her along on his daily quest for a meal.

God knows why, he thought, forcing his words, God knows why.

Luba climbed the hill, full of attention and in a festive mood,
pressing her heels so hard into the ground that her calves and her
buttocks hurt. The road was so steep. Slowly it led to the Kasbah,
higher and higher. First the broad streets, where the Europeans lived
and walked, climbed out of breath, just like them. Small burros ran
down, carried away by their momentum, clicking their delicate
hooves, Arabs shouting behind them, hitting their scurvy flanks with
their sticks.

Along past the fish market, where the last fish was doled
out to the poor for a pittance. Along by the Spanish school, where
small boys in black aprons, not wanting to go home, noisily played
in the falling dusk.

They traversed the open market, passing the late women who
still wanted to sell the last egg and what remained of the bread. Past
a story teller, all by himself, inducing listeners with dull beats on his
drum. Underneath the gateway, by the Jewish butchers, who with

lazy gestures chased the flies from their kosher chopped meat. By the moneychangers in their narrow shops. And then suddenly to the left into the Kasbah.

There was a sharp smell of urine around all the corners. The blue smoke of fish frying, olive oil, Spanish pepper, herbs, camel leather, decay and human smells.

They shuffled along past each other through the narrow passageways, Arabs and Europeans.

Luba remained close behind Manus, her little hand pressed in his palm, her feet all the time hitting his heels. But she did not feel the pain. There was contentment throughout her body and little thought in her head. She was tired too, so that she neither looked up nor around, but let herself be taken along.

They ate in one of the Arab eating places, half European, with unpainted tables and small benches, and a swinging door. A small place, where the owner was also the cook. The sizzling of the oil, smacking of lips, and silence. The Arabs paid full attention to their food, sometimes throwing a curious glance at the European and the ragged little girl. Did they recognize in Manus a deserter to their camp, from the way in which he ordered his food and joked with the proprietor?

Luba with her bare little feet dangling over the floor, her arms resting on the table, sucked at the fat little fishes, and laughed at Manus to show her gratitude.

Manus had no appetite. He was immersed in his thoughts, and drank one glass of tea after another. He looked at the child's hands on the table. Tanned small fingers, gleaming with oil, that picked the bones out of the fish with small gestures. Looked in the large, dark eyes which closed again and again as a sign of confident happiness, at the narrow shoulders that shrugged from inner pleasure when he had burning-sweet Arab pastry put before her. Thin little body under the taut dress, a blue-white rag with washed-out little flower patterns.

It was the first time that Manus had eaten here, contrary to his habit of eating at certain, definite places. He did not want to be seen with the child.

Still silent they went on their way home. Shadows now threw sharp corners on the walls. Houses, yellow, white, blue, pink, as they were continually painted anew by the Arabs. The doors were open, floors made of diamond-shaped tiles, shrill voices. The small shops now were closed, the shutters put on. Here and there a tired Arab lay sleeping on his counter. Women in white haiks and with dark eyes glided through the passageways. Men sauntered by hand in hand on their way to amusement. Spaniards in rags, Spaniards in flashy clothes, on the way to the boulevard for the nightly parade. On the stoop of the Mosque, rows of yellow slippers. Around the city's fountain, buckets, and women with tired gestures, little boys spilling water from the heavy pails they carried.

Luba took Manus' hand, looking after them. She was very sleepy now, but those children carrying water were part of her.

"I am not going home again," she said suddenly. "I shall stay with you."

From the Mosque the hour for prayer was called. A water carrier, the empty ox skin on his shoulders, and a few fishermen walked in the street towards the harbor. The sun sank over the sea and left a purple sky.

Manus crossed the boulevard and went down to the beach. He walked over the wet sand. Luba, sleepy, satisfied, let herself be pulled along. But when they got to the last cabin, she stopped resolutely, and pulled at his arm.

"Didn't I tell you that I won't go home?" she said reproachfully.

When he laid her on his mattress she fell asleep immediately, even before he had spread his coat out over her. She did not awake when Manus threw off his pants and shirt before he went to bathe in the sea.

Salt, the disinfectant that Lies used in spite of the protests of victims and counsellors, this time had failed.

Pierre woke up crying, his leg alarmingly swollen, his small body shivering with fever.

"Now we know for sure at least, that that dog did not have the rabies," Hans remarked. "This is a normal infection."

"Brute," said Maria.

Hans laughed, "What is the matter with you this morning?" He looked searchingly into her white face with burning red spots around the eyes.

Lies felt the pulse of the sick boy, counted, moving her lips.

Aart, resenting her show, as he thought it, drove the other children before him to work.

"Where is Luba?" he asked, suddenly noticing that she was not there.

"Gone," said Maria. The word shot out of her mouth, as it had lain ready there to escape during the evening, all night and morning.

"Gone where?" snarled Aart, annoyed by her aggressive tone.

"Just gone," said Maria, ironically, "just gone, since last night."

He was beaten, suddenly helpless, as Maria accused him clearly.

"I don't know where she is." Maria faced him, her face drained of all color and with hatred in her eyes.

"Well, Goddamn it," Aart cursed, "why didn't you tell me before?"

"I didn't know that you cared."

"Where did she go?"

"To that Hollander."

Hans, who was carrying his first load of water, pushed her. "Hurry, will you? Do you think I can do it all by myself?"

"Leave me alone," said Maria.

Aart stood bent over the soil, stroked with the hard tips of his fingers over the green shoots, looked absentmindedly for weeds.

When Lies came on the field he looked at her searchingly, tried to say something, but didn't know how. He could not draw her attention to the fact that Luba had been gone since the previous night. That would not only accuse her but him as well.

Maria too was looking at her. She does not notice anything, she thought. Lies, who is supposed to be our mother, did not even notice that Luba was away. Luba, poor Luba, my little sister. Pity for herself, and a feeling of being ashamed of Lies, were mixed up in her thoughts.

The night before nobody had noticed Luba's disappearance. At sight of the nasty meal of gruel, which Lies had put before them after Berthe had come with empty hands from the village, Hans had furiously run off—he would get his own meals in the future. In the confusion from this and the bellowing of Dolf, who though hungry, did not want to eat the gruel, Luba had not been missed.

But Maria had sat there, waiting until somebody should notice it, in a corner of the house, brooding. First she had been indignant, afterwards filled with pity for Luba and herself. Nourishing her pity, she was the center of all this misery. Vague remembrances of the past crossed her mind. The always watchful eye of Fräulein, then a burden, but now something to held onto as she suppressed the disagreeable part. A vision of white gloves, and reading from storybooks if she had been a good girl during the day.

After waking up this morning she had patiently waited for the moment of general consternation: Luba is gone . . . ! Where is Luba . . . ? And she calm, but with emphasis: Luba was gone last night. Why didn't you say so before? Nobody cared . . . ! Aart and Lies with a feeling of guilt, submissive to her, immediately going to get Luba. That was the way it would be.

She had not expected that they wouldn't notice it in the morning either. However, they had not been all together at breakfast. The children had been scattered by Lies' scolding. After a sleepless night she had not been able to meet the food problem directly. There had only been a bit of bread. The children got their share of dry bread, which was hard to chew, although they washed it down with water from the well.

Hans had now finally found the explanation of Maria's strange behavior, and asked teasingly: "Lies, isn't anybody missing?"

But Lies' thoughts were with Pierre and she did not understand him. "I put a cold dressing around it," she said.

"Do you miss somebody?" Hans repeated.

Lies looked around, but she still did not notice anything.

"Oh, oh!" Maria was suddenly in tears, with her hands before her eyes.

"Luba!" said Lies. "Oh, God, Luba. Where is Luba?"

"Luba is the most intelligent of the whole bunch," said Hans. "Luba beat it."

Lies threw a quick glance at Aart. "Where did she go?" she asked presently.

Aart did not answer, his lips forming a narrow line.

"She is with the Hollander," Berthe burst out suddenly. She had missed Luba, but had not uttered a word. Berthe very seldom took the initiative when she discovered or noticed something.

"What made her do that?" said Lies helplessly. She stood for a moment absorbed in thought. She looked at Rainer, looked at Maria, looked at Hans, but avoided looking at Aart. She tried to take Maria's hands from her face. "Come, be yourself," she said. "Nothing will happen to Luba. I shall go to town to do errands after awhile, then I'll fetch her at the same time. Manus is a nice man, perhaps he'll bring her back himself." She said this somewhat hesitantly. She still avoided looking at Aart. "What a crazy child, what will Manus think of us!"

"The truth," Hans proffered soberly.

"You shut up," Aart burst out. "You keep your mouth closed, you son of a . . . . . , do you get me . . . ?" He was angry and at the same time helpless at Hans' amused face.

"Come on, Aart," said Hans. "You know yourself how things are here; this is a hopeless undertaking, and the rest is likewise." He included them all with a gesture of his arm.

They all stood motionless.

"Get to work," Aart ordered hoarsely. "To work."

Maria slowly put her hands down, Rainer grasped blindly for the pails. Lies stood next to Aart and put a hand on his arm. He shook her off in a temper.

Then they all grabbed for their tins with a savage display of energy, sweated and trudged, spilled the water over the eager soil.

The sun shone hot now, it was the end of May.

Luba did not come back.

Manus had given her a broom. She swept out the corners and the holes, always busy when he came home after he sometimes had gone out alone. She played house.

Lies had not got around to fetching her the following day. Pierre, with a vicious red mark reaching up to his groin, had had to be taken to the hospital. Little Dolf came along in the sport cart, a box on wheels. At the French hospital the sisters had said that it was blood poisoning. Pierre had been carried away through the white varnished door.

Lies, talking to the nurses, had then feebly admitted that little Dolf had never been vaccinated and they had given him the vaccine right then and there. Lies was one of those people who lose all resistance in a hospital, the will had been abandoned in the halls, the cold white halls where life is held cheap; there are even some who can offer no defense to the doctor behind his writing desk. This had never happened to Lies, because she protected herself beforehand by denying everything.

The violent red stripe on Pierre's leg, however, was a sign, even to the most stupid and averse. In a panic she had run over the hot asphalt road, the rattling cart behind her, little Dolf, her personal possession, with her, which indicated that she actually looked for protection from the sisters. Away from Aart's thin-lipped mouth and burning eyes, away from Hans' mocking and growing protest. Away too from the hungry children, the pails filled with dirty diapers beneath a swarm of flies, away from the counsels of Arab women friends. Away from it all. She and her little Dolf. And as she pulled the children in the bouncing cart under the broiling sun, she felt as if Dolf was lying in the hollow of her bent body. Her very own boy.

"Those damned sisters," she would say the next day to Aart, "they did not want to vaccinate the child, but I told them off." Now she was talking confidentially to the sisters in the confusion and disorder of the Moroccan hospital.

Patients who were wandering around were sent back to bed. Old Arabs with all their clothes on immediately after an operation turned in prayer to the East, sitting on the prayer rugs, too feeble to get up again. Children, in voluminous unbleached calico gowns, played between the beds with rolls of bandages, which they had found only heaven knew where.

The animal-like groans of a woman in labor behind an open door. Women, visiting, who refused to understand that they had to go away. A row of children along the wall, painted from top to toe with black salve against scurvy.

On the way home Lies did her errands and bought an extra piece of meat for Aart. It was too late then to fetch Luba. Dolf in his cart with his first toy, crowing wildly with joy, and Lies talked out and happy, suddenly filled with yearning for Aart and the kids.

4

IT WAS STRANGE without Luba and Pierre. Only now that they were away did the others notice how accustomed they had become to each other.

Berthe spoke about Luba as if what she was saying concerned somebody she had known a long time ago, as grownups speak about some one who has died too soon, or some one whom they have neglected during life.

"Do you remember," Berthe would say, and then talk about some event in which Luba had played a principal part. It was embarrassing, especially when Aart and Lies were there.

After failing to bring Luba back the first day, they seemed to lack the courage to go to Manus' beach cabin. Lies worried over it, but she didn't do anything about it. Every day she covered the long distance to the hospital to find out how Pierre was getting along, and to do errands, but something always prevented her from going for Luba. Was it because she knew that Luba would refuse to return? Or did she suspect that Manus wanted to keep the child with him? Most probably she expected an argument with her countryman, something she did not feel able to cope with. Aart, too, was silent on the subject.

Maria wandered around with a set expression on her face and stiffly closed lips. Even more than the departure of Luba, Hans' attitude seemed to upset her. He disappeared every evening immediately after work, answering Lies' questions with a shrug of the shoulders.

"Where are you going, Hans?" Berthe asked one evening, running after him.

He teasingly pulled her hair, called her a nosy girl, and gave her a lump of sugar out of his pocket. He acted towards her like a grownup towards a strange child. Hans had disassociated himself from the household.

Maria was stirring the porridge over a small fire in the house. Apparently unconcerned, humming a tune, she sauntered over to the hedge, deaf to the calling of Lies, who needed her help with the cooking.

Maria followed Hans along the road. When he heard her footsteps he waited. "What do you want?" he asked rudely. During the last few weeks they had had continual difficulties in their relationship. Maria was always on the defensive and that irritated Hans.

"I don't care a bit," Maria would say, or, "Don't act as if you were the boss; you can't tell *me* what to do." She enraged Hans with these unreasonable remarks which she made all through the day, as, for example, when he passed her with the filled tins. Once she even pinched his arm hard as he went by.

Now she stood next to him on the road, embarrassed and awkward.

"What do you want?" Hans repeated impatiently.

"Nothing," said Maria.

"Why do you follow me then?"

"Just because."

"Doesn't Lies want you to help her with the cooking?"

"Yes," she said. She looked as if she were about to cry.

"Then why don't you go?"

She kept her eyes fastened on the road and did not answer.

Hans did not know what to say. He dug his hands deep in his pockets and stood there, turned away from her, impatient. Still, he didn't want to leave her standing on the road like that. Then he noticed that she was crying. She honestly tried to keep her tears back but couldn't. She sniffed, shaking her head, ashamed of herself for crying. So pitiful, he thought. Then she gave up and sobbed loudly.

"Now, what is the matter?" he said awkwardly.

She tried to wipe her nose on her too-short sleeve. Neither of them had a handkerchief. He suddenly realized it. No handkerchief since he had left Germany! Yes, handkerchief, he thought, handkerchief; he had forgotten such things existed.

It seemed as if he had been away for a long time with his thoughts, handkerchief, home, Germany, but now he came back to Maria.

"What's the matter with you?"

She shrugged her shoulders.

"Listen," said Hans, with some hesitation, "I'll come back tonight, later. Wait for me behind the field, where the dunes begin."

"I don't care," she said suddenly. "I just don't care at all." She ran off, flying hair, skinny swinging legs, her arms stiff against her sides. Hans followed her with his eyes. Slowly he walked up the hill towards the village.

Maria did not return to the field, but ran along the asphalt road in the direction of the city. Somewhat further on she knew suddenly that she was on her way to Luba.

Maria could not speak, she was so out of breath with running. She was glad that she couldn't catch her breath, because she did not know what to say. Luba was so far away, so strange. She was busily sweeping out the cabin until the last grain of sand had disappeared from the corners. And then fussing with a can, getting water from the sea and washing a plate, a fork or spoon, a man's shirt. With a piece of soap she rubbed the shirt, the way Arab women do.

Maria sat on the steps with her back towards Luba. Peered for a moment over her shoulder.

"Now," said Luba finally, with importance, "that's done." She sat down next to Maria and folded her skirt neatly over her knees. A new dress; Maria had seen that immediately. White material with violet and yellow embroidery, a high collar and little buttons, and narrow sleeves over the elbows.

"You've got an Arab dress on," said Maria.

"Brand-new, from the shop." Luba stroked the small bodice with stiff fingers.

"Ugly," said Maria.

"Why, child!" said Luba contemptously, and gave her a push.

"You look funny," said Maria. She scrutinized Luba. Not funny, she thought, pretty. And she suddenly realized how clean Luba was. Her hair washed, softly gleaming, every hair hanging free, not tangled as it used to be. Clean neck and ears, small brown feet with shining pink toenails. Maria squirmed on the steps, curled her feet, hid them between the steps, and sat on her hands so that she would not scratch her head. She was embarrassed, embarrassed before Luba!

My hair, she thought confusedly, my little sister, I smell.

But Luba did not seem to notice anything. She talked incessantly.

"I have been to the bathhouse," she related. "Hot water, buckets full!" She indicated the size of the buckets. "And nothing but women and children. Smell," and she pushed her arm under Maria's nose. "You can still smell it and that was yesterday. Manus washed my hair." She said that bashfully, hesitatingly pronounced his name, swallowing her words. "With some stuff," she continued. "Strong, it hurt an awful lot, and then with soap and then again, and I cried. But he said he would cut it off if I wasn't quiet."

She nodded importantly. "Awful pain, but now I'm clean."

Maria did not say anything. Strange sickly feeling in her stomach, an urge to cry. Thoughts of long ago, home, the bathroom, the big copper geyser, white tiles. Saturday night, and Luba for the first time together with her in the bathtub. The small child's body opposite her in the bluish water. A celluloid frog, full of dents, a piece of pink soap. Luba beating the water with the flat palms of her hands. Laughter and jokes. The warning voice of the dark figure next to the bath. "*Nie ro'b tego, nie, nie, przestań!* Don't do that, Luba, don't!" Mother with the big rough towel to wrap Luba in. Luba making a little pool in the water on account of her excitement. And mother laughing, laughing. . . . The man's voice at the door: "What's going on there?" Then father and mother would carry Luba to the nursery and she would be left alone in the dirty bath water, until she opened the faucet of the cold shower, ice cold, and the salty taste of tears in her mouth.

Luba went on chattering about the bathhouse and how she would go again next week. "Have to go next week," she said with emphasis. She also spoke about the good food she'd had, so that Maria's mouth started watering. She had eaten chicken, Luba related with shining eyes. Mmm, so tremendously good. *Tremendously,* she said.

And then she lowered her voice to a confidential whisper. "I make money too." She motioned Maria to come inside, went down on her knees next the mattress and pulled a sheet of paper folded over ten centimes from under it. "I am going to save these *sous.* When I've saved a hundred, I'll buy . . . I'll buy . . . I'll buy a dress for you!"

Maria nodded helplessly. "Yes," she said, and then she went home. Luba waved after her. They had not exchanged a word about the field. They had mentioned neither Aart nor Lies nor the other children.

She walked home over the asphalt road, slowly now and suddenly calm. She sang a little tune to herself. From the sea came a cool breeze, the first stars appeared in the lilac sky and the chilly evening fog crept over the fields. The trees on the fields, the cacti along the road, the little houses far away and the telephone poles, all seemed to be born out of that mist and to lift themselves towards the broad cleanness of the sky.

In front of her was a rich man's caravan with two camels, horses, mules, and many women, a long trip before them.

Behind her, Arabs from the village were scattered along the road; heavily laden women, their burdens well balanced over the uneven rocking of their tired bodies; men with burros; children playing on the way home because it was so long a way.

From afar sounded the klaxon of a car, a regular hooting that drove men and animals to the side of the road. The noise approached quickly.

Just imagine, thought Maria, if there should be somebody sitting in that car who was going to change everything. Could it happen? Father . . . mother . . . a reality lost, but a toy for dream thoughts.

Often, too—as now—a manifestation of the ego. There was no war. No pogrom. Mother and father just pretended there was, to teach her a lesson. Murder and arson weren't real either. She thought of small sins, masturbations, stealing candy, lies, and that time in France when she had eaten the last piece of bread while Luba was asleep, sins of the past, for which she had paid now. Now father and mother would come to fetch her. And as the car approached, her heart started to beat, until she could no longer bear the thought that the great event was behind her; she waited for it, standing on the side of the road; but she lowered her eyes, because she did not dare face the disappointment. Disappointment! She knew that in spite of all her dreams it could not be that way. That the car would rush by. Looking down, she saw the Arabs' feet like old shoes, flattened out, full of cracks and folds; women's feet, like flat, limp fish, *caplunk, caplunk* on the asphalt. Father—Mother. God, let it be Father and Mother. Please, God, please.

"Maria!" The Consul's wife stuck her head out of the car window, "Maria!" showing astonishment and distrust.

"Hop in, I am just going to your place." They both moved away from Maria, the Consul's wife in her corner at the wheel, Ina, her daughter, next to her, to let Maria pass by. Smell of soap and toilet water, which made Maria conscious of her own smell again, just as before with Luba.

"Taking a walk?" The Consul's wife displayed a friendly curiosity, but her eyes were on the road watching the camels, the mules and the trudging human beings, her hand on the klaxon.

As Maria sat down she felt now how tired she was. A heaviness filled her body. Cramps in her stomach; she hadn't eaten anything.

"Well, Maria?" the Consul's wife was waiting for an answer.

"I was just out on an errand," she lied.

"You must always be careful to be home before dark," counseled Mrs. van Balekom.

"Yes," said Maria.

"Look beside you, there is a surprise for you people." Her eyes were still on the road but her head was half-turned, to miss nothing of Maria's reaction.

"A surprise? For us?" Maria, meek, answered as was expected of her. Discreet with an intonation of I-can-hardly-believe-it. "Really?"

Mrs. van Balekom and Ina, now satisfied, relished the thought of all those grateful faces later as they would unpack the trunks of clothes. Oh, to give was bliss indeed.

Lies sat on her haunches by a panful of diapers which she was washing. The reflection of the kerosene lamp near her on the floor danced over her face with a play of dark and light lines. She was thinking of Pierre, whose leg had been amputated in the hospital. It still was her secret; too heavy, however, for her to carry alone. How could she tell it? This morning when she arrived at the hospital it had already been done. The French doctor, grasping her muscular shoulders firmly, said, "*Ma petite, je regrette*—" and right then she had seen the little boy in her imagination, on the field. A small wooden leg . . . such a small wooden leg.

The Consul's wife, who had gathered them all together around the trunks of clothes, could not be avoided. "Where is Pierre? And Luba? Hans isn't here, either."

"Pierre is in the hospital," said Lies.

"In the hospital! No! Oh, dear, not really?"

And Ina, well brought up: "No, really? In the hospital? Nothing serious, I hope?"

"I don't know," Lies lied. "I have no time to go there."

"Oh, then we must go at once. Tomorrow, Ina."

"Yes," said Ina, "we must go at once, tomorrow, and see him."

The Consul's wife, who wanted them all around the trunks, every one of them, now asked about Luba.

"Out on an errand," said Lies.

Against her will something made her look at Maria and she saw relief and also surprise on the girl's face.

"It is dangerous to be so late on the road," the Consul's wife said in a well-meaning sort of way. "Dangerous, Lies. There are so many sinister elements." And then in an important, confidential whisper, "Yes, even in our colony, among the Hollanders, there are untrustworthy elements. Degenerates—Oh—you can find anything among them. The children are not safe after dark. So dreadful—one would suspect the Arabs, eh?—No, in fact the Europeans here have to be watched."

Berthe was listening, open-mouthed. "Hans is out too," she suddenly said.

Lies' hand shot out, smacked Berthe hard in the face. "Keep your mouth shut till you are spoken to!"

Berthe slunk to her knees, put up her arms to protect herself. It was an automatic gesture. Lies' outbursts of rage were nothing new to Berthe, who had felt her mother's hand before she had been able to understand the scolding. But she was ready to revenge herself; that she had also learned before. She got up and at a safe distance she shouted teasingly, "Luba is gone, Luba is gone. And she won't come back, either. Luba is with Manus. . . . Luba is with Manus. . . ."

"Shall we unpack the trunks now, Mother?" asked Ina, shocked and embarrassed.

Rainer brought the oil lamp; it had grown dark suddenly, and they all formed a circle round the ladies. But Mrs. van Balekom had lost interest in her surprise. She unpacked the clothes with weary movements and handed them around without a word, her head inclined in deep thought. She avoided looking at Lies. After a few minutes she seemed to have come to a decision. She finished the distribution as quickly as possible and without paying much attention to the children, who were trying on the new clothes, she herded Ina in front of her towards the car on the road.

"What did that child say about Luba?" she asked as she was starting the motor. "Where did she say the child went?"

"Manus," said Ina. "With Manus. Was that the man from the South about whom Father spoke?"

"I really don't know, my dear," said Mrs. van Balekom, evading the question. "I don't know."

Ina was surreptitiously scratching her back. "I believe I have got a flea," she said, and then complaining, "and those flies, and that dung heap!"

"Now, Ina, you knew about all that beforehand. Don't be tiresome."

Ina kept her mouth shut tight; she was offended. Mrs. van Balekom drove fast, as if she were in a great hurry.

"I must speak about it to your father at once," she said. "That won't do any longer. Those children must be taken care of better. Oh, good heavens, but how? Just when I am so busy with that new room. Oh, this war is terrible, terrible!"

5

HANS FOLLOWED the asphalt road until he came to the place where a path to the right led over the hill to the village. A path that had been hollowed out by feet and winter rains. For a moment he stood at the crossing, deep in thought. Maria's outburst of tears a little while ago had upset his composure. It was a nuisance when girls cried, but when they cried on account of you it was a rather pleasant sensation. With Maria, however, one never could be quite sure why she was sad. He decided to kiss her that night. He had wanted to for a long time. On her mouth, or perhaps in her neck, her warm neck. Perhaps they would swim first, naked in the sea in the moonlight, as they had done before in Oran, when they lived on the beach. This time, however, it was not on account of the swimming but because they would be naked that he looked forward to it. Now that he had decided on that he no longer felt depressed. Of late he had often been out of sorts. It was not so easy to make a decision, to choose between two positive things: between staying or going away. To stay gave him a small opinion of himself, because he would then be just stupidly walking in Aart's footsteps.

At the very beginning, when they were still turning the soil, he had lost confidence in the undertaking. He had observed Aart, how he would force his spade into the earth, sometimes groaning with the effort, but without being aware of the exertion. It was not the desire for the field to bloom that seemed to urge him on, but something else, something that Hans could not identify. He was driving himself to the utmost, towards physical exhaustion, and it was not easy to watch. Rainer had let himself be dragged along, although Hans had been able to persuade him to work at a slower pace. This, however, seemed to give Rainer a feeling of guilt; his sidelong glances at Aart proved that. Hans always smiled when he

48

thought of Rainer, an understanding smile. I know your kind, he often thought, and he felt far superior.

Later, when Aart put Lies and the girls to work, Hans had decided to leave. The drudging of Maria, Berthe and Luba hurt his self-respect, he wanted to have no part of this. The decision made him happier, gave him a feeling of independence, for a few days at least, because afterwards he began to weigh this feeling. Aart had taken him along last year after the surrender of France. Yes, "taken him along," that was the right expression. He himself had no choice in the matter. The friends in Paris who had sheltered him were afraid the Germans would keep him as a hostage for his father. They had handed him over like a parcel in the mail, as Hans expressed it, to some trusted friends south of the city, who in turn had sent him along with Aart.

When he had arrived at the trailer, only Berthe had been there. In a few days the other children had been picked up. In a whim Lies had decided to take the children along; she had refused grown-ups. Lies had looked on it as amusement; the more the merrier. Hans had thought even then that it was something connected with her pregnant condition. Having termed her as being a friendly, awkward-looking person, with strange eyes and ideas, Hans had been quite proud of his insight.

No matter how selfishly he might look at things now, he probably owed his life to Aart. This fact only added to his antagonism towards him. He was conscious of the unreasonableness of this feeling, but he could not overcome it. And that was why he did not carry out any plan to leave. He stayed, and only the certainty of his inner resolution to leave at some time in the future, gave him the courage to persist.

Finally he had arrived at a compromise with himself. During the last argument he had decided to continue working for the present, until he had found some other means of supporting himself. In the meantime he would free himself from the household, free himself from Aart's motives and plans for the future: he would become a sort of day laborer. The decision had made him restless however; he was afraid of the future; for the first time in his life he had not been able to fall asleep.

He now slowly climbed the steep path that led to his friends in the village. They lived on the slope, where there were a few houses, squarish buildings with a courtyard surrounded by walls. He found them in the courtyard, people and animals. The smaller children shrieking and laughing as they played in a circle. The four cows placidly stretched out, their bodies wrapped in the evening fog as if they were wearing veils, pensive creatures, indifferent to all the noise. At the back of the court the women under a shed, where they baked the flat loaves of bread above a charcoal fire. Silent and patient, kneading the hot dough in the flat plates, their impassive shadows on the wall.

Hans chatted with them for a while and tasted a piece of the bread which they tore off for him. "*Mezian, Mezian,*" he praised the bread, and they shrieked with laughter when he burned his mouth.

In the house, the father sat alone, eating his evening meal by the light of the oil lamp. His two sons sitting on their broad bed were holding a conversation in whispers. Hans, tip-toeing his way in order not to disturb the master of the house, joined them. They were pleased to see him. The eldest was a farmer, quiet and reticent. The younger, Achmed, was always gay and ready for a laugh. He was Hans' age, liked to talk about women, went to sleep in the city while he waited to marry a neighbor girl whom his father had chosen for him. He asked immediately how it was that Hans came so early in the evening, and Hans told them with some hesitation what he had decided to do.

The elder boy did not understand it very well. "If you continue working for the Hollander," he said, speaking in Spanish in order to be understood clearly, "he should give you money."

"He has no money," said Hans.

"Then he must give you food."

Hans was sorry that he had broached the subject. It was impossible to explain this conflict to the boys, it was too complicated for Arab understanding; so he said, "I am looking for other work."

The elder boy nodded seriously; he could understand that. Hans was certainly not a farmhand. But what else could he do? And moreover, there was between the Hollander and Hans a father-son relation, and it would be extraordinary in the eyes of the Arabs to break this off.

But Achmed, without having given it too much thought, had a proposition. Could Hans become a teacher? There were rich families in the city whose sons would go to study later in Marrakech or Madrid, or even Paris. Achmed did not know much about it, though his greatest ambition was to go himself to Europe and study. With a vague gesture he pointed in the direction of Gibraltar. But then he had an even better idea. He smiled slyly. Hans was a German. Then the problem was solved, as some Arabs wanted to learn the German language. He jumped down from the bed and took Hans along in a great hurry, a protecting hand on his shoulder.

The host turned the shiny-white pottery between the pointed tips of his fingers, round and round, so that the golden curved letters on the belly-like middle lost all sense. "*Klaus, trink' deine Milch*" was inscribed on it. "Klaus, trink' deine Milch." The Arab, his face impassive, went on carefully handling his possession amid the respectful silence of the rest of the family.

"*Mezian*," said Hans, but his host remained silent, humble.

A long time ago Hans had drunk from the same beaker. By an extraordinary coincidence there was a German cup here in the house of an Arab in Spanish Morocco. Here, the household articles of Moroccan handicraft—crocks and cans, glazed wealth of life and color on vessels with playfully painted figures, outlined glitter of gold on copper plates—were not appreciated because the eye had become satiated. This European article, shapeless, gleaming, bulging, obnoxious, was different and consequently a more valued possession. "Hans, trink' deine Milch" stood on the cup out of which

Hans had drunk when a child. Golden, elegantly elaborate letters he had loved to look at, but only when he had emptied his cup. Never before.

Already as a child he had had a clear conception of what had to be done or was irrelevant. And because of his background, the excessive rules and discipline of the *Hitler-Jugend* had had little influence over him. *"Selbstverständlich"* or *"Uberflüssig"* were the answers the youth leaders got from him. He gave so much evidence of his discernment that his arbitrariness, as it was called there, had never gotten him into difficulties. He soon became leader of a group. That served him well as he had been an alibi for his father. And this too had never harmed his character.

For the heroes of the Third Reich Hans had never felt more than a somewhat cold curiosity. The hero worship in which the other children tried to identify themselves had been directed towards his father. His father, a member of the underground movement in Germany—the stepchild of the world, as he called it. Without bitterness his parents had understood that the fighters for freedom in Germany stood alone and therefore were helpless.

Father, mother and child realized that their paths would separate. With this realization they lived as three entities, their relations to each other always dominated by this possibility. And to this end Hans' education was also directed. Without undue sentimentality, but with enough warmth to make each other happy, they lived in anticipation of a destined separation.

It gave Hans a strange feeling to find this cup here; he grew restive on his cushion. Achmed seemed to notice his discomfort and turned the conversation back to the businesslike proposition that had been made earlier that night in Hans' name. Twenty-five francs per lesson and a meal. The host had not yet given his answer, and there was nothing to indicate whether or not he was considering the proposal now. He remained standing in the center of the room, turning the cup round and round in his hands. The members of his family sat among the half-empty plates on the floor and looked up silently to him and Achmed. Hans would have liked to stand up too, though he had gradually become accustomed to sitting with legs crossed on a cushion. But the meal had not agreed with him; he was not used to such rich food any more and he had eaten too much anyway. He tried to avoid looking at the women, which caused him to have an uncomfortable feeling in his neck. It had taken a great deal of persuasion on the part of Achmed to induce the women to take off their veils. And before they had allowed him to come in, Achmed had entered and he had waited at the door of the narrow little passageway with the softly tinted house surfaces, which grew grayer as the evening became darker. From afar came the hum of the Souk, the tinkle of the little bell of the water carrier, and the high voices of the women behind the door. He had asked himself why these Arabs wanted to learn German, and a vague suspicion grew in him. Shortly after the Spaniards had taken over the government of this League of Nations city, the German consular employees had returned. Hans had heard this and also that the Consul distributed money and favors among the Arabs. He knew only what he had picked up from the talk he heard in the village. When he was told that the old Mendoub, the Arabian regent, had been sent away and that his house on the large Souk had been given to the German consul, he had laughed bitterly. And what were the English and Americans doing about it, he had asked. Nobody knew, and he understood that no attempt had been made to prevent it. In the old days his father had always known the right explanation for such incomprehensible happenings, but now Hans was alone with his problems. Right opposite the English fortress on the Mediterranean, while the Allied armies were fighting in Africa the Germans were spreading their spy net. He seldom went to the city, but he had heard that the Hotel Ritz was filled with German tourists. Hans did not understand it; it gave him a choking feeling of powerless fury. "*Verbrecher, Idioten,*" he mumbled, as he had heard his father say when he spoke about diplomatic indifference, stupidity, and corruption.

Yes, he had an inkling of the reason why these Arabs of Tangier wanted to learn German. This suspicion was confirmed when Achmed had called him in at last and portraits of Franco and Hitler stared down at him from their silver frames.

The family sat at the evening meal, men and women together, as was the new custom. There was only the head of a sheep on a plate between them.

"*Erras del H'aouli*," said the host, excusing himself. "Mutton. Yes, I know English, too!" He laughed in self-approval. Making quick gestures over the dish, he had explained to Hans that something else would be brought for him. It was a dish of chicken and sweet pastry, which the women offered him zealously. They had taken off their haiks and wore little pointed hoods, the long blue-black braids wound round with cord, and light dresses under which the shape of their breasts was visible. At the hems of their gowns the edges of dark wide trousers showed. Their graceful hands and feet were painted with henna, but their faces were as colorless as grass under a board, so different, thought Hans, from the peasant women with their sun-tanned faces, dressed in red, black-and-white-striped loincloths and ragged bodices, their calves wound with sack-cloth or leather, and on their heads the coif of the much-coveted bath towel, imported by a clever dealer just for that purpose.

Hans felt the consternation he caused among these women; they avoided his gaze, giggled and whispered. At the same time he felt something quite different, an internal excitement, as if a door had opened on a familiar room and his father had come out, placed a hand on his shoulder and said, "Here I am, the companion of your youth. Do you see the pictures of Franco and Hitler on the wall? Who has urged these people on to take German lessons, and to what purpose?"

The memory of his father was now as vivid as if he were actually there without drawing attention to himself. Not with crossed legs on the floor—that Hans could not imagine—but at his study in a broad leather armchair, unobstrusively looking at Hans to catch his attention, "Look out and take care!"

The master of the house still had not answered Achmed's proposition. Now he was squatting on the floor again, picking his teeth, and his other hand caressed the cheek of one of the children that sat in the hollow of his arm, eating from the leftovers.

Achmed joked with the women and their daughters, who laughed out loud and stole glances at Hans, timid, but still enticing. Hans tried to find out which one of the sons wanted to take lessons. There were three; they wore the fez of the Nationalists, speckled white and black. The eldest had attended the University of Marrakech. The second son was with his father in business. The youngest would leave for Paris during the latter part of the year to go to the Sorbonne. It turned out to be the eldest, a small, oldish-looking boy with the beginning of a beard and restless eyes. Finally the father forced a decision. They had quarelled in loud voices in a dialect that Hans did not understand. He knew the Arabic spoken in the village on the hill, but he barely understood the language that was spoken in this family. In order to counteract the nationalist movement various spoken and written dialects were encouraged in these French and Spanish colonies. Hans knew that and resented it.

It appeared that the son considered the twenty-five francs, that Achmed had asked, adequate payment, or that he had a special reason for not trying to lower it. The father consented and the hours for the lessons were decided upon.

Hans left the house of the Arab with the image in his mind of the portraits of Franco and Hitler, and underneath them the small cupboard and the mug with the gilt letters. "*Klaus, trink' deine Milch!*" he mumbled. "Empty your mug." As quick as thought comes he knew that this was his father's message: "*Hans, trink' deine Milch!*" He tried to make this symbolism seem absurd. But the thought captivated him. From now on he would keep his eyes open.

Achmed was satisfied with the way things had gone during the evening, but he convinced himself that his task was not yet finished. They had often talked about the night life of the town and Achmed had exaggerated his stories, though at the same time showing casualness in relating his experiences as if the part he played in them was the most usual thing in the world. Now the evening Achmed had anticipated for a long time had come, he would be able to give real proof of the veracity of his stories. Secretly, however, he was afraid that the reality would be somewhat disappointing.

He nudged Hans, who was deep in thought and was barely aware of his actions and surroundings as he accompanied him with lagging steps. It seemed to him as if he had actually left his father behind in the house of the Moor. He felt lonely.

Achmed led him through the somewhat wider streets below the Kasbah down to the small Souk where there was no merchandise, but only drink and amusement for sale, a district where the Occidentals and the Arabs mingled—Europeans and Americans, seekers after sinful pleasure and devotees of untrammeled passion, fugitives from the law and from fascist persecution, Spanish inhabitants and officers from Gibraltar, and hundreds of women, European as well as Arabic, who had turned here only through dire necessity.

Achmed stopped at an old Spanish house, with a red light out front and shadows behind the windows. Behind the door hung a curtain made of beads, that Achmed pushed aside as with some pressure he shoved Hans in front of him. At first Hans heard the sounds —dance music, voices, the tinkling of glasses and women's high laughter; then, when his eyes had become accustomed to the stinging tobacco smoke and the dim light, he saw the row of people standing at the bar, Spaniards, collarless and unshaven, attentively bent towards each other; an Englishman in a grey sweater, shamelessly sunk in a drunken stupor such as an Englishman only indulges in outside his native land; next to him his companion for bar and bed, her peroxide blond head above a glass of absinthe; some Hungarians spouting torrents of words, political argument, of course; and at the end of the counter the three members of the ladies' orchestra of the Hotel Victoria and a drunken Arab. Achmed was busy with whispered comment, in which he did not shrink from emphasizing the dramatic.

The barman, Hardy, stood at the cash register. It was still early in the evening—after midnight he rarely knew which side of the bar he belonged on. He considered it a happy coincidence that the owner owed him money, but as Achmed said, his hours were accounted for in front as well as behind the bar. Hardy, product of American parents and English education, was unconcerned. He had found his Sodom and happily proceeded towards his delirium tremens.

"Achmed," he called when he noticed the young Arab, "you've come just in time." He put his arms around him and vigorously slapped his back. "Allah sent you," he said in order to flatter him. He pulled aside the curtain of a small kitchen with towering stacks of dirty dishes. Achmed grinned and introduced Hans and Hardy to each other. Hans proffered his hand rather absentmindedly. He was fascinated by the spectacle at the bar. This was the first time he had been in a bar at all. He was rather disgusted with it but he was also curious. At the same time thoughts ran through his head like moral tracts: you lived in order to attain and accomplish something; these people spent their time in emptiness; they were in the grip of decay. He looked at the face of the Englishman, puffy, completely devoid of expression. His head swung back and forth. Then suddenly he woke with a start, and loud as the crack of a whip his hand came down on the bar. "Goddamit." The blond next to him did not pay any attention. Hans had to laugh. At the piano in a corner a woman was playing. She looked so attentively at Hans that it frightened him and he quickly joined Achmed and Hardy in the little kitchen. Hardy stood leaning against the sink, somewhat dazed, but when Hans came in he started a sort of jolly complaint. It was meant rather to enlist their sympathies and to assure himself of their help than to give vent to his anger. "Those Arabs are a scurvy lot," he grumbled, "you can never trust them. On Monday they accept a job and on Tuesday they don't come back any more." Hans looked at Achmed to see what kind of impression these words would make on him, but Achmed stood by indifferently. *"Allons, mes petits,"* Hardy continued, "do me a favor, wash up that stuff. Twenty-five francs for both of you." And then to Hans, "I know you have not been brought up to do this sort of thing, but Jesus, what can *I* do!" And he elevated his voice: "I am a doctor!" Then humming a tune, "Arms, legs, arses, bellies, from the cradle to the grave!" Suddenly he whispered importantly: "And here I stand. Do you think that I ever complain? Never!"

"Thirty francs," Achmed said indifferently.

"It comes out of my own pocket, do you know that?" Hardy whined.

"Thirty," said Achmed. He was already taking his *djellabah* off, convinced that Hardy would give in. The barman looked at Hans for help with eyes grown pale through alcohol, but Hans avoided his gaze. Somebody at the bar yelled for Hardy and he disappeared behind the curtain. Achmed began stacking the dishes and lit the oil stove.

"Is he going to give you thirty?" Hans asked. Achmed shrugged his shoulders to signify that it was self-evident, that he no longer wanted to waste any words on it.

By the physical activity required to replace the plates and the glasses, Hans was completely awakened and realized the absurdity of the situation. He could not forego the pleasure of a teasing re-mark, *"C'est comme ça qu'on passe la nuit, hein?"* But Achmed, without moving a muscle of his face, declared that he usually made money that way in order to be able to amuse himself during the rest of the night.

They continued their work. From where Hans was standing, he could see the bar, the long, soiled counter, where people came and went, where they either quickly tipped their glasses to their lips or slowly sipped, staring dully at the wall or conducting quarrelsome, jovial or confidential conversations. He did not see any pleasure in it and was astonished at the women who seemed to enjoy it. All these people must have some place they call home, he thought, a room, where they had their possessions and a bed. What were they looking for here? In the cast-iron cabin in the field the evenings were unbearable. Aart and Lies when they were home argued about the field until they found an end in bed to their squabbling. At their reconciliation, Hans would go outside to take a walk, irritated and filled with shame. The children groaned in their sleep because of the talk, the eternal carpentering and hammering of Rainer, or a lamp whose light shone in their eyes; sometimes on account of the heat when they closed the door because of the evening dampness. It was comprehensible that you walked away when a home was like this. But even so, he thought, he would not go into a bar. It was boring there, and it smelled bad.

Every now and then Hardy would stick his head through the curtain and ask how they were getting on. In the course of time his remarks became disconnected: "Those damn Huns have Paris. Still they won't know how to enjoy themselves there. But I, boy, I knew how. Here!" He put his hand on his heart and grasped Hans' hand, "Feel there, boy, how it beats. My father was a doctor." He let Hans' hand drop. "Thirty francs—that goes against my conscience. I will make it fifty. Fifty, dear boy." A slap on Hans' shoulder, then confidentially, "Not another cent to that scurvy fellow." And then loudly, in Arabic to Achmed, "Listen, you son of a bitch, are you almost ready?"

Achmed continued his work without paying any attention. After about ten minutes Hardy brought in a number of soiled glasses which he had jammed into each other to make two tottering towers, which, as could be expected, fell noisily to smithereens on the tiled floor, into the sink, and upon Achmed's naked feet. In practically no time at all the young Arab had put on his *djellabah*, had thrust his feet, one of which was bleeding badly, into his *babushes* at the door, and had disappeared. Hardy grinned stupidly. The pianist shoved the curtain aside and looked with an expression of amused resignation at Hardy. "Fetch the broom," she said not un-friendly, "get a move on, *gaffeur*, before the boss shows up." She turned to Hans, "German?" She had a curt way of speaking, as if she did not consider it worth the trouble to know more than a set number of words. Her French had a strong accent. Hans, suddenly turning a fiery red, and afraid of cutting his sandaled feet on the splinters, stood in a corner, and nodded in confusion. "Yes, German."

"Have you been here for a long time?"

"Five months." Maria, he thought suddenly. For the first time this night he remembered his appointment with her. She would be waiting for him in the dunes. Strange, how he should suddenly be thinking of her now. Surreptitiously, he was watching the pianist, but she did not seem to mind and introduced herself: "Marga, Hun-garian, for four years in this from-God-and-civilization-forgotten land."

Hans did not know what to say. Luckily, Hardy came stum-bling in, swinging a broom, his movements uncontrolled. Marga took the handle with a rough gesture, and started sweeping up the splin-tered glass, her long blond hair falling over her face.

The glass crunched and broke under her slippers. She first swept along the sink, so Hans could continue washing the dishes. She made a threatening gesture with the broom in the direction of Hardy and chased him out with a curt remark. Then she asked Hans, "How did you get here?"

"Over Oran," said Hans, expert at avoiding questions.

She uttered a short laugh, in a voice hoarse with smoke, drink and late hours; there was a complete life story in that voice. Hans felt helpless and timid, and wished that she would go.

"How much is Hardy paying you?" she asked, no longer pursu-ing her previous question and his evasive answer.

"I don't know, first he said thirty, then fifty. But to share with Achmed, and now Achmed's run away."

She laughed again: "That fellow won't come back," she said, "Arab pride."

Again Hans did not know what to say. He stood with his back towards her, heard the swish of the broom and the soft tinkling of the glass and smelled her perfume.

Say something now, he ordered himself. But what?

After some time he heard her go away. Thank God, he thought. But after a moment she came back. A small Moroccan boy was with her, to whom she gave instructions, in Arabic, to carry away the broken glass. She came and stood next to him at the sink, lit a cigarette and crossed her arms over her chest.

"Gymnasium?" she asked suddenly. Bewildered, Hans looked up. It was such a long trip in his mind from this filthy little kitchen in a Moroccan bar to the rectangular dark building, as it had stayed in his memory, the red building with its large classrooms and shiny benches. What a strange question! Why did she ask it? He looked up at her, unsure. Had he understood her rightly? She held the cigarette in the corner of her mouth, her long hair hung along her cheeks. She had pencilled dark shadows above her eyes and a deep red, broadly painted mouth. But she was indifferently dressed, in a white blouse and dark skirt. Like a jig-saw puzzle, in which the pieces fitted, but the picture didn't.

"Are you incognito?" she asked with a jolly expression in her eyes. Suddenly they both laughed. It was good to laugh, Hans thought. He stood leaning against the sink. He laughed until tears filled his eyes.

"Ça se passe," she said laconically, and later, "They can't take away from us the sense of humor, but that is the only thing they can't take." She said it without self-pity, without sentimentality or pride, even without sarcasm.

Somebody called for her, to play a piece that he wanted to hear, but Marga did not answer. She stood in a corner with her arms crossed, on her left cheek a thin yellow line along which the smoke of her cigarette travelled.

"Did you go to the gymnasium?" Hans asked. He thought it a ridiculous question. Her remark, their understanding laughter, had already served as an answer. But what else could he say? He was very conscious of how much older she was than he. He felt awkward and bashful.

She nodded. "Long ago," she said. "To the university too. Law."

Hans put the last glasses in the rack. He dried his hands in his trouser pockets. He shook his head.

"It's all so strange and mixed up," he said, and more confidentially he added, "I live outside. At Quinze Kilomètre. That's what the Arabs call the village," he explained.

She nodded, smiling. "With your family?" she asked then.

"No," he said, "with Hollanders. They have a piece of land. We work there. There are nine of us."

Again somebody called for Marga. She grabbed something from the pocket of her skirt.

"Here," she said and gave him a key. "Câla Magelan 34, top floor. My room. Wait until I get there. Then we shall be able to talk. I'll bring you the money from Hardy." She slid away through the curtain and a moment later her piano music began.

Hans left the bar unnoticed. Hardy was sleeping with his head on the counter, and another man filled the glasses. It was chock-full of people, and noisy. Outside it was quiet in the light of the moon. From the Mosque the midnight hour was called. Hans stood for a moment thinking, the key in his fist. Maria had certainly gone home by now, he thought.

He sank into reflections of how it would be at Marga's. They would talk. Talk: the world had suddenly acquired a particular significance. But images obtruded themselves between him and his thoughts. Satin draperies, lace curtains, rugs, a woman, soft in a transparent negligée, the book "Nana" by Zola, that he had read halfway through.

"What madness," he said aloud, "Hans, *Du bist ja plemplem.*"

He went in the direction of the Câla Magelan. But suddenly the cold sweat broke out in the palms of his hands.

6

He awoke when she came in.

"Hello!" she said. He looked at her as she took off her coat, prepared the primus and measured out water and coffee. Suddenly the room seemed warmer. Before, when he had hesitatingly opened the door, it had been cold there, as cold as North African nights can be. A room filled with women's things, he had thought, with the stale smell of powder and cigarette smoke. But a table near the window, strewn with paper and documents, a couple of books on the night table had given him confidence. He had sat down on the edge of the bed and immediately fallen asleep. For as long as he could remember, even as a small boy, he had thus sunk into a deep sleep even before he had undressed. They had always sent him to bed with the admonition, "Undress first." But repeatedly the tiredness after a full day would overwhelm him. In about twenty minutes his mother would look in. Then the same little drama would take place, every night anew. He irritable because she disturbed him in his first sleep, and she filled with tenderness, gentle, patient.

"Come, Hans, get undressed, let mother help you."

"Go away, leave me alone."

"Come on, boy. Look here, mother will undress you."

"Go away, go away," with his eyes closed and his feet pushing her legs.

She would undo his tie, take off his blouse and pull down his pants, as he resisted and moaned with his eyes closed. When he got older, and came home late from meetings of the party, it was still the same thing. "Oh, darn it, Mother, you old bother!" And when she had undressed him except for his underclothes, "Come on, Mother, get out of the room." She would then come back later and tuck him in. Always, every night. Until the very end, when he sometimes came home after midnight and she herself had already gone to bed. And even the very last evening.

The memory of it stood out so clearly that it hurt him. He cursed. Leave me alone, he thought, don't think about it, oh Jesus Christ, damn it, first Father so plainly visible, and now Mother again.

"The coffee will be ready soon," said Marga. "That will set you up. Or would you rather go to sleep? You look tired. What do you do all day?"

He got up from the bed, went to the window, where she stood. Above the sea the sky was already growing lighter, a dirty yellow, that seeped through the grey night sky. Across the boulevard, of which they saw parts in between the houses, the first caravans were already on their way to the market. The palm trees, heavy with the morning dew, stood like closed umbrellas along the boardwalk.

Hans pressed his face against the pane, thought before he answered. Always when people asked him what he did, he had to face the same problem. Tell them about Aart and the field. He hated it. He was ashamed about it not because of the fact that not the refugees but only the Arabs and the poorest Spaniards, mostly escaped loyalists, worked here on the land. No, he hated to talk about it, for he had had part in the failure, the blind, stupid, hopeless efforts of Aart. And like many children of his age, children with personality and deep feeling, he felt responsible for the actions of his elders.

"You don't have to tell me," she said.

"Oh, it is nothing in particular. I work in the fields. We raise vegetables and potatoes."

"I envy you."

Nobody had ever said that. I envy you. Hans laughed.

"Would you rather work in a bar?" she asked. He noticed the condescending tone, as if she were talking to a child. She seemed to realize that too, and she added hastily, "You must not always have the feeling that I am older than you are. I like to talk to you." She laid her hand on the back of his head, and mussed his hair.

He shuffled away from the window and sat down again on the edge of the bed. From here the room looked familiar, here he felt more at ease. His eyes closed again. It was torture to stay awake. . . .

He awoke because somebody took off his sandals, opened his blouse, pulled at his sleeves. "Let me alone, I am tired," he said sleepily. "*Lasz mich in Ruh', lasz mich.* . . ." He heard her kind laughter, some comforting words, felt a blanket pulled from under him and then spread over him.

He was staying with his grandmother on a farm at the Polish border. The bed was large and square. Under and over him was down; he lay buried in a soft hollow. The smell of the old bed, where an eternity of nights had been lived, where the passing days had thrown their shadows, where life had been created, given, lost. Soft, warm hollow with the sweet air of bodies, and lavender from the old linen closet. In this hollow he made himself small, pulling up his knees to his chin, as if he wanted to return to his embryonic being.

But noises penetrated the depth of his slumber. The stamping of horses that were hitched, rattling wheels, the alluring voice of his grandmother as she fed the geese.

The enticement of the soft hollow fought with his desire to be outside sharing in the breaking day.

He stretched his legs along the smooth old sheets, the downy cover, that moulded itself to his body. The luxurious warmth enfolded him, strange things were happening to his body. He investigated with his hands.

The awakening from this dream was frightening. He tried to sit up, but he couldn't disentangle himself.

"Were you dreaming?" she said.

He did not answer. Dumb with fright and shame.

"Go to sleep again, it is still very early."

"You must not be afraid," she said later.

"I am not afraid," said Hans.

"Then everything is all right."

It had never yet occurred to him to neglect what he thought his duty. He had never been late for school. He had worked, till late in the evening, at his geometry problems, trying to discover the logic that other children seemed to have found. He had done his part in the *Hitlerjugend*, not because he had been forced in, but because he found it necessary in view of his father's position.

Now he was having his breakfast in the sunlight, and he chased the thought of the field away like a bothering fly.

They had opened the window wide. Outside, the working day was in full swing. Arab merchants and market women were jogging along behind their donkeys. European housewives, with their shopping baskets hanging from their arms, passed, preoccupied with the problems of where to find oil or how to go about bribing the bâkal to let them have some rice and sugar.

In front of the hotels on the boulevard the street was swept, the red fezzes of the houseboys were a brilliant color note in the pastel-tinted morning. In front of an Arab teahouse, a donkey was impatiently braying. A beggar suffering from elephantiasis shuffled past on his pillar-like legs, his voice rising and ebbing like a grey elegy. On the roofs the Arab girls spread the laundry under the sun.

Refugees dwaddled past, carrying a newspaper or a book, something to hold on to. On the terrace of the Hotel de Bretagne a few guests were having breakfast. A Spanish policeman went by on his bicycle.

Hans saw it all from the window. At the same time, he felt extremely proud of himself. He found it difficult, however, to look at Marga. He knew that she was completely at ease, heard her quiet voice and accepted the food that she offered him. But he avoided her eyes.

"Do they know where you are?" she asked. "Won't they worry?"

He shrugged his shoulders. "I am no longer a baby." It was his usual remark and he was afraid that she was going to laugh. But she continued smoking quietly.

"Luba was away for a whole night and a morning, before they noticed she was gone."

"Where was she then?"

He pointed out of the window towards the right. "With a man, who lives there in a beach cabin."

"With Manus?" she asked.

"Yes. Do you know him?"

"Of course. Who doesn't?" She looked at him thoughtfully for a moment. "What did they do, when they noticed that she was gone?"

"Nothing," said Hans. "She is still there."

She threw her cigarette out of the window, and lit another. "How old is that child, Luba?"

"About eight, I think."

"Do they know Manus? Have they ever met him?"

"He called on us once."

"When you go home in a little while," she said, "go past Manus' cabin and give him my regards. And take that child, that Luba, along with you."

"Why?" asked Hans. Now he looked straight at her, forgot his embarrassment. "She is probably better off with him than with us. Do you know what it means to carry buckets of water in the broiling sun, all day long? And not half enough to eat?"

"Still, I would take her home."

"Listen," said Hans, now highly excited, "Luba ran away, she was fed up—see? That child is the most clever of us all."

"Still, I would go and fetch her."

"I haven't the slightest intention of doing it."

She kept quiet for a while, gathering the plates and the glasses.

"Why do you stay, if it is that bad?"

"I won't stay. I am leaving as soon as I can earn enough money to take care of myself."

"Washing dishes at Hardy's?"

"No," he said, "of course not."

"How will you make money?"

"It does not matter how."

"Oh God!" she said.

He suddenly hated her. Hated the night that was behind him, hated her wide, painted mouth, her long, red nails, all the rest that now repelled him. He got up. "Well, I guess I'll be going," he said.

"Don't be so unreasonable. There are a few things in life yet you don't understand."

In his head a thought, deeply buried, suddenly took shape. Still vague, but already taking hold of him. A slobbery, disgusting something, like the birth of a mollusk. First the image of little Luba. Then of Manus as he had sat that night with Rainer in front of the shack. Items read in the paper, which had never become real to him. The little red volume with stories of Maupassant in his father's library.

He looked for his sandals underneath the bed and got into his clothes.

Marga was still sitting at the table; she had not even turned around.

He hesitated for a moment at the door, as he didn't know what one said in a case like this. "*Au revoir*," he then said.

"*Bon chançe, mon petit*," she called.

That evening Hans and Maria walked along the road.

"We'll have a sirocco," Hans predicted.

"Let's not go to the beach then," Maria said. "It is horrible to get sand in your eyes."

She held her hands behind her back, which she thought gave her an unconcerned air. She didn't want him to know that his invitation to go for a walk had made her happy. She wanted to appear sophisticated. "The valley behind the village," she said, "it is simply beautiful there."

"Simply beautiful in the dark, eh," he teased. "Come on, be yourself."

She didn't respond as she realized he had seen right through her.

Still Hans turned in the direction of the valley but for his own reasons. He wanted to avoid Achmed as he didn't feel up to a meeting with Achmed, who certainly would ask questions.

Maria had made up her mind not to mention Hans' absence in the night, but she had a hard time keeping still.

Sometimes when she had made a decision like this, it seemed as if she was forced to do just the opposite, and when she did it then it would upset her and make her most miserable. She was forced to do the strangest things, she thought. In the morning before she took her dress from a nail in the wall, she felt compelled to touch that nail three times. Three times she would knock against the nail; she had to, but at the same time she hated to. Later before she ate her breakfast, she would touch the hollow of her knee three times. And every time she lifted the full buckets she would have to count three. Otherwise terrible things would happen to her. Sometimes three times three and add one to make an even ten. But doing that she really resisted, because she feared that going on this way she might become insane. Once, she remembered, when she had been out with her mother, she had seen a lady who suddenly stopped in the street, put her handbag on the ledge of a shop window and then rolled her arms around, quick, quick, like a child playing a game, but with a serious face and with her eyes closed. Then she had picked up her bag again and gone on.

"What is that lady doing, Mama?" Maria had asked.

"She is sick, but you mustn't look, Maria. Don't look around now, *nie ro'b tego.*"

Why was she thinking of that lady now?

Last night she had waited hours for Hans. It had been cold in the dunes. Today she had had to make water repeatedly. Now it was cold too and she had no panties on. She had asked for them tonight, but Lies had laughed at her. "Why tonight, child? Are you going on a date?" And seeing Maria's pained expression, she had said kindly then, "Panties is a luxury. We don't have panties any more. Be glad that Mrs. van Balekom gave you such a nice dress."

"I wish she had given me panties and shoes," said Maria. "And the dress is much too big. Does it look funny on me, Lies?"

"Come here, lamb, I will fix you up." Lies had sewn a fold in the dress with long stitches and Maria had gone to her date feeling warm inside as this was the first time Lies had really *done* something for her, a thing mothers do. Hans had not shown up, however. She had been in a dark well of waiting, until she almost choked with a mixture of anxiety and fear. Finally she had run home, as fast as her legs would carry her, and always with the feeling that somebody was behind her and would grab her.

"Where were you last night?" she now asked Hans. See, she has asked it. Oh, why did she have to do things when she didn't want to? She would try not to touch anything three times. Tomorrow she would start. Tonight she had to as otherwise things might turn out wrong. Three times her hand pressed against the hollow of her knee. Why was she doing it again, instead of listening to Hans' answer?

"What did you say?"

"I said it is none of your business." He put his arm around her, in order to take the edge off the answer. Maria held her breath, as she felt her shoulder in the hollow of his hand.

"You don't have to tell me," she said meekly.

"I can't tell you." Her shoulder was so small, he thought. So much smaller than that other one, the soft flesh to which he had pressed his face dizzily.

"But I have no secrets from you," came the voice next to him, so small in its urge to be caught in the warmth, in the desire to be submissive.

He laughed goodheartedly, held her against him.

Where might he have been, she mused. Probably with his friends. And now he acted important to make an impression. But she would not show him that she could see through him. She would not be catty this evening. Sweet and natural, like sweet, blond girls—sweet, blond girls, that was what boys wanted. Girls who didn't have strange thoughts and crying spells. It was wonderful to walk like this, divine, she thought. At last she was with someone, belonged to someone. She could have walked all night. She didn't want to go back to the field ever.

Hans followed the asphalt road and went around the hill, which was covered with cacti, dangerous in the dark. And between the grass, wet and burning-cold to her feet, grew hard stubble. But if she suffered all this without complaint, she thought, the evening would turn out to be wonderful.

Once they had found a spot against the hill, she had to go for a moment, and as she sat hunched behind a bush, she was suddenly terribly worried that Hans would come to look. But she was really very astonished for thinking this, because she had never had such a thought before.

Hans was quietly lying on his back and looking into the sky, so wide, stretching out so tremendously far over the land and the sea that all worries seemed puny and ridiculous. The small doings of people, who crawled like ants over the earth. Eternity, he thought. He formed the word with his lips and let it go like a soap bubble. "*Ewigkeit.*" What did it mean? What was it? Looked at from above, the people on earth were nothing more than a big ant heap. This war, the whole mess, in a few centuries nothing more than a few lines in history books. Completely forgotten in a few thousand years, because there was no author of the stature of Homer to formulate it for eternity, or rather relative eternity, he corrected himself. Homer at the typewriter, war correspondent, the idea amused him. In school they were reading the Iliad when he left. He had not had a book in his hands since Paris. Marga had books. Marga. His skin started to tingle, the blood seemed to gather in the lower part of his body and to engulf him.

"How do you like my new dress?" Maria asked as she sat down by him. He had not noticed that she had come back. He bent over her and kissed her on the neck.

"Do I smell good?" she asked. "I snitched Dolf's soap."

He did not answer, but pulled her back and kissed her again. She struggled to get up. "What are you doing?" she said breathlessly.

"Not a thing," he said. "Don't be frightened." He put his hands around her small breasts. Maria started to cry.

"You mustn't do that," she sobbed and flung her arms around his neck.

"I won't harm you. Don't cry, Maria."

"I'm not crying," she whispered.

He moved his hands over her thin body. Now he knew how to. She pressed herself against him. He put his hands under her dress.

"Don't, don't," she implored.

"I won't do anything to you, you don't want me to do. Don't be afraid." He lay very quiet now, tried to breathe regularly.

"I want to, but it isn't right," she whispered.

"Many things aren't right," he said. For some time they didn't move as Hans was thinking how wrong everything was. Here under the wide, clear heavens it all showed so plainly. How miserable Maria's life was. Such a skinny, lonely girl, with big, hungry eyes. Hungry she was, hungry for everything. How much love she needed, and care and understanding. . . .

Tomorrow he was going to give his first German lesson. And the money he was going to make would be spent on the children instead of on himself. After all, it wouldn't be so bad to keep living on the field. Any day now Aart would come to the realization that he was fighting a useless battle. Then he, Hans, would get his chance. In the future, maybe, he would be able to provide for all of them.

"Come here, little goose," he said, drawing Maria against him. "And don't cry, or I'll spank your bottom."

7

MARIA AND BERTHE trudged back and forth between the well and the field. Children, performing the work of adults, looking so forlorn, so cast off, as if they carried the wrath of all mankind on their shoulders.

Hans was helping Rainer with the sprinkling, Aart was planting potatoes further on, and Lies, at the well, filled the buckets. Little Dolf and Pierre were sitting next to her under a small tent she had rigged up for them and over which she poured water at regular intervals in order to keep them cool. Lies didn't speak at all, because, God help her, she was pregnant once more. Besides, she felt Pierre's presence under the sailcloth; now and then she caught sight of the little wooden leg, saw it moving along the ground as Pierre crawled around while playing. He still couldn't manage his artificial limb; he couldn't get around very well and when he wanted to get up he had to be helped. But the few times when he did manage it all by himself, he glowed with satisfaction.

Yes, Lies had become very quiet. Aart missed her exuberant laughter. Because of that he sometimes put his arm around her shoulder, even during the day, though showing his affection didn't come easy with him.

"We would have done better to leave them behind," she once said. "They are really not so well off with us. And we don't get any pleasure from them."

He let his arm drop silently and went to work again.

One afternoon when the sun was beating down so fiercely that the children remembered Oran, and talked about it, Luba came stepping into the garden. A strange Luba, the children thought, neat as a pin in an Arabian dress and slippers and with two stiff tails along her ears. And with "such black eyes" as Berthe said later, opening her

73

pale blue ones wide, trying to show just how Luba's eyes looked.

Luba had made up her mind to pay this visit. Why had she come? . . . Inborn honesty? Formerly acquired social manners? Loneliness? Manus now left her alone until late in the night, being gruff and uncommunicative when he returned, handling her roughly before he went to sleep. He frightened her with his restlessness. Now he always took care that the door was locked. And sometimes in the middle of the night, he would get up, go on tiptoe to the door and jerk it open suddenly. He no longer took her along to the Kasbah, but brought her food. In a way he was kind to her. But was it kindness, what he did to her and asked her to do? It couldn't be; or could it? She brooded about it with lips tight and intense eyes, which seemed to grow bigger daily.

But on the field she spoke enthusiastically about all the good things she got to eat so that everyone's mouth watered. When she had told all, Berthe in turn related what had happened to them. They put their arms around each other and suddenly they were very close again. They sat near the house, played who could hold his breath the longest, till they got blue in the face, rattled off: "*Vingt-et-un, vingt-deux, trois, quatre, cinq.* You are cheating, you are cheating, you must say the complete numbers."

But then a disagreeable incident occurred. When Luba crawled under the canvas, where the small boys were, to play with Dolf, she saw Pierre's wooden leg. She burst into tears, pressed Dolf closely against her and cradled him back and forth, as she cried spasmodically. They all stood around and did not know what to do. Pierre, more confused than the others, shook with nervousness, even his lips were white.

Maria too started to cry, but Hans pinched her arm.

It was the first time that anyone had reacted so violently to Pierre's injury. When Maria and Berthe saw the boy after Lies had fetched him from the hospital, they had started to giggle nervously. Hans, being told by Maria what had happened, had indulged in swearing and cursing and had avoided Pierre for many days. Rainer had first looked for Aart's reaction and went back to the field as fast as he could. Aart's jaws were closed so stiffly that his face seemed a mask. "Why didn't you tell me?" he asked Lies. "I couldn't," said Lies, greenish-pale through her tanned skin. "I simply couldn't." And Aart had lifted the child carefully, carefully, out of the little cart, and taking long wearisome steps, he had carried him into the house.

Pierre himself was contented getting everybody's attention. First from the sisters and the doctor, then from Aart, Lies and the children. When the interest in him waned, he felt a longing for the hospital, the nice sisters, the clean bed. But he was a well-mannered little fellow and too polite to show it.

In the evening, before he went to sleep, he thought that he would get his leg back through a miracle. What this miracle might be he did not know and here his imagination gave out, but then there was another dream picture. The doctor could do it. He had taken it away, and now he was curing the leg and would put it on again. Well, that leg had then become a wonderleg. He won all the races with it. He won over Hans. He pursued the dog that had bitten him, caught, and kicked it until it was all flat, like the rabbit on the road that had been run over by a car. Then there was a parade, like the time of the inauguration of the new Pasha. Men in white burnouses or gold-and-red uniforms, on white horses that reared and stepped sideways; flags and banners. The horse of the Pasha got out of control. The Pasha, who was terribly strong, awfully strong, could not hold it. The people yelled. The horse started to run away down the Boulevard Pasteur, the hooves clattered, sparks sprang from the concrete. Then he, Pierre, jumped forward. Now he suddenly had a wooden leg again—that was strange. He grasped the horse's reins, let himself be dragged along for some distance and saved the Pasha.

In the morning when he woke up, he wanted right away to crawl from the mattress, but then there was that short feeling as he called it, and the whole misery would weigh him down. Those were moments filled with anguish and an urge to shriek out and to beat his fist against the wall in a fit of anger, just as at the time when he came out of the anaesthesia and the sister told him that they had taken away his leg. Yes, just like then. With the bustle of everybody's getting up and the breakfast with the other children his somber mood disappeared. Everybody was nicer to him than before. The Consul's wife brought him soup and meat. Berthe had gathered shells for him and Rainer had made him a little cart with high wheels along the sides, so that he could maneuver it with his hands. For Hans and Maria, however, he felt some fear. Pierre did not feel at ease when they came to see him. He did not understand, of course, that Hans and Maria, more sensitive than the others, suffered personally from his tragedy. Hans included the mishap in his resenting of Aart's undertaking, the life that they led generally, the war. When he came to sit next to Pierre, because pity and a sense of duty drove him to it, he did not know how to behave. He forced himself to appear "as usual," but the small boy felt, behind everything he said and did, the forced action. *"Bonjour, mon petit bonhomme,"* Hans would say, for instance, "how is life treating you today? Did you fight any important battles?" Pierre would look at him, smile somewhat embarrassed. "You're a lucky fellow," Hans would continue, "sitting here so nicely in the shade." At the same time Hans hated himself for his artificial jocularity.

"I am playing soldier," Pierre would help him in his friendly way. "This is the trench and there where little Dolf is sitting is the fortress. He is a paratrooper, you understand. I have nobody else," he excused himself for his lack of playmates. The little fellow tried to put Hans at ease, tried to hold him with lively conversation. Then Hans would get down on his knees, fire an imaginary machine gun, cursing inwardly as he watched the small boy crawling around, moving the stump of his leg awkwardly. "Now I have got to get to work again," he would say after a few moments. "Give the enemy hell!" And Pierre would suddenly sit very quiet, looking up at him, not knowing what to say.

Maria put herself in Pierre's place. She imagined that it had happened to her and during the night her mattress would be moist with tears shed out of pity for herself and the small boy.

She had an irrepressible curiosity about the operation and the novelty of the loss of a leg. How did it feel to lack a leg? She came to sit with Pierre, tried to put all the warmth and pity she felt into her eyes. Pierre, made restless by her staring, squirmed back and forth, looked past her into the garden, avoided her glance.

"What is the matter?" she would ask. "Does it hurt?"

"No," Pierre would say dully.

"Sure not?"

Pierre shook his head.

"Did it hurt?"

"No." '

"I mean at the time."

"No," said Pierre, stubborn now and irritated.

"Not afterwards either?"

He shrugged his shoulders and, giving in under her steady glance, he admitted, "a little bit."

"Did you see the leg afterwards?" she asked, but then she was ashamed of her question, which she had not been able to hold back and blushing furiously, she said, "Don't be unhappy, you know that Maria will always stay with you and help you." Then she ran away and Pierre remained behind, perplexed and upset.

After Luba had said goodbye and left, Aart said to Lies, "I am going to get the child back here."

"After all this time?" asked Lies mockingly, "the man will think that we are nuts."

"You are so damned naïve."

"I understand more than you think I do," she said, insulted.

He looked at her searchingly, penetratingly, until the haughty expression disappeared from her face and was replaced by one of honest doubt, and slowly, an expression of understanding.

"Jees! Aart," she said helplessly, stretching one of her hands out towards him, "you don't think . . . ?"

"I don't think anything," he snarled. "I'm going to fetch her back. She belongs with us. That's all."

"Oh, Aart," Lies wailed; hidden shame and thinly veiled lust appeared in her eyes. Then she gave him a push, as she snapped bitingly, "Oh, go on, you, you get the craziest ideas. Manus was such a nice man."

"Did I say anything?" Aart asked threateningly.

"Men always have such thoughts," she said. Then after a moment, "Why didn't you get her back right away then? You're a fine mess!"

"I have waited," said Aart, concealing his anger, "I have waited until you would do it. You are the mother here."

"You said it," said Lies sarcastically.

He wanted to answer, but he held his breath for awhile, looking at her searchingly, "What do you mean?"

"That," she said gruffly.

"You don't mean to tell me . . . ?"

"Why, you don't mean to tell me?" That he should ask it in this manner, she could not bear.

He laid his dirty, rough hand on her neck, and rubbed his thumb over her skin.

"How is that possible?" he asked, beaten. "I don't understand."

"I don't understand," she mimicked him. "If I had a hundred francs, it wouldn't have happened. Do you get me?" Tears stood in her eyes.

"Lies . . ." he started hesitatingly.

"Yes?"

"Has that . . . did it happen . . . at the time . . . that evening after Pierre came home . . . when I was drunk?"

She shrugged her shoulders, pressed her face against his arm. Then she jumped backwards, gave him a slap on the back. "Come on, boy, what the hell, the more the merrier." She laughed uproariously, bent over the well and let the pail fall down with a plop.

That evening Aart put on a clean shirt and went to look for Manus' beach cabin. He followed Berthe's confused directions; she had explained to him with an important expression, stumbling over her words, where it could be found. Over the dunes and along the beach.

The moon hung in the sky, low, orange and round, like a Chinese lantern above a garden party. Caravans of human beings loaded like animals passed him, going in the other direction.

If I had been born an Arab, he thought, life would have been less complicated. He put himself in the place of an Arab peasant who had just passed, and whose following train of women and children now shuffled by. Small demands and primitive thoughts. He knew that it was impossible, though he still did not want to admit it. His youth, the complications of an education that went straight against his character and aptitude, prevented it. When he had come to that point, he was seized by fury, hatred for society, hatred that confused his thoughts. Hatred for the stupidity in his country, the short-sightedness, the sanctimoniousness, the lukewarmness, the division, the spasmodic clinging to antiquated systems, to the past. All the attempts at self-preservation of a toothless, blubbering monster, that could not resign itself to dying. That stretched out its withered tentacles and with the iron grip of a fleshless skeleton tried to crush that which would have hastened its death. That is the way he saw it. He was not a fighter and he had built his trailer and had left. Away, away, away. He could bear it better detached from his own soil, wandering in his own trailer-island over alien soil.

What he had missed himself he wanted to give to his children and to the poor things that he had picked up along the way, victims of a rotten society. Victims of those who had their mouths filled with big words: Build a better world for youth. . . . The future belongs to youth. . . . The responsibility, that we owe to those who come after us. Those words were the banner that covered the freight, he thought. Under this banner the greatest crimes were committed against them, against youth, against their future. Neutrality, diplomatic relations, commercial treaties, cartels, monopolies—such was the load they carried. Away, away, away from it all.

He would prove to the children that it could be different. Next year they would no longer need to work; they would grow up healthy, independent individuals who had forgotten the past. He would prove it to little Dolf and the child that would be born in eight months.

In tempo with his excited thoughts he had accelerated his steps. He was now suddenly aware that he had already passed the first beach cabins. He turned back to where, according to Berthe's description, Manus' cabin ought to be. And to end his meditations, came the self-reproach that he had left the child to Lies' indecision, that the child had become the victim of his own stubbornness and indifference. He clenched his fists in his trousers pockets. "Son of a bitch," he said half aloud. The epithet was directed against both himself and Manus.

Aart stood looking helplessly at the cabins. He had already walked back and forth for several minutes, looking for the Hollander's cabin, but he could not be sure which it was.

He decided to call out. "Manus . . . Luba . . . !" It sounded funny in the silence and he felt ridiculous, as if he were calling to a passerby who didn't hear him and continued on his way. He knocked at several doors, but all remained closed. He plainly heard the rushing of the waves and behind him on the boulevard the hooves of the donkeys and the cries of the Berber women. Aart sat down on one of the small flights of steps and rolled a cigarette; he sat smoking for awhile, looking over the moonlit sea. It would be a good idea to live here, he thought. If the field failed. . . . But that supposition he suppressed.

To the right, out of the dark, a figure appeared, slowly plowing along through loose sand. He recognized Hans. What was the boy doing here?

"Eh, Aart!" said Hans surprised.

"Hello," answered Aart, "are you looking for somebody?"

Hans hesitated for a moment. "Luba," he said. He sat down next to Aart.

"Cigarette?" Aart offered.

"Me?" Hans asked astonished.

"You don't smoke yet, that's right," said Aart absentmindedly. "What do you want with Luba?"

A direct question from Aart was so unusual that Hans was put off for a moment.

"Well . . ." he said, "I thought it would be best for Luba to come back to the field."

"So, that's what you thought?" Aart asked sharply.

"Yes," said Hans, "that's what I thought."

"So, that's what you thought, eh?"

"Yes," said Hans, getting angry.

"And why, may I ask?"

Aart spoke sarcastically, but Hans noticed the unsureness in his voice.

"Just because," he said airily. "Give me a cigarette anyway."

Aart spread the tobacco over the small piece of paper and licked along the gummed border. They sat smoking silently, Hans ineptly with short drags and awkward gestures.

"You always know everything," Aart said sarcastically. "Perhaps then you know which cabin that fellow lives in?"

"No, do you?"

Aart did not answer. He rolled a fresh cigarette.

"Luba looked like hell, didn't you think so?" Hans began again.

"Did you think so?"

"Yes, didn't you?" Hell, what nonsense, thought Hans. Why couldn't Aart ever speak to him as one man to another? Here they were playing hide and seek and time was passing. Though he had

put the thought of Luba aside for a long time he was now suddenly
worried and wanted to do something about it immediately; as if
after all these weeks something might have happened to her only
now, at the very moment that he had recognized the possibility and
as if he could still save her from the things that in fact had already
happened.

After Luba had left that afternoon, a small slight figure, walking
away through the hedge to the road, hesitatingly but without looking around, he had impatiently awaited the end of the working day,
because when he saw Luba, Marga's words had jumped to the fore
in his thoughts like a devil from his little box. He had kept the cover
closed, he knew now, but the devil had wanted to get out and was
now grinning at him in all his vile-colored ugliness. The dirty, rotten
truth, he thought. Now he had come here to do something—yes, do
something—and he was held up by this silly conversation with Aart.
Aart, who of course had the same aim, but did not want to
admit it.

When Hans got up to look at the beach cabins from a distance,
Aart called mockingly, "Well, Doctor Watson, what do you think?"
Imagine being so mixed up inside, thought Hans, so tied in a knot.
He started banging on doors, tried to open them.

He had wandered some way off, when he heard voices, and
looking around, he saw two men standing beside Aart. Hans walked
towards them, but when he recognized the leggings and the shiny
uniform buttons, he pressed close to the side wall of one of the
cabins. Policemen still called up a reaction of self-preservation in
him. He still felt the anxiety of a traveller without a passport and
he instinctively knew why they were here. They had been sent to
arrest Manus. But the Hollander had apparently got wind of it
and had disappeared.

The conversation between Aart and the two men sounded inimical
and became louder every minute. Hans slunk along the wall of the
small building and looked round the corner. They stood facing Aart,
who was still sitting on the steps. One of the two tried to seize Aart's

arm, but Aart pushed him back with force. *"Ne me touche pas,"* he said with concealed anger.

The other Arab, somewhat more polite than the first, said:

"Bgiti dji m'aya?"

"I wouldn't think of it," said Aart. "Why should I go with you?"

"Aji, aji!" cried the first one now. He was a rough fellow, and in the moonlight Hans saw his beard and a shining medal. *"Aji, aji,* we have orders to arrest you, we have orders to arrest you."

"Where is the girl?" the other broke in. "Where is the child?"

"Fools," said Aart, "you have got the wrong man. Let me go!" he then roared furiously at the Moor, who again took hold of his arm. He kicked him in the shin. "Let me go, dog."

The Arab went raving mad and broke forth in a flood of invective, of which Hans did not know the meaning. But the other admonished him to remain calm. He now took the initiative.

With a triumphant expression on his face, like a magician who produced a rabbit out of his hat, and after a proper moment of silence, he asked, "Who are you? Where do you come from? Where is your land?"

Aart looked from one to the other. He knew he would have to give up in the face of their stupid determination to carry out their orders. They had been sent to arrest a Hollander and, with the absence of Manus, Aart would serve the purpose. There was a look of bitter resignation in Aart's eyes, but also of hatred, a hatred that encompassed everything, everything that had been, was now, and was still to come.

His previous arrest in Oran had made him wise. These Arabs wore uniforms and carried rubber truncheons; they had been given power, a small amount of power, for all that had been taken away from them during centuries. The traditional red fez covered their heads and underneath it they were no wiser than their brothers, who had never learned anything but a few rules from the Koran.

Aart looked at them and did not answer. He was probably weighing his chances of escape and perhaps he thought about the story he had heard of an event the whole city had laughed about, the arrest of the British admiral who, plunged in admiration of the horses of the Pasha's retinue, had stepped down from the sidewalk; an arrest symbolic of the lack of discrimination of the Moorish police, as the British Consul had said, and against which agreement the Spanish Governor had maintained that an admiral can be recognized only by the gold on his coat.

There was a moment of silence, a laden, intense silence in which the sea could be heard and the parade of the little donkeys on the boulevard.

Again the policeman with the beard put his hand on Aart and again Aart kicked him away. Then as if by a pre-arranged signal the Moors produced their truncheons.

"I am somebody else. You are looking for somebody else," said Aart hoarsely, and then he was up in one jump. Like an animal that does not know its strength after having long been confined, he sprang upon the men. It was so unexpected, that they both fell back, barely keeping their balance. It was a struggle of bodies, choked cries, and dull thuds of sticks. Hans, for a second dazed by Aart's violence, came out and threw himself against the Moors. But when Aart saw him, he shouted: "Beat it, get away, get away, the Consul!"

It did not take long. Aart, semi-conscious from the blows on his head, was dragged away, and Hans, wildly indignant, the bitter taste of injustice in his mouth, ran over the dunes. His feet sank in the soft sand, he grasped for ground to support himself. "*Schweine*," he said half weeping. "*Schweine*."

It was only after a few minutes that he realized that he did not know where to find the Consul at such a time of night. Still he ran to the consulate. Perhaps he would find the *shous* there.

8

THE CONSUL was looking out into the garden. He could not see much of it because the window was small and barred. What he saw gave him a certain amount of satisfaction—the little flower bed with a few discolored tulips, painfully kept alive by the gardener, and half-hidden behind a laurel bush, the Dutch flag, gently waving in the morning breeze. Further away, near the fence, he saw the brightly white *djellabah* of the *shous*. He knew that visitors were waiting on the verandah but he did not feel inclined to receive them. He was chewing his cigar and listening disdainfully to his lady assistant who was thinking out loud. Opened up before him, as always, lay the three cashbooks, the register of his own possessions, that of the Government and that of the possessions of the Catholic Church Community.

When Zus van Lennep was excited she spoke Dutch less distinctly than she usually did for the Consul. He had trouble with the language. At home they talked French, and for years he had not been back to Holland. "I have unlearned it," he used to say. "I was living here when the Place de la France was still a desert and in the evening, when we went calling, we carried a lantern and my wife rode on a mule to the Souk. Those were the days." The Consul preferred the old times, the new ones caused him too many headaches. Since the war had broken out, and every day saw new refugees waiting on the verandah, he hid behind a mask of unwillingness. "I did not ask for this," he said. "I don't have to do it, that is not my job." And the Dutch subjects walked bewildered out of the gate, as the polite *shous* waved after them.

"You are not listening," Zus admonished him. "I said that if those people can prove that they are refugees they can claim a decent

85

allowance and the liberty of doing what they please with their money. Proof that they are refugees, money at their disposal," she repeated with emphasis.

"You are a communist," said the Consul mildly, "and who is ever able to prove that he is a refugee?"

"Better a communist than a philanthropist," said Zus. But that escaped the Consul.

She shrugged her shoulders and continued with the letter she was typing. She typed slowly, letter by letter, because she had never been taught how. A consular job was a position of standing; intelligence and even technical skill on the typewriter were minor requisites. But the ticking irritated the Consul; he often waited for the down beat of the next letter and sometimes it would go on like a tune through his head: tedum-tum . . . tum—tum—tum—tedum. . . .

"Go and see who is sitting outside," he asked.

"You call the *shous*," she said, "I have no time now." The Consul pressed the button under his desk and a moment later he saw the guard shuffle towards the house, along the tulip bed, and past the Dutch flag, which he saluted elaborately.

The first visitor was a Dutch painter, to whom the wife of the Consul had given a commission, a panel above the fireplace in the new room that they were building to enlarge the house. With the invasion of Holland they had stopped work on it, not because of lack of funds, thank God, no, but as Mrs. van Balekom said, it would have been bad taste to indulge in pleasure while the Dutch people were suffering. For months the Consul had to look at mounds of cement and unfinished walls. After the first excitement had let down somewhat, the family had dropped their scruples and the masons had resumed their work. The painter had brought some sketches along, which the Consul spread over the cashbooks. It had to be a sala-mander. Why, the Consul had forgotten, but it meant something or other. He would rather have had a Biblical scene but had given up the thought when his wife drew his attention to the complications that might spring from it. In time they would have to give a reception for the new Arab authorities.

After the painter had left, the Consul said: "A nice boy; he has never asked me for money."

"What has not happened can still happen," said his secretary. "And I don't like his wife."

"You're jealous," said the Consul teasing, brushing the ashes from his vest.

She turned around to give him an answer, but the *shous* admitted the next caller and she took up her typing again. She did not even bother to listen; it was the daily routine. She could dream these interviews. Friendly refusal on the part of the Consul, pleadings by the compatriot. Finally Mr. van Balekom would give in, as he always did, and he would disappear into the little side room where the safe stood. Then there was always an extra dish of light political discussion, as if the visitor wanted to display his patriotism and wanted to give assurance to the Consul that good money wasn't spent on disloyal people.

"They won't get the Hollanders down," said the visitor.

"*Pas de chance*," said the Consul. "Certainly not. Never, never."

"Have you heard anything new?"

"Nothing. Have you?"

"No, not since the last letter. You know, from my mother."

"Oh yes, that's right; nothing else, eh?" The Consul looked longingly at his cashbook. "Yes, yes," he said.

"They say that people here are continually disappearing, the Gestapo working close together with the Spaniards," said the visitor. Do ask the Consul, the refugees had begged him on the café terrace. He looked somewhat doubtfully into Mr. van Balekom's face.

"You must not believe that, Mr. Wagenaar; that's gossip. No, no. People are all in . . . in . . ."

"Infected," Zus van Lennep suggested.

"Yes, infected," said the Consul. "People don't have enough to do," he added with a glance at his cashbooks. "Gossip, that's all. Why would the Spaniards give away people? And the Gestapo! Why, Sir?" The visitor, somewhat abashed now, made preparations to go. "Well, several people have already disappeared, a German journalist and a Hungarian. They have been dragged off to Tetuan or to Algeciras."

"I don't believe it," said the Consul, angry now.

"Did you read what they are doing to the Jews in Holland?" asked the visitor, who wanted to get to a safer subject.

"Yes, yes," said the Consul. "It's sad. A hopeless affair. That's the way it is. The good along with the bad."

"The good must suffer with the bad," Zus van Lennep interrupted sarcastically. "Then it does not look so rosy for the good Christians either."

But in the meantime the Consul had pressed the bell under his desk and the *shous* came in with a trumped-up errand.

"Listen, Zus," said Mr. van Balekom after the visitor had left, "You mustn't always . . . mustn't . . . the people might, *il faut être . . . on se. . . .*"

"All right, all right," she said, "I'll shut up." She thought again about going to the British Consul to apply for work with the Red Cross or something of the kind. She would have to decide soon.

It was a relief to the Consul when he saw his wife enter the gate. Though she could not see him she waved in the direction of the window.

"Well," she said, coming in, "any news?"

"News?" asked the Consul. He looked at his three cashbooks and then at the portrait of Queen Wilhelmina facing him on the wall. "News? No, not that I know of."

"But darling," she looked at him reproachfully.

"Yes, of course, I have been so busy," mumbled the Consul. He unhooked the telephone and spoke in Spanish while his wife listened eagerly.

"They got him, eh?" she said when he had rung off. She sat down in the wicker chair opposite the desk and drew off her gloves.

"Yes," said the Consul, "offered resistance at that. But the child isn't there."

"Isn't there? Good heavens, where is she?"

He shrugged his shoulders. "They tried to get it out of him, but he refused to speak. He wants to see me, the Dutch Consul."

There was a moment of silence. Zus had turned around in her chair and said, "That poor lamb."

"Are you going to see him?" asked Mevrouw.

"Me? *Jamais! Ce, ce . . . salaud, ce. . . .*" The Consul looked for a better term of invective, but his wife gave him a warning glance. "Darling," she said.

"That poor lamb," Zus repeated.

"They will get it out of him," said the Consul. "The girl will be found. Besides," he continued, suddenly calming down, "that child is Polish. After all, I can't look after the whole town."

"Eh darling," said Mevrouw van Balekom reproachfully, "that sounds very strange coming from you."

The Consul, embarrassed, brushed the ashes from his vest, and closed the cashbooks.

"Listen," he said, "I am fed up with that whole family. I wonder why I . . ." He turned to Zus, "We must write again to Lisbon, remind me of it. They must have news from London by this time. That family must be taken over by Lisbon or by Suriname or by the Indies." He made a vague gesture toward the portrait of the Queen.

"One of the boys is outside waiting right now," said Mevrouw van Balekom. "That Hans. He has probably come for the allowance, instead of Lies."

"Let him in," said the Consul jovially. "Let him in; the money is ready for him."

His wife went around the desk and pressed a kiss upon his cranium.

Hans saw no reason to wait any longer with his story. Since the night before, when the *shous* had refused to give him the Consul's private address, more than twelve hours had passed. An endless night. He had told Lies white lies which she had immediately detected and she had got the truth out of him. And now he had been waiting over two hours—others had been called in before him. His impatience and anger were at the bursting point.

The shock and the confusion which his story aroused gave him at least some relief. The Consul, however, did not immediately reach for the telephone. It was a painful complication, and as he asked Hans for the particulars, his diplomatic brain sought for an easy solution. Finally, after covert urging from his wife, he telephoned the Spanish authorities. During the conversation his face became more serious and his confusion was painful to see.

"Well," he said after it was over.

"Well, what?" asked Mrs. van Balekom.

"He has resisted the police. Attacked the guard. They can't release him."

"They can't release him? But that is the limit," Zus van Lennep shouted indignantly. "First they arrest the wrong man and when the poor devil protests . . ."

"But, Zus," Mevrouw interrupted.

The Consul looked at the picture of the Queen. "We can't do much. I'll try. . . ."

He thought of the "mañana, mañana" of the Spanish authorities, the delay of measures and decisions, with which they tried to gain time until the general confusion, caused by the taking over of the government, should diminish. With the inauguration of their regime in the city the Spaniards had cleaned ship, so thoroughly, however, that the vessel threatened to founder. The Consul liked that kind of figure of speech. That was the way things stood. And the pressure of the Germans, which caused panic among the refugees and urged the fascist elements to terrorize, necessitated severe police measures. Once a man was in prison. . . . The Consul toyed with the cord of the telephone, looked longingly at the closed books on his desk. The policy of watch and wait of the English and Americans did not make it any easier for the diplomats of smaller countries. They had no power at all, thought the Consul. Resistance to the police, *mon Dieu*. He could not ask for any favors for such things . . . *des bagatelles* . . . there were more important problems. The Consul laid one hand upon the cashbook of the Church community.

9

THEY CONTINUED working in the field as if Aart were still there. Wearisome! The earth absorbed their labor and did not produce. In the neighboring fields, sprinkling had ceased. There everything showed a young and fresh growth.

Again the Arabs came to watch, hesitating somewhat at a distance, fascinated by the stubborn persistence, the slaving of Lies and the children under the burning sun. Weekdays, Sundays, endless days. The marionette-like movements of Lies at the well, the tripping of the girls back and forth on the little path, continually stumbling over their own feet; and the boys, ceaselessly emptying their watering cans over the parched earth.

The women of the village stood motionless in their wide white haiks, and called a greeting more formal than the usual: *"Labas?"*

"Allah isa 'ad shabek!" they called out.

They had heard what had happened. Wise through experience they knew that Aart would have to wait a long time for a hearing. They had of course informed themselves why Aart had been arrested but it had made little impression on them—mistakes occurred daily. What they found more astonishing was the fact that they had wanted to arrest Manus. If the Spaniards followed such precepts, there would soon be no more room in the prison, they giggled. Also Manus' escaping in time struck them as funny. Driven by a healthy curiosity they had come to the field. But nobody came over to talk to them.

Lies had changed. She waved absentmindedly and paid no further attention to them. Lies didn't care about anything now. Her spirit closed to the outside world, her body a shrine in which her child was growing. For the first time since her marriage to Aart she felt an inner peace, to which she submitted without asking how or why.

She left everything to Hans, the care of the children as well as the supervision of the work. They all looked on him now as Aart's substitute. Even Rainer followed his leadership, though he plagued Hans with the questions, "Can't we do something for Aart? Is there no way to get him out of prison?" Yes, Rainer felt guilty because of his helplessness; he labored unceasingly.

Hans, with the money he was earning now and with the daily allowance from the Consul, bought food. He went to the market at six o'clock in the morning before other people made their purchases, and though the prices were rising, he was able to buy enough food to still the children's first hunger. Little Dolf got milk and on several occasions Pierre had an egg. The girls were allowed to beat it up for him, and while he ate it with a spoon, the children stood around him as if they were witnessing a miracle.

But Hans was brooding. Could he take advantage of the opportunity that was offered him? Could he use the time that Aart was spending in prison to move Lies and the children to the city? He had seen how his father acted without scruple when he wanted to achieve his aim. He had told him that if the cause was worth it, conscientious scruples and ethical considerations were a curse.

Hans tried to draw an opinion. He wanted to make them share some of the responsibility. He didn't get anywhere, however, for they were by this time so accustomed to the life in the field that an alternative never occurred to them.

He first went to Pierre. The small boy was getting fatter partly from the better food but more because he sat idly all day. In the morning, as soon as he had been installed under the protecting sailcloth, he put the wooden leg beside him and would then sit with his other leg and the stump crossed underneath him or would crawl around a bit. The children teased him goodhumoredly about his weight, because they didn't know what else to say to him.

In answer to Hans' question, Pierre blew up his cheeks, thumped his fists on his stomach and said, "I'm a Japanese wrestler." In order to hide his embarrassment he would now indulge in clownish jokes and gestures.

"*Un lutteur japonais, hein?*"

Pierre nodded his head, showed the horizontal fold in his stomach, and laughed uproariously. He grabbed for something behind him and produced a soiled illustration from a calendar with a German inscription underneath it.

"*Haisha le m'a donné,*" said Pierre proudly. "Interesting, isn't it?"

"Yes," said Hans, and then in a confidential tone, "You mustn't take off your seven-league boot. Come, let me help you." And attaching the wooden stick to the stump of Pierre's leg, he said, "And now get going, walk around a bit."

"It is too tight," Pierre protested.

"I bet it is," said Hans, "but you'll get used to it, see. And when you go to school in a few months from now you'll be able to walk like a giant. Because this is your seven-league boot, didn't you know?"

Pierre allowed himself to be helped and looked at Hans with the wise eyes of a child who has learned to submit to the inevitable.

"You want to go to school, don't you?"

Pierre nodded absentmindedly and he seemed to have come to a decision. "Listen," he said, and whispered into Hans' ear: "Dolf, *il m'ennuie terriblement,* he cries so much and he does not have any diaper on and he smells."

There was so much to take care of, so much to change in their lives. Hans did not want to make irrevocable decisions; this way of life was only temporary, he thought. Why make a fuss when they would be leaving within a short time anyhow? He must ask Berthe to bathe little Dolf and to wash his diapers, because Lies was unapproachable. And Maria reacted to every gesture, every word like a . . . he looked for a comparison . . . like an alarm clock. That was it. The slightest contact produced an outburst, which made you blindly grab for some way to make her shut up. How could such a skinny, underfed body bear such tension? When he held her in his arms in the evening she trembled like a spring that was about to unwind and talked excitedly without rhyme or reason until he started to caress her; and then she invariably burst into tears, cried fretfully like a child with her hands over her eyes, or like a woman with dry sobs, her head against his shoulder.

"What is the matter?" he would ask. "Do you want to go away from the field? Shall we move to the city?" She would shake her head because she did not know what she wanted.

"Do you want us not to meet any more in the evening?"

She lifted her head and looked at him as if she were terribly frightened, her eyes wide open. Then she threw her arms around him, mumbling, "Don't leave me alone, don't leave me."

He knew that making love to her was wrong, increased the tension in her. Still he meant to go no further; she was only fourteen years old; that he must not forget although he was tempted to.

He approached Rainer too, acting as if he valued the boy's opinion highly. "What do you think, shall we move to the city?"

Rainer was shocked at the idea. *"Aber das wäre ja doch die gröszte Unverschämtheit Aart gegenüber!"* He defended his way of looking at it with the most violent expressions: Shamelessness, lack of respect, acting behind Aart's back, the gratitude they owed him. Hans listened quietly to him, and then elaborated on his point of view. "It is senseless, Rainer. That you must have realized long ago. Look at that field. Monk's work. Here working the land is based on family tradition. The secret of the soil is a legacy. We do not know it and nobody will ever tell us. In the meantime it is wrong to expose Berthe and Maria any longer to this beastly life. Maria is completely exhausted. And look at Berthe."

Rainer declared that he had nothing to say about it. It was Aart's land, and the decision, if any had to be made, would have to wait for Aart's return.

"But that may not be for weeks! He has resisted the police; the affair has still to be settled in court. There is even a possibility that he may be convicted."

Rainer, upset over this new point of view, did not know what to answer. He sought refuge in work, intensifying his efforts, carpentering during the evening hours, a sand trough for little Dolf, a set of crutches for Pierre; and finally after lengthy calculations he fiddled with the motor of the car until it worked. It was characteristic of him that he wrote a letter to Aart in prison. He wanted to haul loads of manure in the car and asked for permission to change the chassis in order to do it. He waited for two weeks for an answer and then he went with the same question to Lies. "Go and ask Hans," she said indifferently. After some struggle within himself he went to Hans: "Do you want to help me?" This was a compromise with his pride.

Hans was happy because of Rainer's initiative and because getting manure to the Arabs should be profitable. Rainer found satisfaction in the dirty work. It was his idea, his enterprise, and he did not realize that he had humbled himself in the eyes of the Arabs. In the morning at six he would drive away, behind him the rattling bed he had built on top of the chassis. He fetched the ordure of the city from steady clients and delivered it before eight o'clock at the fields. This little business completely engrossed him. It gave him self-respect, even a certain importance. With a pencil stub he entered his receipts. The little cashbook in his back pocket was a possession, and sometimes without knowing he did it, put his hand upon it. He kept none of the money for himself. He accounted for every centime to Hans.

Hans now gave lessons three times a week to the young Arab. At the beginning he felt positively ashamed over the direction of his thought during that first evening. Overwrought nonsense, he called the symbolic significance he had given to the earthen mug. But in spite of himself he remained on guard.

Jilali ben Mohammed was a good, serious pupil. And sensitive too. During his first lesson he had known how to put Hans at ease. He had even suggested how to go about giving the lessons.

"Let's talk," he had said. And thus they had soon acquired a great skill in the game of questions and answers. As Sidi Jilali's German vocabulary increased, Hans got more pleasure out of their conversations. Later, because it was so noisy in the house with the curious little sisters, Jilali proposed that they continue their lessons outdoors. They wandered through the streets, sat in front of Moorish tea houses and Hans got acquainted with the Kasbah. Ptetty soon he learned to distinguish the streets by their earmarks, a pump, a small shop on a corner, a doorway with particularly beautiful carving. He was really sorry when the hour was over. But he never stretched it out, not only because Maria was waiting for him at the hill, but also, as he convinced himself, because this was a business arrangement. Jilali was always discreet in his questions, he never became personal, though his eyes, always restless, would look for more information in Hans' face than he got out of the answers. Hans talked to him about Germany, of the school system, of life in the city where he had lived and of the part youth played in "the new order." Jilali spoke of his student days in Marrakech, his youth in Rabat, his plans for the future. Sometimes Hans laughed inwardly. He remembered the social game that had amused him when he was a child. There were little cards with questions and others with answers. For every question there was an answer, but both were thoroughly shuffled before the game started. What would happen if he forgot to shuffle the cards and he gave the correct answers? He had once sorted the cards for curiosity's sake—every child who owned such a box of cards did—and this required some patience but was satisfactory in the end. Now he did not need to look for the corresponding cards. He had them right there. Sometimes, however, he was so impersonal in his communications that he asked himself whether he still knew the truth. He could not accept his own hypocritical cleverness.

One evening they had climbed to the top of the Kasbah. Here on the highest point was the most peaceful spot in the whole town, a square paved with round uneven stones, a small palm tree in a corner; all around the square were ancient Moorish houses, the museum of Arab culture and the prison. At the eastern side an old archway led to a small terrace with a magnificent view of the Strait of Gibraltar, the harbors; and, when it was clear, of the southern coast of Spain.

There stood two ancient cannons, fired on holidays, by which, as the story had it, an Arab soldier always was either being wounded or killed. In the blue light of dusk the little square had a fairylike and mysterious beauty. It was then that Hans came to the unpleasant realization that he was standing in front of the jail. But Jilali sitting on his haunches near the tree, his hands crossed over the sleeves of his *djellabah,* said "Wunderschön," with a sarcastic smile, imitating tourists. At that moment an inhuman roar came from the prison, followed by dull sounds of beating. Hans stiffened, he felt the blood leave his face.

"Don't be afraid," Jilali said at his side, "that isn't your friend."

It only occurred much later to Hans that he had never talked about Aart to the Arab. But at the moment he was completely absorbed by the horrible thought that in the building from whence came that dreadful sound Aart was kept a prisoner.

"That is the section of the insane," Jilali comforted him, "*Verrückte.*"

"Insane?"

The young Arab laughed timidly as he stroked his short beard. Then he continued in French, "We have as yet not adopted the new methods for the nursing of the insane."

"New methods! My God!" said Hans as the roaring resounded anew. "Do they lock these people up? Are they beaten?"

Jilali made an apologetic gesture with his hands. Then he pointed at the Moorish houses at the other side of the square. "The inhabitants don't seem to have any objections . . . ! The British, Americans, Frenchmen . . . !" He indicated each house separately. "No objection either to torture or chains on the prisoners' ankles," he concluded with a delicate smile.

"Straps, chains, good God!" said Hans. He walked away distraught in the direction of the town and the Arab followed him.

When they sat later on the small terrace of a tea house high above the roofs of Arab dwellings, Hans asked, "What do the Arabs do towards changing that? The modern ones, like yourself?"

"Very little," said Jilali laconically.

"But why?"

"There are things that are more important at the moment. It is not only the insane that suffer. Millions of sound mind do. . . ." In a sweeping gesture that included the houses, sharply silhouetted against the moonlight, the Arabs in the tea house—slope-shouldered, faces furrowed by a hard day's work—noisily gulping their tea. "Have you seen the breadlines?"

"Breadlines here?"

"Stay for an evening in town. Look in at the baker's. At midnight the women and children are already waiting there. The nights are cold. At six o'clock the first bread is sold. There isn't enough for everybody. The importation of grain from Portugal has stopped. Spain has not enough for itself, and most of what comes in is taken by the Spanish coast guard."

Hans was silent; he felt embarrassed.

"And who else comes first?" Jilali continued bitterly. "The servants of the Europeans and the Americans, the cooks and the house boys—for their masters' breakfast. Breakfast! But bread is the only thing a simple Arab can afford. It now costs four francs and I assure you that it'll be six or seven francs before the year is over. The daily wages of a laborer are seldom more than five francs. Bread and a little fish are his meal."

Hans still kept silent. He realized that he had been so absorbed by his own worries that the thought of the needs of the Arabs had never occurred to him. The small amount the Consul gave him, added to what Rainer and he earned, kept them alive. There wasn't enough. But the Moroccan population had even less. After all that the Mohammedans had suffered, at the hands of European imperialism, they were once more indirectly the victims of the war.

Later on his way to the hill, he realized that he would have to attach still another significance to the portraits of Hitler and Franco that hung on the wall of Jilali's home. He realized what these pictures meant to Jilali. The young Arab expected help from their side since he had found out that there was nothing to be expected from the other.

Misled and betrayed throughout the centuries, the people allowed themselves to be misled and betrayed again. And this betrayal would continue until, one day, they would realize their strength, their combined strength. This strength they were still not aware of. That in itself was incomprehensible. Millions upon millions allowed themselves to be abused and trampled upon by the few, by the more privileged, by those who assumed leadership. Why? he had so often asked his father, but even his father could never give him a satisfactory answer.

In part it was ignorance, that he knew; but also indifference, laziness of mind and selfishness. Most people, as they received just a bit more than those they had shared with, crossed the dividing line. In order to quiet their consciences, they handed small gifts over the hedge to their former comrades. You might think about it as long as you wished but you were forever running into the same gigantic question mark, he thought.

He himself was not much better. In order to protect himself, in order to avoid difficulties, he had given Sidi Jilali half-truths. From now on he would tell him the truth. But would Jilali believe him? For a moment he stood still on the road. Would the Arab laugh at him? That delicate, bitter smile . . . ?

Oh damn, he cursed, what was the difference? Had the truth helped his father? His voice had been drowned in all the noise. They had not listened to him, not in Germany, and later certainly not outside of Germany. "*Die haben doch Angst,*" he had said of the Americans and the English. "They are more afraid of the truth than they are of a lie." Now his father was a fugitive in his own country, a price on his head. And he did not exist, so far as the world was concerned. Hans' bitterness turned upon the Consul. Tomorrow he would tell him that he refused any longer to come each day for the money. Once a week he would come to get the dole. And if he, that mutton-head, refused, he, Hans, would smash his windows . . .

and go . . . yes, go to whom? He did not know. He felt so powerless that he broke into a sweat. And then he suddenly wept, filled with shame and fury on account of his tears. It lasted but a moment.

Next week we are going to move, he suddenly decided. Next week! It does not matter where, only away from the field. He beat his right fist into the palm of his left hand. It was a decision that relieved him.

10

AT THE UPPER END of the Rue Marrakech, next to the gate leading to the market, the money changers had their booths. Narrow little cages in a row. Between the counter and the safe there was enough space for one man. Money changers stood talking in the street, broke into a run towards the side streets, where the banks were. Quibbled over money, fought over money, cheated and lied.

Against the back walls of the cages hung a row of exchange quotations. Rates from London, Paris, New York, Rio de Janeiro. Refugees milled around—Poles, Hungarians, Czechs, Austrians, French and Germans—read the quotations in one place, and compared the figures at another. They walked with hasty steps, busily gesticulating down the street, where at the end two more brokers had their places of business. Then they would come back, go to the bank and come back again. They sent telegrams. They sat waiting in the cafés behind their coffee and their aperitifs. They peeled shrimps, large, pink shrimps. The waiters came with brooms and swept the shells away, raising clouds of dust. The refugees paid and went to their consuls—the American consul, Portuguese consul, Spanish consul. They again stood in line. Then they went to the travel agencies. They scolded and they shouted. Then they ran back to the brokers, to the bank, to the post office, until three o'clock, when the little businesses in the Rue Marrakech closed up. Thereupon they returned to the cafés.

"What did the Consul say?" "Tomorrow perhaps."

"I cannot get my travel permit."

"I got mine, but my Portuguese visa has not yet come."

"For how long is it good?" "Six more days."

"Have you got your American visa?" "I'll get it tomorrow."

"Don't you believe it! I was supposed to get mine three weeks ago." "What will you do then?" "I have a visa for Cuba."

"I'm leaving on the next boat." "The *Niassa?*" "Yes." "She is overdue, isn't she?" "Who says so?"

"Have you any money left?" "I can still hold out for another two months." "I know of a way to get money. Come, sit closer."

"The dollar is a little better today." "Shall I buy it or not?" "No, wait."

"There is no longer any correspondence with France." "I received some mail only yesterday."

"Watch him." "A cat, driven into a corner makes queer jumps." "I'm just warning you."

"When my visa expires I'm lost. Within a few weeks they'll start the registration of aliens. The next step is the concentration camp." "I am going to the police station. Do you want to come along?" "That does no good any more."

"The American vice-consul is an anti-Semite." "The new one too?" "Much worse even."

"Do you know where I can exchange some *Kronen?*" "How many have you got?" "Do you want some?" "Perhaps."

Rats in a trap, making desperate attempts to free themselves before it is too late. Hunted men, trying to assure their future, run smash into a wall of diplomatic finagling and hyprocrisy, the lowest form of barter, stupidity, prejudice, indifference; quotas, affidavits, visas, steamship tickets, travel permits. The intelligence becomes sharper like the instinct of a fox during the hunt. Speculation, bribing, cheating. Money is the last resource. They hear the barking of the dogs, the hunter's horn. Money, money. . . .

In the rooms of the pensions with the rickety bed, the oil burner on the table, the sleeping children on the mattress on the floor, they whisper until deep into the night. "What's going to happen to the children? I have only one hundred francs left."

A desperate voice, choked into the pillow, "I can't stand it any longer. . . . I can't . . ."

"Be quiet, the children, there is still a chance . . . the next boat. . . . I am still with you . . . we are still together. . . !"

In the bars the lone women. Behind them is Constantinople, Cairo, Alexandria . . . this is the last harbor city, their last station.

In the restaurants and the cafés in the Rue Marrakech strange bargains were struck, promises made good prices. Intermediaries are highly regarded. Mohammed el Kbir was such a one. The refugees sought his help, they trusted him, he spoke French, German and a bit of English, he had as yet cheated nobody, he was resourceful, pleasant in his relations with people, reasonable and patient with the desperate, the neurotic. A blond Arab was not uncommon, said the know-it-all refugees as they drew their friends' attention to the many blond, blue-eyed Berbers at the market. Mohammed el Kbir, slender under his grey *djellabah*, even drank a glass of wine with them and smoked their cigarettes. And in the meantime he listened to their bitter complaints, their excited tales. He was a good listener. Then he consoled them. They freed themselves of the furious seething indignation that filled them. Were they criminals? Why couldn't they obtain a visa? Without an American visa no Portuguese visa, without a steamship ticket no Portuguese visa, without a Portuguese visa no steamship ticket. Without a steamship ticket, American or Portuguese visa, no permit to leave the country from the Spanish authorities. Why did they torture them? Why? Why had Palestine been barred to them? Why had the British army refused their services? They had enough references. Why? Why? Why? The city was full of German spies. Didn't the English in Gibraltar know that? What did Sidi Mohammed think about it? Had he seen the fortifications along the coast? The Spanish refugees, the loyalists, who built the fortifications and were treated like beasts? Did he believe that they would have concentration camps here as in French Morocco? Would they be sent back? Would the Spanish boat stop here? Did he know that that Belgian, that Vermylde at the steamship office, was a swindler? How much did he want to get a passage? Could Sidi Mohammed arrange it? He would get two thousand francs. Trembling hands opened portfolios. Worn letters of recommendation, letters of credit, affidavits, passports. See, here were all the papers. Everything shipshape. All right? Tomorrow at the same place.

It was a masquerade Manus enjoyed. Now he was no longer himself, but represented somebody else, an Arab, discreet, silent, worthy, now for the first time in his life he was respected by others and himself. He played his rôle to perfection. He had clad himself in the gray *djellabah*, put on a *fez* and *babouches*. Therewith the world had completely changed, from him towards the outside world and from the outside towards him as a focal point. He was superior to the struggle around him; the martyr's road of the refugees delivered him from all his burdens. In him was peace, a pleasant feeling. He was contented because he found satisfaction in the troubles of others, not because he enjoyed their sufferings but because they had exchanged parts. They now implored him to help them. The Arabic clothing had not changed his character, but it had given him another place in life. Now he leaned back in an easy chair and they sat on folding chairs. It had been so easy, without any internal conflict, without hesitation. He had always thought that he suffered more than others; he had not been able to conform during his youth; circumstance had made him as sensitive as an open wound. Now he had suddenly changed. He was the conqueror. And at home in the little Arab house that he had rented was the child, Luba, in whom he still found pleasure, and the Arab boy Ali, a new sleeping companion.

Mohammed el Kbir. That meant Mohammed the mighty. In a paroxysm of joy and daring he had called himself that. And when now he saw how it succeeded, this masquerade, this complete, crazy change, he had gone home and in the enclosed space of his small house he had surrendered himself to the pleasure that he had felt all day. The restrained laughter had broken loose savagely, inexhaustibly. Luba, at first somewhat astonished and afraid, also began to laugh, threw herself on the mattress with childish abandon, rolled on it, threw her legs in the air and raced countless times around the room. Ali had grinned rather timidly, embarrassed by this uncontrolled hilarity that he failed to understand. For him Manus was one of those strange Europeans who had put on Mohammedan clothes in order to mix more freely with the Arabs. A man with a great deal of money, so he thought, whose favor he wanted to keep.

Luba stood in front of the little shop, a small cubicle on the narrow street. Her nose was just visible above the counter on which the merchant was lying asleep, his head in the palm of his hand, his knees drawn up. His face was close to hers, a pale yellow rotundity with little black hairs and a border of pimples framing his cheeks up to where his turban started. At the corners of his mouth little globules of spittle burst as he exhaled his breath. Flies buzzed around him and fed on his greasy looking skin.

"Sidi!" said Luba. Then louder, "Sidi!"

He opened one eye, looked drowsily from left to right, and continued to sleep. She went inside along the counter and looked for the bag of bread. The grocer turned around on his back and chased her away with a shout, keeping his eyes closed.

She stood thinking for a while. Manus had forbidden her to go further away from the house than this *bakal* but she was hungry. Around the corner, where the narrow street went up in steps, it was crowded with people. There was sunlight and the children played along the steps. There was the cobbler's; you could smell the camel's leather all over the street. And the tailors. Little boys stood outside the workshops and wove the tresses for the *djellabahs* that were sewn inside. She was forbidden by Manus to go there. Lately she had gone there just the same and Ali had seen her and grabbed her wrist. The children in the street had laughed when he took her home. She did not like Ali, he was mean.

She went out of the street on tiptoe, around the corner, remained standing in front of the tailor's boy and watched how his nimble fingers wove the cord, as quickly as the tailor in his workshop stitched it to the material. She could stay watching that forever. Forever. The boy gathered the threads, his hands flew about as if they were chasing each other. The hands of the tailor trembled and his head moved up and down as if it were attached to the needle. He sewed black cord around a grey *djellabah*. Manus had one like that. Soft, grey stuff like the skin of a mouse.

The boy had scabies, a white crust of mould over his bare skull. Filthy! But she could not help looking at it. He pulled the hood of his *djellabah* over his head. She stuck her tongue out at him. He was a little boy, smaller than Pierre, she thought. She began to hop on one leg, holding the other bent back. She hopped around in a circle. The little boy was watching her, but the tailor chased her away.

Further on was the large loom with the nice men. They called her, pinched her from behind or caressed her arms. The bobbin shot through the loom like a rat, *rrrtt, rrrtt*, just like that time when Rainer had caught one in the house and Hans stood ready with a stick. How scared that rat had been. How they had laughed. Here in the city there were also rats, dead rats in the gutter. "Bah," she said, "bah." And once more, "Bah."

Two boys played with a hoop. One standing at the top of the street sent the hoop to the other. Shaking and bumping, the toy came running down. Imagine, if they would let her play with them! She, Luba! Throwing and catching. A swing with your arm, so that the hoop would sail high in the air, circling against the blue, and come down right in the center of the street. And you down there, your feet firmly planted, your body bent over and the hollow of your hands ready. Oh, to play with those boys!

Further on a few girls stood in a circle. She started to hop again, around and around with her eyes on the girls. They looked at her and giggled. Hop and hop, now embarrassed, hop and hop until she became dizzy under the burning sun and got out of breath.

Later on she stood before the counter of the big *h'anout bakal*. Other people were ahead of her. She stood there looking very small with her shopping bag, above her the raucous voices and grabbing hands of the Arab women. She stood on tiptoe, planted her elbows in the soft bodies around her: "*Sidi, khoubz!*" The women laughed. But there was no more bread. She bought some dry cakes and half a pound of beans. On the way home she nibbled on the hard pastry. She ducked under the rope at the tailor's, stuck out her tongue at the boy, offered him a cake and then quickly withdrew it. Then again she stuck out her tongue. . . .

At home it was cool. The small hallway and the high room, a cool dome around her solitude. It quieted her down inside and she sang a ditty. She made a neat little pile of charcoal in the stone oven, topped it with newspaper rolled into small balls and held a tiny flame to it from a distance, her arm stretched out because she was afraid of it. She scooped some water out of the pail into the stone vessel and shook the beans into it. She took a pinch of salt between her thumb and index finger and sprinkled it over the beans, all quite seriously and attentively. Then she sat down on the mat. The days were long. She had cleaned up before and now she was waiting for Manus and Ali. She waited until the sun went down and the shadows came crawling slowly over the walls. She sat thinking in the tall, cool room what she could do until the beans were done and she could eat. In this way she divided up her whole day, from this to that, because there was really only emptiness, because Manus had forbidden her to go out and also because she was not allowed to go around with the children on the little street. Looking at pictures in a book, counting the pennies she had saved, hopping on the black and white tiles. Standing on a soapbox, looking out of the little high window. But there was nothing to see but a piece of sky, violet blue in the heat, and sometimes women on the roofs. She would like to go back to the field, but Manus had told her that they had gone away. Maria gone, little Pierre, Lies, all of them. To America. Manus had told her how it all had happened suddenly, but that Maria would write to her. That was what she was waiting for.

She did not like it when Ali came home before Manus but that often happened. When he looked at her, he would have a sly expression on his face—laughing with one eye she called it. And he entered unnoticed, he wore no mules. Without a word of greeting he would sit down on the mat and look at her. She pretended to continue with whatever she was doing, but her hands pricked from misery and she would have liked to go outside.

"*Aji,*" he ordered.

She hummed softly and continued with what she had started quickly when he came in.

"*Aji.* Come here!"

"Pooh," she said and shrugged one shoulder with a disdainful gesture.

"*Aji.*"

She continued playing—now with a doll that Manus had given her. She really did not know how to play with it; she could only dress and undress it. She would do that then. But Ali teased her, using dirty words. Belly and buttocks she knew in Arabic, she could only guess at the other parts of the body he mentioned.

"You are dirty," she would say. "Don't."

Once he came in more friendly than usual. He said that the weather was fine, asked her if she had had a pleasant day. Then he unexpectedly pulled out a dead rat from under his cloak. He held it by the tail so that it dangled heavily, monstrously swollen.

"I'm not afraid," she said, staring steadily at him. "You're bad, Allah will punish you."

She could not say much to him, because her knowledge of Arabic was limited, but these words, from which it appeared that she had followed his train of thought, and also the manner in which she said them, were sufficient to prick him. "I am powerless, too small to be a match for you," he understood from what she said, "but there is somebody who is watching you and certainly disapproves of such vileness."

Ali threw the dead animal into the room, got up and left the house. After a few moments he came back and removed the rat without looking at her.

Another time he sat opposite her and opened his pants.

"Why do you do that?" she asked him. He was completely non-plussed by this question and suddenly doubted what he felt he knew for sure about her relation to Manus. He took this question for innocence and did not perceive that instinctively she had found the right defense.

"Why do you do that?"

They looked at each other and then he let himself fall down backwards on the mattress and turned to the wall. She went out and sat at the front door to wait for Manus, sang softly in the manner of the Arab children, flat, on a scale of few notes. She made up the words herself, a mixture of Polish, French and Arabic.—I am a little girl, she sang, my little sister, my little sister—I have a bed—a bed have I—it is wide like a ship—and the waves are high—my little sister lives in a house and at night the lights are lit—pancakes with syrup, pancakes with syrup—one and two and three and four and a hundred—silver and round—bah—bah—bah. . . .

She sat dreaming in the shade of the door until Manus came home. She thought about Maria, who she believed was in America. What America was, she did not know. Manus had told her about skyscrapers, but she still couldn't imagine them. She had a vague picture of tall mosques and Oriental gates, and Maria in a fur coat, such as she remembered her mother had worn. When they were together she had paid little attention to Maria. She felt herself superior, as every well-balanced child feels towards another who is over-sensitive, though the other may be older. Now Maria had achieved complete dignity in her imagination—an older sister in America, something to hold on to.

This evening too she was waiting at the door. At the end of the little hallway a tiny section of the wall and the tiled floor was still warm from the afternoon sun that shone inside through a crack. She crouched down there and looked into the street. Manus would come from the right. She did not for a moment lose sight of that side of the street, as if the looking would bring Manus home sooner. If he came before the boy, they would cook together. The beans were done, he would bring meat or fish and make the sauce. When they were alone together he was more talkative and friendlier.

Manus came around the corner, bent forward against the steeply inclined street, in his hand three silver fishes hanging from a string, and a bunch of bright green parsley.

Now the waiting was over. She thought suddenly about the ball of wool in which her mother had hidden a coin when Maria was learning to crochet, and Luba, too impatient to wait, had undone the wool until it was a tangle and had been punished for it.

While she fastened her eyes on Manus she heard footsteps to the left, and the sound of a voice that made her look in that direction. Two people were turning the corner, an Arab and a European. . . . Hans. It was Hans! Her heart started to pound. She remained sitting there in the hall, she could not get up, couldn't say anything. She felt dizzy and sick. When she was able to react after a few moments, got up and wanted to run towards him, Manus entered the house, pushed her back and closed the door.

'She resisted. "Hans," she sobbed angrily, "Hans!" She fought to get loose, kicked Manus' shins, shrieked, "Hans! I want to go to Hans. Go away, let me go, you . . . you . . . mean . . . I hate you . . . let me go . . . ! Hans!" But Manus closed her mouth with his hand and carried her to the room. She screamed, tried to hit him, freed herself, was caught again, and then she threw herself on the floor and screamed until she began to throw up, painfully.

Manus put the fishes into a pail, and washed his hands without realizing he was doing so and took off his *djellabah*. Then he lifted Luba up in his arms and walked up and down the room with her. She pushed her face against his neck and he felt her tears through his shirt.

"That wasn't Hans," he said soothingly. She sobbed and clasped her arms around his neck.

"He looked like Hans, but it wasn't he. Hans is in America. You know that, don't you?"

She lay against him, emotion shaking her little body.

"It was a boy who looks like Hans. I know him. That boy has another name . . . he is called Roger . . . see? That boy was somebody else. It was Roger." He stroked her head upon his shoulder. "Tiens! Remarkable, how that boy looks like Hans. I was mistaken too when I saw him. But Hans is in America—see? So it could not be he."

He hated himself, but still noticed with a certain satisfaction that her little body relaxed. He had so often been lied to as a child, a fact he had only realized in later years when he analyzed his memories; but ever since he considered lying to children as particularly offensive. He could still evoke the feeling of powerless astonishment and confusion that had hurt him so often as a child. But out of the necessity of protecting himself he had concocted for Luba the story of the departure for America.

"Is that a reason to be so upset? The boy looks exactly like Hans, that is true, but he is taller. Older, see? Didn't I tell you that Hans is in America? Little fool! You scared me, you know that? And no more crying now, do you hear? My whole neck is wet. Look, the water is running down my back . . . !"

She giggled softly, drew up her nose.

"Now she wipes her nose on my shirt! . . . *Voilà* . . . How about that! . . . she is wiping her nose on my shirt!"

He sat down on the mattress in the corner and took her in his lap. She kept her head in his neck.

"Come on, look at me. No? All right, she doesn't want to. Okey with me. And who can wash the floor? Manus, of course. That's a fine thing. Look at the floor, look what you did."

She violently shook her head in denial and pressed herself against him. His hands around her small body felt its feverish warmth.

"Do you know what . . . ?" he said. "We'll lock the door, then Ali can't get in. And then there is just the two of us." She turned her head a bit and rubbed her cheek along his ear.

The boy would be furious, he thought. The reconciliation would cost him at least fifty francs.

Later on he asked her: "Why were you so upset? Are you so fond of Hans?"

She did not answer directly, pretended her mouth was too full with food to talk. . . .

"Well . . . ? Say something. Before you were talking all right."

"What did you say?" she asked, not looking at him.

"Are you lonesome for Hans? Would you rather be with him than with me?"

"No."

"Why did you get so excited then? Did you think I had lied to you?"

"I don't know," she said. "Can I have some more fish?"

He could not stop his questions. He wanted to be sure that she trusted him.

"You don't think I am lying, do you?"

"No," she said.

When later in the evening Ali pounded on the door for the second time, Luba was the first to get up and let him in

II

WHEN HANS told Lies and the children of his intention to move they offered objections. Reluctance to change, fear of the unknown —these were symptoms of their tiredness, their nervous exhaustion. They clung to the present, though they resented it.

"I would not think of it," said Lies. And then violently, as if she were awakening suddenly from a long sleep, "I would not think of it; imagine Aart coming out of prison and unable to find us."

"But we can leave a letter or a message at the police station."

"Listen to him . . ." she said sneering, "They would sure love to hand him a message . . . the dirty swine . . . that trash! . . . Leave a letter! I think you are crazy! Leave a letter, indeed." Lies had had her experience with the police.

Now and then she realized that for some days she had not thought about Aart. She would send Rainer into town, first to the Consul and then to the police.

"What do you want me to do?" the Consul would ask in a friendly manner. But he did not do a thing. *Mañana—mañana*—they promised Rainer at the police station. Lies then would go herself, make a scene at the consulate, cry at the police station, and would come home relieved, her conscience satisfied.

"Leave a letter . . . !" She laughed hysterically, the tears running down her cheeks . . . "Leave a letter . . . !" The children stood around her with pinched faces because she was acting so queerly. Hans laid a hand on her shoulder, "Come now, Lies."

She pushed him back. "Go to hell, you dirty Hun!" Then, as if it had all been in fun, she pulled him towards her, gave him big kisses in order to make the children laugh and to convince them that the calling of names had all been a joke. Berthe shrieked with joy and made a tune of it, ". . . dirty Hun . . . dirty Hun! Hans is a dirty Hun . . . !" But Maria and Rainer turned their backs and went back to work. Pierre with 'a miserable expression on his little face, stumbled behind Rainer, whom he now helped with the weed pulling.

That night Hans found a solution. Achmed drew his attention to a little house this side of the hill. Though Hans had passed it almost daily, he never had considered it with much interest. It was unoccupied—nobody had ever lived in it. The Frenchwoman who owned all the land, had had it built for her, but before she had moved the furniture in, she had changed her mind. Malaria had developed in the valley. The west wind drove the smell of the fish cannery to the house, and anyway it seemed dangerous to live in the midst of her tenant farmers. She rented it to Hans for forty-five francs, because she thought he was a clever boy.

It was a square house, white and clean as if it had just dropped from the sky. The roof leaked no less than the other roofs in the neighborhood, because the mortar was poor. There was one room in the house, and a kitchen and a toilet. A small parcel of land was included in the bargain—very fertile, the Frenchwoman said, but Hans knew better.

After a few days Lies consented to move into the house. She did not say a word about the field, the wasted time, Aart's ideal. Neither did Hans, because he understood that she had relinquished all responsibility, that he alone would have to justify himself to Aart.

So one day as they were sitting outside in front of the shack having their supper, Hans told the children what he had decided.

"We are going to move to the white house on the hill." He pointed, and the children pushed each other aside to look in that direction.

When they had sat down again, or, because of the lack of seats had knelt around the box that served as a table, there was a silence.

"Why are we leaving here?" Pierre asked.

"The field . . . that's no good." Hans explained with difficulty. "I don't know the cause of it, but it just doesn't work. It does not produce enough to sell, and that was the plan. We must make money some other way."

"I wouldn't mind to make money," said Pierre, "but I would rather stay here."

"Me too," said Berthe.

"But why can't we stay here?" asked Maria.

"We must make money," said Pierre importantly.

"I don't want to live in a house," said Berthe.

"That's what you think," said Hans. "A house is fine, you'll see how happy you'll be when you live in it."

Rainer had not uttered a word; he was slowly eating the fried peppers on his plate and he did not look up. "I didn't know you were the boss here," he said.

"I'm not. We are discussing it together."

"Is that so?" Rainer said sarcastically.

Hans put his fork down. "Have you any objection?"

"Yes, I've already told you. We haven't the right."

"The right to starve here?" Hans pointed at his plate, at the children, at little Dolf who was chewing a dirty crust of bread soaked in oil.

"You don't starve that quick."

"It's beginning to look like it. What are we going to do next summer? Up to now we haven't had a thing out of the soil."

"That's Aart's affair."

"But Aart isn't here."

"He is still the boss. He has rented the land. We have no say in it."

"Shut up and die, eh, that's your motto. *Maul halten und krepieren.* You are no longer in Germany here."

Both faces grew white with anger. Rainer was speechless with fury, his hands clenched. The children, in deathly silence, stared at Hans and Rainer.

"It's people like you who have driven Germany to ruin. Slaves! Keep your trap closed and obey, no matter what happens." They now stood facing each other.

"Du, Du Schwein . . ." said Rainer powerless.

Hans laughed sarcastically. "If you hadn't been a Jew you would have made a good Nazi."

"For Christ's sake, Hans!" cried Lies. "Are you out of your mind?"

Rainer turned around, walked towards his manure truck, started the motor and drove away.

They continued to eat in silence. There was no other noise than the scraping of the forks over tin plates and the babbling of little Dolf.

"Rainer will never come back," whispered Berthe in Maria's ear, but loud enough for everybody to hear.

Pierre pushed her. She gave him a push back, so that the boy who still found it hard to keep his balance, even while he was seated, almost fell from the box he was sitting on.

"Da—da—da," crowed little Dolf.

"Oh, you little darling," said Maria. She lifted him to her lap and hugged him.

"Let Dolf go," said Berthe, "he is my boy." She tried to pull him away from Maria.

Lies' hand flew out, slapped Berthe's cheek hard . . . "Sit down!" she said. Berthe, stunned by Lies' action, after she had not bothered herself about her for weeks, sulked for awhile. Then she turned to Hans and said: "She slapped me, Hans. She is not allowed to do that."

Lies piled up the plates, "Rainer is right too," she said. "Hans is now the boss here. I might as well go away. I am of no use here."

The children dragged the boxes and benches into the house. Hans remained seated all by himself, bent forward, his hands slack between his knees. He looked at those hands and saw how involuntarily they balled themselves into fists. It came from a feeling of humility, of being beaten down, of shame, and it was so strong that it separated him from his surroundings and left him bereft of thought until he instinctively sought to regain his balance. He washed at the well, put on a clean shirt and left the field. He took the asphalt road towards town, toward the bar where Marga worked.

The moving of the poor is the same the world over. A few pots and pans, bedclothes—and then the treasure, the one possession that the imagination has transmuted into spun gold. It might be a threadbare dress dating from better times, some worthless ornament, a wornout book or yellowed magazine, a musical instrument, a piece of furniture, the Bible or the Koran. Everywhere in the world it is the same. A broken-down vehicle or a beast of burden, piled high, and often with a child on top of the load, clutching its own indispensable possession.

As Rainer remained unapproachable, coming and going without uttering a word, and would not put his manure truck at their disposal, Hans had borrowed a small mule from Achmed's father. This added interest to the moving for the children. They crowded around the animal, fed him all they could spare, and gave excited counsel on the even distribution of the burden. The heavily laden beast had to make the trip three times, because Lies would not dispense with the smallest household possession.

"I thought that we would have to carry it ourselves," Berthe said, all excited.

Pierre nodded his head seriously. Hand in hand, they preceded the mule, and Pierre, pale, perspiring, would not remain behind and made all of the three trips.

Finally they were installed. The children had explored the house like cats in a new home and had gratefully taken possession of it. The toilet especially was a source of joy for Berthe and Pierre, and when they used it, they left the door open, so filled with pride were they. But quite soon Hans was obliged to deny them entrance to this sanctuary. The house had no running water and the well was about five minutes' distance. They uttered jealous protests when they saw others disappear into the tiny cubicle until Hans forbade them all to use it except Lies.

"I don't even want to," said Berthe then. "It is much nicer outside."

After a week their life had already acquired some regularity. Rainer worked. What he did beyond carrying manure nobody knew, but he brought more money in. Hans gave lessons, washed glasses for Harvey, and only came home towards morning. Now that the others had been freed from the exhausting labor, morale improved. They were still tired, it even seemed as if they grew more tired every day. The children were continually falling asleep and in the morning they did not want to get up. But they no longer quarrelled and they were filled with plans and had fun.

There was a general effort to keep the house clean and beautiful. Little Dolf, who was continually sinning against this, was anxiously watched—and Lies too, who was not quite convinced of the importance of cleanliness, had to learn that the children held their ideals high. She was amused to watch the industry of Maria, Berthe and Pierre, but when she tired of it she threw them out of the house and bolted the door, a privilege that had been denied her up to now for technical reasons, but of which she took advantage more and more.

Lies became bigger and more fond of her ease. She did only the most essential work, left Dolf to Berthe, the cooking to Maria and Pierre, and went often visiting in the village. She now wore the halo of the martyrs. It gave her dignity and importance. She sunned herself in the light of her halo and sang because she was happy. She was received with open arms in the village. They had missed her boisterous laughter, her tales about the emancipated women of faraway countries. Lies now knew every woman in the village and many of the men.

In their urge to beautify the house, as far as their remembrance of former days gave them inspiration, the children planned an expedition to the beach. Maria knew that things would come floating in, things from boats that had been shipwrecked as she expressed it, and if nothing were found, there were always shells and the flowers on the dunes. There was great activity before the departure, because whenever Maria with her feverish excitement was in charge, the preparation always exceeded the undertaking. This time she insisted upon the children being cleaned and their hair combed. Nobody understood why. But they allowed themselves to be handled and Berthe was proud of her braids—though a part of her kinky hair was lost in the battle when Maria had removed the burs. Pierre's shirt was washed; it was still dripping wet when they left, but it would dry on his body. And Dolf, as usual bound to Berthe's back according to the Moroccan custom, had a pink cap on his head, which had been a present from Mrs. van Balekom. They took bread and a bottle of water along and an empty bag for the treasures to be found on the beach.

It was thus that clean and beautifully arrayed, Maria had in the old days been taken out on Sundays and this memory probably had inspired her when she prepared herself and the others for the expedition.

"Perhaps we may find something made of gold and silver," said Berthe, who walked on ahead, carefully descending the hill because little Dolf was a heavy load on her back.

"Maybe," said Maria.

"Or a barrel, on which you can sit down," said Pierre more realistically.

"Is your shirt dry yet?" Maria asked.

"Nice and cold," Pierre boasted, who had violently protested when the wet article of clothing was pulled over his head.

"I'm choking," said Berthe puffing from the heat.

"I once read in a book that a house had been completely furnished with pieces that had washed ashore," Maria invented.

"There was a terrific sirocco yesterday. Maybe a ship has been wrecked," Pierre added hopefully.

"Pooh, that little bit of wind," said Berthe. "No, those ships go down because of the war. Sometimes you can see clouds of smoke; then there are bombs."

"There was a large convoy, Hans said yesterday." Pierre had great difficulty keeping up with them, but when he pressed his hand to his leg it made walking easier.

"I saw it too, an enormous convoy, it lasted all of an hour before it had passed by. You get a fine view from the hill. Rainer is going to try to get a telescope."

"Did Rainer speak to you?" Maria saked.

"He always speaks to me," said Berthe.

"*Ce n'est pas vrai,*" said Pierre, "he talks to nobody."

"But he does to me," said Berthe.

"Naw."

"Yeah."

They crossed the asphalt road and walked along the field.

"Booh," sneered Berthe and stuck out her tongue at their former dwelling.

"Booh," repeated Pierre.

"Bah-bah," prattled little Dolf.

"Oh, do you hear that?" Berthe called out. "He understands everything." And then to the little boy on her back, "Filthy house, eh? Dirty, stinking house. Little Dolf is going to get flowies, flowies for the new house and shells, wee, tiny shells . . ."

On the beach was a troop of boys, young Falangists drilling. When the children stood on the dunes, the first thing they saw was the brilliant red of the berets in a row.

"Oh, what is that? Oh, look, look!" Berthe shouted with joy. She ran down the dune, in spite of the little boy on her back.

"Berthe . . . ! Be careful! Come here . . . !" Maria shrieked. She thought the wooden rifles with which the children exercised were real weapons; the display of the military still filled her with the greatest fear.

"What is it?" Pierre asked beside her.

But Maria did not answer. She was stamping her feet in the sand and shouting, "Berthe . . . here . . . *viens ici*! Oh, that horrible child," she said with tears in her eyes.

"Are they soldiers?" Pierre asked.

"Yes," she said.

From the left side bigger boys came marching ahead and although they carried real guns Maria decided to go there too. She ran down, loudly calling Berthe's name, to draw attention to herself. Pierre remained behind, alone. He slowly let himself down in the sand and stayed seated there, while the Spanish boys paraded back and forth and went through the manual of arms. He looked especially at the smallest ones who were of his age. He imagined that he stood between them, he felt the rhythm of their steps in his legs and the red beret on his head.

After the Falangists had marched away, and they had looked after them until the red and the black of their uniforms dissolved in the hazy colors in the distance, the children began their exploration along the beach. Pierre was silent and Berthe said, vaguely aware why he didn't talk. "Just a lot of crap. They didn't even have real guns."

But Pierre exploded: "They were real too; the big boys had real rifles." And Berthe, mad, now said, "You can never join them. Do you hear? You can't."

They wandered along the edge of the sea, their feet in the cool wet sand. First they picked up everything that attracted their attention. Small softly tinted shells, like fingernails, as Pierre said, and other shells with grooves that had the shape of snail shells. Some had holes in them or were broken. These they dropped as they found good ones of the same kind. Further on there were pieces of driftwood, in which their imagination saw ornaments or furniture for the house and which they dragged along in the bag. They rested awhile so that Pierre could undo his wooden leg. Maria, partly from curiosity and also because she wanted to be kind, but with a strong feeling of repulsion, massaged the little fellow's stump—a blue stump of flesh with cruel red marks and weals made by his harness. Pierre, usually reluctant to show his deformity to anybody, let her go ahead, as he was dull with fatigue. Berthe fed the baby with bread after she had first removed the sand from his mouth with her finger. She pulled the little pink cap over his eyes and played peekaboo with him.

The sun was shining so fiercely that they decided to bathe. Dolf and Pierre were put in the water where it spilled over the beach and Maria and Berthe splashed around in the surf, Berthe completely naked, Maria in her dress, that clung to her back and legs.

"If somebody sees you," she warned Berthe, "if somebody sees you like that . . ."

"Then what? Then what?" Berthe asked provocatively, and stretched herself out to her full length and let herself fall forward to an oncoming wave.

Maria was splashing around a bit. She was afraid. She convinced herself that she had to take care of the children and walked busily back and forth.

"Whooh-whooh-whooh . . ." Berthe jubilated. She ran through the water, splashing and stamping like a young colt, the water in glistening drops on her body. "Whooh-whooh," she slapped her hips, ran in a circle around the little boys and then threw herself again into the waves.

It calmed Maria down. She came to sit near Pierre and Dolf and looked at Berthe. Always when other children were having fun, Maria became quiet. Then sad thoughts came into her head. Now it was Luba, her sister, who had disappeared and about whom she seldom thought.

"Can Berthe swim?" asked Pierre, who had little Dolf on his lap.

"No," said Maria.

"Won't she drown then?"

"The water isn't deep."

"Can I learn to swim?"

"Later when you are grown up."

"Watch Dolf, will you?" he asked. "I want to go a little bit further into the sea." He went slowly, carefully into the water until it reached his knee. He looked around.

"Go on," Maria encouraged him. She suddenly felt so disconsolate that she wanted to cry. All the excitement had disappeared. Pierre went two steps further and stood still, a little figure, arms stretched out in order to keep his balance, head bent. Berthe splashed towards him, her wet hair streaming in front of her eyes, her mouth agape in an ecstasy of fun. "Come," she shouted. "I'll help you."

"*Attention* . . .!" they suddenly heard. They had not noticed that there were people walking on the beach. "Look out . . . careful, come out of there, boy!" They saw two beautifully dressed ladies carrying canes. The children looked at them, scared. Pierre stumbled back, Berthe plumped down again in the water, and moved towards the beach on her belly.

"Is that your little brother?" one of the ladies asked Maria as she pointed at Pierre.

"No," said Maria. As always when people inquired after their family relationship, the children did not know what to answer.

"This one then?" they asked, indicating little Dolf.

"He is my little son," said Maria snappily.

"Good grief! Did you hear that?" one lady asked the other, whose face was almost completely covered by green goggles.

"Well, here anything is possible," she said.

"But they aren't Arab children!"

"So what . . . ? Probably refugees."

Maria, with little Dolf on her lap, looked up at the ladies. Berthe lay on her belly, let the water spill over her. Pierre stood next to her and watched how his little wooden leg gradually made a small hole in the wet sand.

"Don't you have a bathing suit?" the first lady asked of Berthe. Berthe looked at her but did not give an answer.

"Where is your father?"

"In jail," Berthe said suddenly, pointing to the right, where the sharp contours of the Arab quarter showed above the rocks.

The ladies looked at each other. The children looked at them. Maria took in every detail of their clothing, the white skirts, the brown shoes with thick rubber heels, the colorful silk scarfs they wore around their heads and shoulders, the walking sticks and the handbags. Little Dolf suddenly started to bawl, rubbing his eyes with his small fists.

"He is thirsty," declared Pierre, who was now making a second hole in the sand with his artificial leg.

"Did your little brother get hurt in the war?" one of the ladies asked in a whisper of Maria.

"He's not my little brother," said Maria and after a moment of thought she said confidentially, "The Nazis hacked off his leg."

"Where do you live?" the lady with the glasses asked.

"We live there over the dune, in a white house. You can see it when you stand on top of the dune. We have a large garden and three cows." Berthe, forgetting that she was nude, came closer. Maria handed her her dress. Berthe stuck her arms and head into it, danced around flapping her sleeves.

"Come, let's go," said the lady with the glasses. "Horrible children. The baby is covered with lice."

"Wait a moment," said the other. "I believe I know who they are. They are the protégées of Margaret van Balekom!" The other giggled, "Protégées!" she said. "She is outdoing herself."

"We'll give her a ring," said the other. She winked and both burst out laughing. The one who had first spoken to the children took a banknote out of her handbag and gave it to Pierre. "For your piggy bank," she said. The other hesitated for a moment, then gave Maria a ten-franc note. "Here, buy some candy with this." Arm in arm they continued on their way.

The children crowded around Maria. They had never been given any money and it took a while before they realized that it was theirs. Some Arab boys playing with a football had wandered near where they were, and now came closer. Maria grabbed the banknote from Pierre and closed her fist around it until the boys had passed, then she gave it back to him.

"Have any more water?" asked Berthe. "I'm so thirsty."

"No, what is left is for Dolf," said Maria. She looked after the ladies, then she pressed her head against little Dolf's neck, seeking consolation in its sweet warmth.

Pierre had smoothed out the ten-franc note on his knee.

"What are you going to buy?" asked Berthe, bending confidentially over him.

"I don't know yet." Pierre looked at her absentmindedly. He still had not decided what to buy—either a new leg or a rifle.

Hans says that you'll have to go to school when you have decent clothes," said Berthe. "Now you can buy some clothes. Then Hans won't need to buy them." She came and sat next to him on her haunches, her forehead lined from thinking.

Pierre put the money in his trousers pocket.

They continued their walk along the beach. They did not talk. Their thoughts were occupied with their wealth, so new, so strange. Maria led the way. Berthe again carried little Dolf, who had fallen asleep. His head with the red curls rocked slowly up and down with Berthe's movements. The pink cap had been lost long ago. Pierre dragged the bag with the precious load behind him. They no longer collected shells or wood. They just walked along.

12

As USUAL every morning at sunrise Hans was on his way to the house on the hill. To him this trip had come to be rather like a stroll, for while his feet made headway, he enjoyed the awakening day. Then having refreshed himself thus after the long night in the smoke-filled bar and a short sleep in Marga's room, he summarized the events of the past hours. He accounted for his actions and thoughts, held himself responsible for the mistakes he thought he had made and weighed plans for the near or distant future.

When he had passed the modern suburbs, he always stopped for a moment at the outskirts of the city and took a deep breath to fill his lungs with the moist, bitter morning air. Now the past day was behind him and here he took up the new day. In front of him stretched the hills and the fields—they looked as if they were suspended in the blue morning haze. His eyes rested on the vague outlines of the land, the severe cedars which first detached themselves from the vapor and the naked, dead trees from whose branches the veils were slowly torn. He focussed his eyes on the glow at the horizon which became more translucent and expanded, as if somebody were approaching holding a red lantern; it was the sun, glowing like a red disk which quickly rose and suddenly burst forth in a thousand yellow colors.

This spectacle was his, he thought with secret joy, because he was the only one to leave the city at this hour. The Arabs on their way to the market had turned their backs to the land and would not look around, because they were busy with the donkeys, which had to be urged on for the last stage of the road by shouts and beatings.

Further on he passed the encampment of the gypsies who waited here for their papers for America. All was quiet there because they slept until late into the day. Only a few Arab dogs looked between the tents for refuse; they barked at Hans and came to smell at his heels.

Gypsies! he thought. And with pity he compared their way of life with the desperate efforts of Aart to live in freedom with his clan, a struggle for independence and individuality that had completely failed because Aart was a product of puritanical Holland. Even though he fought against it, and had freed himself from it, it was still in his blood. The gypsies, however, recognized their right to freedom and with it their right to live as they pleased, be it as parasites or thieves. They also allowed for everybody who came in contact with them the necessity to protect themselves from them. Only the survival of the fittest counted and they solved every problem by their light and natural logic.

The image of Aart as he stubbornly bent over the soil, interposed itself between Hans and the landscape. This picture was more steadfast in his mind than the one of Aart in prison, because the first was basic and the second was only an inconsequential incident. Moreover his imprisonment was only a passing phase, as Aart would now soon be released from prison. Marga had put herself behind the fight for his liberation with female perseverance. Hans did not doubt that she would succeed, though he preferred not to think what means she used to achieve her aim. But at the back of his mind he knew that to Marga these were completely secondary, as irrelevant perhaps, he secretly feared, as her relations with a seventeen-year-old boy. Last week he had become seventeen. He had lied about his age to Marga as if he hoped that one year would make a difference in her feelings and consideration. But she had taken him into her arms, laughing "*Dix-huit, hein? Hänschen, Hänschen,* I don't know whether I did the right thing. Eighteen, eh? *Mon Dieu, qu'est ce que j'ai fait!*"

Not only she, but he too doubted the motives and the conditions of their relationship. Always at night there was the image of Maria between him and Marga. The image was more real than the reality he held in his arms. The slight body, trembling under his touch, the small breasts in the hollow of his hands, the strong unformed legs alongside his own, and her hot tears always running down his neck or moistening his face. When the image was not there he evoked it; when he forgot it he felt the lack of it later. Was it because he felt guilty about his affair with Marga? Or the feeling of inexperience that sometimes made him timid and at other times angry? What else? Because his meetings with Maria were a nuisance, a damned nuisance, as he expressed it; though their meetings became less frequent as he had more business to attend to, her hungry eyes followed him everywhere and exercised a pressure upon him against which he needed all his will power.

Since they had lived in the little house Maria had quieted down a bit, but still was certainly not normal, he thought. Normal were the girls of his memory, his girl friends from school and the daughter of his host in Paris. Maria did not fit in that picture. A damned nuisance, yes. If she only had found something to do. Berthe did not want to let her take care of Dolf. Berthe, the little bitch! A kid like that found its way out of any situation. But Maria? Could he send her to school like Pierre? Then she would have to sit in one of the lowest grades. She could barely read. Fourteen years old and she could barely read. "To youth belongs the future." It was as if this platitude was called out to him, an echo that he caught out of the distance. To youth belongs the future. Who spoke about the present? What could youth expect of the future when it was now being spoiled for the future? The youth of Europe was fed on hatred, driven on by fear, and educated for murder. To youth belongs the future. The future—youth—youth. The future.

The words followed the cadence of his steps. The fog moved on tiptoe along the side of the road, fled over the land. When the veils had lifted, round dewdrops glittered on the grass stubble. The moisture on the road dried up, leaving strangely shaped patches.

Aart had tried it, he thought confusedly. Poor soil, no water. That was the way it was. He searched for the right form of simile. Children. Seed. The future. Youth. His footsteps sounded hollow over the small wooden bridge over the gully which had already dried up though the summer had hardly yet begun. He leaned over the rampart, looked into the yellow mud. Aart had tried it. . . . The field. The seed. The children. The world.

Then he knew; the field is as the world and the children are the seed.

Further inland a column of smoke rose from the chimney of the city incinerator. Light was still shining in the building. The donkeys on the grounds brayed dismally.

From the direction of the village a small cart, pulled by a mule, drove up and turned towards the disposal plant. Hans laughed at the small Arab boy who, on top of the carriage, swayed from left towards right with the unsteady movement of the vehicle and the jerky pulling of the mule. The large pompon which decorated the boys icecap—heaven knew where the Arabs got those pieces of clothing —swayed right along with the Arab. *Voilà*, Rainer's competitor, he thought amused. Yes, of all things, this boy had gone into the business, taken Rainer's trade away. Rainer had worried about it a great deal, as the Moorish boy, smart indeed, got the refuse right at the plant. As the farmers in the neighborhood had provision for next spring anyway, Rainer had offered his truck and his services to the villagers on the hill. Now at five in the morning he drove the women to market. Rainer and his harem, as Lies called it. Embarrassed when the women pushed, squabbled and fought to get in the car, he got mad when Lies teased him about it. Now he was looking for work in the city, at the market. He would not find it so easy, thought Hans, knowing himself to be more adaptable than Rainer. Rainer would have trouble gaining the confidence of the Arabs. Distrust of the "Rummy's" increased in proportion to the worsening of the situation.

As he turned away from the rampart of the bridge his thoughts returned to a conversation he had had with his pupil the evening before, while passing by the Café Roma. On the terrace in the evening breeze, the Italians and Germans were drinking their *aperitif*.

Though the heat of the past day still lingered, the wind brought coolness from the sea. As they were passing Hans noticed how piercing
eyes took him in. Going by Café Roma at this time of the evening
meant running the gantlet. This all the refugees in the city knew.
Here the wolves in sheep's clothes, the German tourists had their
observatory. Going by there gave Hans a boyish thrill: if they only
knew who I am, if they only knew whose son I am. . . . But last
night, Jilali had greeted one of the Germans and Hans had felt very
uncomfortable.

"Do you know that man?" he had asked in spite of himself.

"Why would I greet him otherwise?"

"He is a German, isn't he?"

"Probably."

"A tourist?"

Jilali smiled, gave him a sideglance. "*Wahrscheinlich.*"

"*Ohne Zweifel,*" Hans corrected him.

"*Wahrscheinlich* means 'probably,' doesn't it?"

Hans bit his lips. Damned hypocrite, he thought. How long ago
was it that he had resolved to make Jilali acquainted with Nazi
ideology? Some months or was it centuries ago?—*Hans, trink' deine
Milch*—He still blushed when he thought about it. Then he had been
a child, he knew, with contempt for his adolescent attitude. What
could he say to the Arab? No, what could "one" tell an Arab? That
the Germans would be even worse colonizers than the French? That
this war would make an end to colonial policies? That Morocco
would become independent? That Tangier would be a free city
after the war? He lacked the necessary conviction because he
did not believe these things himself. No, he was honest now with
Jilali. Maybe that was the best way to be.

"Why don't the Americans put a stop to the spying even though
the English refuse to do anything about it?"

"They could put an end to it, if they wanted to. Don't you think
so?"

At the top of the street in the Arab tea shop they had rested, looking over the bay, listening to the monotonous sounds from a gramophone. Hans had thought how his father with complete disregard for his own safety fought the Nazis, while here the work he had done was carelessly brought to nought by the Americans and the English. The refugees said with bitterness that the consular corps was too busy with its society doings, but Hans knew better. Marga had clarified the matter for him. She had pointed in the direction of the Atlantic Ocean with a gesture that indicated the other side and then pointed north with a shorter arm. "There they are, the ones who are responsible. Those here, *ces imbeciles ici*, carry out their orders."

Yes, his father. In connection with thoughts about his father, images would rise in his mind, always the same. Remembrance, imagination and worry about his parents had merged into definite pictures. They made their appearance unexpectedly. Or sometimes he realized he had not thought about them; then he felt that there was something definitely lacking and willingly his mind offered him the picture he had been looking for. His father was fleeing down a street in Berlin, always the same street. The road between the house of a little girl friend of Hans' and the music school where he had taken violin lessons. Not the way from school to home, for instance, which he had taken twice a day, not the street where his father's office was, nor the one where the secret meetings were held. No, a side street that he passed twice a week when, after his violin lesson, excited by the playing in which he was fairly proficient, he made a detour in order to continue the mood of the evening in a conversation underneath the stairs with his little girl friend. Why in God's name *that* street? His father was fleeing. It was dusk, a spring evening. He pressed himself against the houses, slid along the portico. He still had his hair—later he had become bald. Underneath his arm he carried his old black briefcase. Then there was another picture. His mother was crocheting in a chair at the window. On her lap was a book. Outside the Hitlerjugend was marching by. She shook her head and said to somebody in the room. *"Das arme Kind wird zo spät in die Schule kommen."* He did not remember that he had ever seen her crocheting at the window. She wore a white scarf wound around her hair as she did during the summers at his grandmother's home. Then there was a picture that he always quickly tried to obliterate, but at night before he went to sleep he evoked it, and sought for Marga's warm, consoling proximity. His father was on his knees, his hands on a large, flat stone. It could be a tombstone. A man in uniform was leaning over him. Hans could not distinguish whether he was an S. S. or an S. A. One of his eyes was covered with a black patch, like the pirates in boys' books. This picture gave him a bitter feeling and he accused himself of hysteria.

He quickened his gait, angry at himself now as he soberly evoked these chimeras. He looked for the starting point of his thoughts. His father. How he had risked everything while here under the nose of the English and the Americans the Germans could do as they pleased. It gave him a sick feeling in his stomach as he realized that his father's struggle and that of his little group of collaborators, looked at from here, with the present circumstances in mind, were simply ridiculous. A little bunch of idealistic *schlemiels* as his father had called himself and his group with ill concealed pride. But Hans knew for sure that the diplomats here, if they were to hear of them, would speak about these attempts with pity and disdain.

Last night at the bar he had been introduced to an Englishman— Johnson was his name—a man, tall and skinny, and with a strong British accent, as if he tried out the correct pronunciation of every word before he allowed it to pass his lips. An untrustworthy individual, Hans had thought, too friendly, and proud of the new scar on his forehead, which according to what he told Hans, had been acquired in Ethiopia and which had earned him his discharge from the service.

And what was he doing here, Marga had asked him curtly. That was a secret, he said, lifting his eyebrows and coquettishly smiling at Marga as if she were in on the secret. Marga wanted none of him, though she later laughed at Hans because he said he did not trust Johnson.

One distrusted everybody now, he thought, but joked about the lack of confidence as if one were ashamed of it. One hesitated, too, to express one's opinion because every utterance was tagged, and that tag then wore forever like a proper name: fascist, nazi, reactionary, communist, anarchist, war profiteer, anti-semite, capitalist. . . . Every word was weighed and classified as belonging in a certain category. He wondered how they would label each other after the war.

"Are you French?" Johnson had asked him, as if he did not recognize Hans' German accent.

"No, Hungarian," he had answered, ignoring Marga's astonished expression.

"Ich war einmal in Budapest, schöne Stadt."

Hans had mumbled an excuse and had disappeared into the kitchen. For the first time since he had left Paris he felt fear, a feeling that completely possessed him, so that afterwards he found himself washing the glasses without any conception of his thoughts or his actions during the preceding moments. He saw the sink on his right hand filled with glasses, but did not even seem to remember he had put them there. There had been a vacuum of fear. And then for a fleeting moment, too short to be fully aware of it, there was a feeling of liberation. He was then completely calm, though looking around in his mind for the significance of the feeling just experienced.

"I do not trust that Johnson," he said later to Marga, and when she answered him teasingly, he didn't react to her joking.

The short conversation, however, was etched in his mind: Are you French?—No, Hungarian.—*Ich war einmal in Budapest, schöne Stadt.* An answer given jokingly in perfect German but of threatening significance.

Later that night looking through the curtain between the bar and the kitchen, he watched Harvey talking to Johnson, confidentially with heavy drunkard's hands resting on Johnson's shoulders. Comforting himself, he reflected that Harvey did not know anything about him.

Now, in the light of day his mistrust and fear seemed silly, and he gave himself a talking to: So, the disease of mistrusting everybody, got you too. You better watch out for yourself, don't get involved with that nonsense. And annoyed about his brooding, he thought: Oh, to be able to get rid of your burdens, to do what you would do under normal circumstances. To be the one your parents had planned you to be at your birth, just a boy . . . to have a youth of freedom without any other worries than the worries of a boy.

He began to walk faster, broke into a trot. Oh, run, run with other boys, over hurdles, jump, skip rope. . . . He made a gesture with his arm, of throwing, something creaked in his shoulder, he had become stiff. His shopping bag heavy with food for the children, bobbed up and down on his back. Perspiration ran along his temples. "*Verdammt noch mal,*" he swore.

Reaching home he found Lies and the children still in a sound sleep. Only Pierre was awake and crawled noiselessly to the door where Hans stood waiting. As usual he was allowed to accompany Hans to the village to get milk before the others woke. He considered this an honor and he did his best to conduct an intelligent conversation.

"How was business yesterday at the market?" he asked in a man-to-man tone.

"Pretty good," said Hans, "I sell for somebody else, see. I get just as much whether I sell many or a few vegetables."

Pierre sought for an observation that Hans might think worth while. "But you would rather sell much than little?"

"Of course, *ça va sans dire.*"

"*Dios,* it is hot already."

"Next month will be worse."

"When I am in school, it won't bother me."

"Yes, school," said Hans laughing because of the clever way in which Pierre reminded him of his promise. "Only I don't know how you'll get there."

"I'll walk."

"It's too far for you." Involuntarily Hans grasped Pierre's hand as the little boy tried to keep step with him along the steep uneven path, to walk evenly, as Hans had taught him, and watch out for his own safety.

At the top of the hill they rested a few minutes.

"High, isn't it?" Pierre pointed towards the bay, which looked farther away and smaller seen from here because his eyes were used to the view towards the water from the house. "A bird can fly straight down," he said, and as Hans did not seem to be listening, "when you fire a cannon from here, you can sink a ship."

"Why do you want to sink a ship?" Hans asked.

Pierre looked up at him. He suddenly burst into laughter.

"I don't want to sink a ship, silly!"

Hans looked into the child's face lifted towards him with an expression of affection.

"Pierre, listen," he said suddenly, "if I should no longer be here, if I have to go on a trip or something, then you must go to the American consul. The American consul, do you hear?"

"Yes," said Pierre, now very serious.

"Come on, don't stare at me like a dope," said Hans, dissatisfied with himself and feeling suddenly ridiculous. "We have to get on, I can't stay here all day!"

They walked between the houses along a small road with deep gullies from the spring rains, where offal was rotting. Pierre walked along and looked with interest at the evil-smelling diversity of objects.

"Hans!" he called out standing still, "Look!" And he pointed at the carcass of a dog, a yellow African dog, half covered with the refuse which had been dumped out later, and next to the dead animal a slippery, blood-drenched mess. "What's that?"

"I don't know," said Hans. "Come." Then thinking it over, "It's a dog, a dead dog."

"Oh," said Pierre. He took Hans' hand. "Why are you going away?" he asked.

"Who says that I'm going away?"

"You said so yourself!"

"I didn't say anything of the kind." They turned into the alley between two square white houses and Hans opened the door to the yard of Achmed's home. There was a beehive of activity there; the women and the daughters were busy with their work. The children were milking the cows before they turned them into the valley. Hans went into the house to talk with Achmed who was still in bed. Pierre watched the can which they had brought along being filled with milk. He spoke to Suleika, a nine-year-old girl whom he liked most of all the children in the village.

"Did you see the carcass?" he asked in order to show his knowledge of the difficult word.

"*Què?*" asked Suleika, on her haunches underneath a cow's heavy body, stretching out her neck towards Pierre.

He pointed behind him where he knew the nasty interesting thing was.

They both went to look. Suleika walked in front of him; he looked with satisfaction at the long braid entwined with yellow cord that softly bobbed upon her back as she moved with a springy step.

They stood next to each other above the slippery mess on the path. Suleika sticking out her naked foot, just touched the dog's intestines, but she did not say a word. The sun burned fiercely upon their heads, in their faces, as it was reflected from the whitewashed walls that hid the yards and the houses from their view. Loud, throaty voices sounded from everywhere. An Arab woman on her way to the well yelled something that Pierre did not understand, but she kept on going.

"It is a dog, *kelb*," he said to Suleika, and then as a result of deep thinking, "just like the other one."

She did not answer, but walked back to the house.

Later, at breakfast, Pierre threw up and Lies and the children were indignant.

"What did you eat?" Lies questioned him. But Pierre went outside, where he sat down at the side of the house, sick and ashamed, struggling with the picture of the carcass that he could not get out of his mind, and, strangely with a sudden deep sorrow because he had only one leg.

"What's the matter with you?" Hans came to him after breakfast. "Are you sick?"

Pierre stubbornly shook his head.

"Come on, tell me," Hans urged, bending over him.

"Don't go away," Pierre suddenly sobbed, hiding his face against Hans' arm.

Hans stared down at him dejected for a moment. "I never said that I was going away. You act like a baby! Listen! If you stop crying, I'll tell you something. Listen! Are you listening? Achmed has promised me a donkey. You may use one of Achmed's donkeys to ride to school on. Now, what do you say?"

But Pierre put his head between his arms and would not answer.

13

MARIA WAS now living with the van Balekom family. Just when life in the house on the hill had become more pleasant, she thought regretfully. Things always happened at the wrong time. Some weeks ago she would have liked very much to go with the Consul's wife, but now she had followed her with reluctance and hesitation. She was disturbed, too, because she did not know the reason for it. One night after supper they had fetched her in the car—the Consul himself and his wife. They had talked to Lies and Hans and that was the way it had been decided. Without asking her whether she wanted to. Yes, without asking her opinion at all. That made her furious. Hans surely wanted to get rid of her, she thought later. Was he really glad to get rid of her? The idea absorbed her. She tried to remember how their last meetings had been. She tried to think of what Hans had said, because she suspected him of conniving with the Consul.

When she thought of the house, she had a picture of sun and light, the hot sun on the little flight of steps and a hard light in your eyes so that it was mostly impossible to look out over the bay. And Lies, the child in her belly—you could already see it—crocheting socks of rough sheep's wool in the manner of the men in the village. And just when Maria was also learning to crochet and would earn a few cents, they had taken her away.

In her imagination the little house was a better place to live than the Consul's comfortable dwelling. The little table and the chair that Rainer had obtained in some way or other represented a luxury that was closer to her than the shiny pieces of furniture in the Consul's house, because she felt part owner of the treasures found by Rainer. The flower seeds that Hans had brought were wonderful; they held greater promise than the precious bulbs in the garden of Mrs. van Balekom. The mattress on the floor looked like a safer place to sleep than the bed with the clean sheets here. The tastefully prepared food that the servant put in front of her she could barely swallow. She longed for the porridge and the peppers in oil, the things concocted by Lies which she had eaten without much attention.

The security she had enjoyed for a short time in the little white house, the shelter of Hans' care, had been taken away from her. She was alone again.

On the first morning she had run crying from the breakfast table because of all the strangers and the embarrassment and confusion she had felt when they bent their heads to pray. She had tried to hold back her tears until she almost choked. After breakfast a nun had come from the hospital. She had put on a big apron with sleeves and busied herself with Maria's head,—a nun, with lips stiffly pressed together, "and the church in her eyes," as Zus called it. Maria had never before seen a nun that close; she did not know that nuns talked like other women. She had met them on the street in Warsaw and had asked, "What's that?" as if she were talking about an inanimate thing instead of a person.

Crouching over a stool in the bathroom, she had undergone the treatment. The nun had wound an oil-soaked cloth around her head and pulled a sock over it. For days Maria had had to walk about like that and there were mirrors in all the rooms. Her right arm had been smeared with black salve, because there was an itching spot on her wrist. And she had been so ashamed that she never dared sit down on the beautiful chairs. She had stayed in the garden with a picture book.

There they came to see her, Mrs. van Balekom and Ina, with their knitting and later the Consul and Zus. "Isn't it lovely here outside?" the Consul's wife exclaimed, "So nice and cool, eh?" And when Maria did not answer, she went on talking in order to put her at her ease. "Nice pictures, eh? All painted by Dutch artists. And do you know what we are going to do as soon as your wrist is healed . . . ?" Just as if she were talking to a baby, thought Maria. Wrist! Maria knew better. As soon as you are deloused, that's what she meant.

"Now, can't you guess? We'll go shopping! Yes, sure. To the big store. And we'll buy shoes, and ribbons for your hair."

Maria looked down at her dress, her own dress, which at least was clean now, and the *babouches* they had given her until she went to the shoe shop.

"I used to have ten dresses," she said. But she still couldn't risk saying anything, because already the tears welled up in her throat.

"Ten dresses . . . !" Ina exclaimed. "Even I don't have that many. Say, that was a lot of dresses!"

And then they sat in silence, while Maria turned the pages of the book, fighting to keep her tears back.

Mrs. van Balekom, who noticed—she always saw everything, Maria knew—started off on a light conversation that was intended to include Maria. The stork on the roof of the barn, the donkey on the field of stubble, the color of the flowering cactus against the wall. . . . Maria tried to think of pleasant things, but it did not help, and tears fell on the book.

"I am going to bake cookies for tea. Who's coming along?" Then Maria shuffled in behind them, stood helplessly in the kitchen leaning against the table while Arab servants walked back and forth to bring flour, eggs, milk, and salt. Mrs. van Balekom handed her a wooden spoon and Maria stirred the batter clumsily with her left hand, because the salve-covered right one was stuck into a glove. She looked timidly at the Arab girl and the cook, who tolerated their presence with impassive faces.

There was one person in the household in whose company Maria felt more at ease. With Zus, who in a way ignored her, she felt better. When the nun had come for the last time in order to shampoo and cut Maria's hair, Maria's bed was put in Zus' room. The relationship between the two events was noticed by Maria. She understood why during the first few days close contact with her had been avoided. . . . What she did not know though, was that Zus purposely left her alone in expectation that Maria would seek her out on her own initiative. Still she had insisted that Maria share her room.

"Put the girl's bed in my room," she told the servant after Maria had run from the breakfast table crying.

When, coming back from the office in the afternoon she found that on the order of the mistress of the house this had not been done, she spoke her mind.

"All right, granted the child has lice. Is that her own fault? Is that a reason why she should be isolated?"

"Why Zus . . . !" Mrs. van Balekom was never equal to the straightforward utterances of her niece who had become her husband's assistant through unforeseen circumstances. She felt that she had struck a bad bargain with Zus. As if she had ordered something from "*Au Printemps*" in Paris and had received something of a quality inferior to what the catalogue had promised.

Zus' family was one of the oldest in Holland, a noble one, but she really had revolutionary ideas, so the Consul's wife worried. No, the ticket on the goods was wrong.

"Moreover," Zus went on, "lice and charity belong together, because what would happen to charity if there were no longer any lice?" The subject seemed to please her and she pursued it. "I wonder what came first, the lice or charity. Charity probably. But then it bore another name. Yes, that is very interesting. . . . Remarkable under how many different names charity is practised. And you'll still see what they'll call it in the future. . . ."

At first Maria considered her roommate with curiosity, then with envy, and finally Zus became her ideal. She deified her privately and she looked forward to the evening when Zus came home from the office, her days just a waiting.

Maria was always outdoors, and spent her time in loneliness. The Consul's house was on a plateau with a view over the valley through which small paths, arid stretches, and the bed of a river wove a pattern, and the hills on the other side shaped themselves into a funnel running towards the sea. The low house and the surrounding quarters for the servants and the domestic animals were of bright red brick. Cedars, palms and tall shrubs kept the sun away. The garden on the south side had been laid out in terraces. The care of flowers and vegetables was entrusted to an old Arab who had no faith whatever in the agricultural advice of the lady of the house and thus achieved miracles. Cows and donkeys fraternally shared the dry field covered with stubble, at the front, chickens and geese walked unharmed among the cacti and sharply pointed crassulas. A deliciously sweet smell blended with the rural and peaceful odor of the Africaland. Maria mostly sat on a chair that Zus used for Sunday sunbaths when the others were at mass in the city. The chair stood in a sheltered place, invisible through the shrubbery. She sat there dreaming for hours, occupying her mind with fantasies in which she was the central figure, and in which Hans and Zus always played large and friendly parts. She did not walk about much because since her stay here, she imagined that the weeds on the paths and the wild grass in the field suffered beneath her footstep. On her way to the chair she avoided everything that was green and growing, which made her way of walking so strange that the Consul's wife asked her whether her feet hurt. Everything was alive now and was crushed beneath the weight of her body. She identified herself with the grass and the weeds and the smallest insect life, and felt, as it were, her own crushing footfall. In the same way she considered the relation between herself and what God represented to her, sometimes as "something" without dimensions, but more often as the primitive picture of the old man with a white beard.

She was small and powerless. God saw everything—though her mind disputed the possibility that God could be everywhere at once and could watch everybody. During a thunderstorm that broke loose after the drought of the past months she upset the whole family with her hysterical fear.

She had never occupied herself with God until she was now brought suddenly face to face with religion and the church. The Consul especially was pious, he had even had a small chapel built near the house where he went to pray in the early morning. Her confusion and embarrassment when they said grace before a meal, disappeared after a few days and gave way to curiosity. Her attention was particularly directed towards the Consul, and it astonished her to the highest degree to see such a grown-up, fat gentleman folding his hands in prayer. Later on she turned her attention upon Zus, who with a studied pose of indifference and boredom waited for the end of the procedure.

Nobody spoke to Maria on this subject. They knew that she had been a victim of the German pogrom and on the principle that one does not speak of the rope in the home of a man who has been hanged the subject was carefully avoided. The Consul and his family belonged to the category of the well-meaning, who, if the occasion should present itself, provide an alibi by declaring that some of their best friends are Jews and that Jesus was a Jew too; who think the persecution of the Jews "most unfortunate"; who, however, are convinced and bear witness to it, that bad Jews for a large part are responsible for all the misery. What they mean by "bad" Jews they have never been quite clear about. They have formed a vague picture in their minds in which money plays a large part, paired with shrewdness and noisy manners. When they are encouraged the least bit, they'll cite examples. Their Jewish friends are always those who, if they had the courage, would have themselves baptized, who anxiously avoid the subject, and who if the subject is mentioned, agree with everybody or blushingly turn their heads. They are those who hate Zionism. And who consider Hitler's persecution of the Jews his greatest "mistake," "because otherwise he would have got on much better."

Maria's parents had belonged in this category. Maria had therefore only vague ideas about her religion, a confused mixture of shame and pride. She was suddenly conscious of being Jewish. Thus she made them aware that she was not allowed to eat pork, though this was completely founded on fantasy. She had been brought up unorthodox.

"Oh, of course, how stupid of me," said Mrs. van Balekom, who felt that she had done something tactless, and she had the cutlet taken away from Maria. This reaction caused Maria great satisfaction. After that day Maria always got something else when the cook had prepared pork. This in turn filled Maria with regret and shame and after some time she declared timidly that she had resolved to eat pork.

"I won't hear of it," said the Consul's wife very decidedly. "It is no bother to us at all; we can understand it."

After Maria had been provided with her new clothes she appeared on Saturdays in her best dress and walked around on Sundays in her slacks and blouse. When they entrusted her with small duties, she did them industriously and willingly, but avoided them on Saturdays, which everybody noticed, of course. The particular position that she thus created for herself gave her more self-confidence, though very soon the comedy began to annoy her and she would rather have forgotten the whole thing.

In order to furnish her distraction Ina gave her a child's illustrated Bible and Maria looked at the pictures with a great deal of pleasure, especially at those of the New Testament. The picture of Jesus in the manger filled her with tenderness, and with longing for little Dolf. But she showed her greatest interest in the crucifixion. Its representation she examined repeatedly.

"Did they put nails in his breast?" she asked Ina.

"Yes," the older girl answered, not knowing very well how to go about the subject.

"Didn't he die then?"

"Yes, of course."

"Why did they do that?"

"They were very wicked."

"Who did it?"

Ina, who never gave a thoughtless answer, looked for a way out, but Zus, who was in the room, said, "The Jews, but that was two thousand years ago and we won't hold you responsible for it. *Allons*, put that book away and come for a walk with me, the sun will do you good."

Maria felt the division in the household: the Consul and his family against Zus.

It never came into the open, but there was always a certain tension. Zus, who had come to visit her family, had been stranded as a result of the occupation of Holland and was looking for some other occupation, a change which was tactfully encouraged by Mrs. van Balekom and which the goodhearted Consul hopefully anticipated.

Zus' somewhat confused but certainly progressive ideas weren't at all appreciated by the members of the family, who had spent twenty years in Tangier in blessed ignorance. The sarcasm and irony, through which Zus sought distraction and relief, confused the others. Her observations and remarks jarred with the pastoral disposition of the Consul and his wife and daughter.

Without realizing what caused the friction between Zus and her relatives, Maria instinctively chose the side of the niece. She enjoyed Zus' remarks, though of course she didn't understand their implications. She felt protection in the aggressiveness of Zus, protection against the outside world.

From Zus she received the first lessons in social thinking. Although the instruction was confused, without foundation, and more emotional than intellectual, it influenced Maria's thoughts to such a degree that it distracted her from herself.

But weeks passed before Maria had recovered sufficiently to understand anything outside herself. During those weeks she groped her way through a dark tunnel wherein everyday things acquired exaggerated and frightening proportions.

Maria had anticipated the purchase of new clothes with eagerness, but when the moment came to drive to the city, she was reluctant. She stood by the car in her light cotton dress, slippers on her feet. Her hair hung in irregular fronds around her pinched face, which in spite of good food still had kept its unhealthy appearance. She held her arms stiffly by her sides, in her eyes an expression of unwillingness to hide her timidity and fear.

"Must she come along dressed this way?" said Ina, about to get into the car, a white gloved hand on the handle of the door. "Mother, why didn't you give her a dress and some shoes of mine?"

"Oh, I hadn't thought about that. No, she actually can't go this way." The Consul's wife looked pleadingly at the Consul next to her at the wheel. But he said impatiently: "*Allons*, it is already nine o'clock. Let's go. Zus and I must get to the office."

Maria, who while Ina talked had looked straight ahead towards the donkeys and the cows in the field, said in a shrill voice: "I would rather not! I'll stay home!"

"What is the matter, Maria? No, really . . ." the Consul's wife looked quite upset.

"I don't need new clothes," Maria whispered.

The Consul, suddenly red in the face, started the motor.

"Come on, get in," Ina urged.

"No," said Maria. "I would rather not." She cast a quick glance at Zus in the back seat of the car. Then she looked at the stubble field with the animals which moved before her eyes in a haze, as if it were flooded with water. The Consul stopped the motor with an ostentatious gesture and leaned out of the window on the other side, as if he were only interested in the view.

"Come on, Maria," the Consul's wife implored, "the Consul wants to get to his office."

"I'll stay home. Please . . ." said Maria. 'I hate you,' she thought, 'I hate you all. Let me alone, I don't want any new clothes. I look ugly. I am ugly.' She suddenly had the picture of Lies before her, as she often used to see her. The body walking behind the head which was carried on a pike, Lies' body in the worn printed dress with the dirty spots at the sides where she rubbed her hands. And the belly swollen, because that was where the baby was.

"Don't you want any new clothes?" asked Mrs. van Balekom.

Maria shook her head. Lies was often nice, she thought. She wanted to go home, to the hill and the flowers that Hans had sown.

"Why didn't you say so before?" asked Ina. "We are going to the city specially for your sake, see?"

"What nonsense, Ina," said her mother. "The child can't keep running around this way. We can't have any guests."

"Thank God," said Zus.

'I hate you,' thought Maria, 'you with your crazy nightgowns that almost make you look naked. I hate you.'

"*Alors, qu'est-ce-que c'est que ça*, couldn't you have argued that out before?" asked the Consul, consulting his watch.

"Come, darling, be patient, Maria will go along. Won't you, Maria? She'll come along like a good girl."

Maria did not move. She stared at the ground; her hands were moist with perspiration and her heartbeats shook her whole body. 'If I were dead, you people would be sorry,' she thought. 'If I were dead.'

"You might be nicer, Maria. Why are you so stubborn?" Ina laid a hand upon Maria's arm. "Instead of being grateful . . ."

But Zus interrupted her. "That's enough, Ina." She got out of the car and hung her short white coat over Maria's shoulders. She pushed her with soft insistence into the car. Then she said to the Consul, "Go on, Uncle Niek, we are ready." She got in, Ina followed her, and the Consul started the motor for the second time. He drove the car carefully down the hill. The chickens and the geese went clucking and chattering to the side of the road.

In the car Zus exchanged her shoes for the babouches, Maria was wearing. But Mrs. van Balekom protested, "Zus, please, you can't walk around on slippers."

"Why shouldn't I?" she said airily. "Maria did, didn't she?" Upon which remark the Consul suddenly started to laugh—the chuckling of a good-hearted fat man. His shoulders shook and they saw his neck swell.

On their way to the shopping section Maria was presented to the acquaintances of the Consul's wife, doing their shopping at this time of the day: "The little refugee we have taken in with us." And as the ladies looked Maria up and down, she would add, as if she were apologizing for Maria's appearance, "We are going to buy clothes for her. Just now. Yes, lots of fun." And then affectionately pinching Maria's arm, "*Hein, Maria, ma petite?* We have two daughters now. No, we did not adopt her. In due time she'll go to Lisbon. We have written to a committee. . . ."

Maria, feeling like a sacrificial lamb, tried to give a friendly smile because this she knew was expected of her. But she was shy, deafened and confused by the noise around her. People rushed by in a great hurry, pushing her to the side.

Everybody was trying to get ahead of the others in her buying. Since the stoppage of the importations from Portugal, shopping had become a real problem even for people with money to spend. It had come to be a question of ingeniousness and agility, of influence and power of persuasion, of flattery and hidden threats. It was a chase after groceries and clothes, after practically everything. The provisions were exhausted and what was imported and reached the stores without the Spaniards confiscating it for the coastal garrison was sold for double the price. People used all their power and beguilement. It was an exhausting state of affairs for everybody. They comforted each other by stating that it was even worse in Tetuan and Ceuta. The people who went there with a one-day pass brought back bread, grey as clay, hard as rock, and as indigestible. Here only the Arab population suffered from hunger though the poor Spaniards were miserable. So it wasn't so bad, they said. It was much worse in Tetuan and Ceuta. Even the better classes got nothing but stomach ulcers, as the jokers said. No, here it wasn't so bad, after all. With some influence and skill. . . . In a certain way the ladies and gentlemen enjoyed the chase after food; it broke the monotony and formed part of the new existence: Red Cross work, war relief, parties, concerts for the British this or the French that. . . . .

They ran past each other on the street with a greeting or a joke, having hardly time for a chat. The porters dragged heavy baskets behind them. The ladies no longer dared leave their shopping to the servants. Oranges and potatoes were counted, the weight of rice and sugar was checked. They were cheated by everybody, by the merchants, by the porters, by the servants. And then the refugees! They had taken possession of the town, they-pushed to the front in the shops and the market. They upset the standards; they paid more to the porters, to the servants. One had to struggle to keep ahead of them. Yes, life had become more interesting.

Maria, walking behind the Consul's wife and Ina, wanted to stretch out her hand for support, but she didn't dare to. All noises had meanings different from their real ones for her. The shrill voices that met her on the Socco Grande, shouting *"Porteur?"* sounded like a menace. The call of a beggar was accusation. The braying of a donkey a complaint. The question of a market woman a mockery. In the tooting of an auto she heard a shriek. The sounds seemed to possess her senses so that she became almost blind to the colorful life around her. She saw just spots, white sunshine, movement of shadows, suddenly an outstretched hand with an egg in it, a large white lily, a flag, a gate, a broad black umbrella, a child, a bicycle. . . .

The somber coolness of the department store enveloped her as if she had been rescued from a furious, seething sea.

"First the dress," came the matter-of-fact voice of the Consul's wife. First the dress, it echoed in her head. She let herself be handled—first one dress, then another. She stood limply, sticking out her stomach, with slumping shoulders, her eyes helplessly turned towards Mrs. van Balekom.

"Too long, too short, not the right color, haven't you got anything else? Nothing at all?—Hello, *comment ça va?* This is the little refugee that we have taken into our house. How is your husband? Maria, stand straight. Will see you in a while at Perrod's. Hot, isn't it? Which dress would you like, Maria? Tell me. Shoes—two pair. Heavens, how expensive! Do they fit well, Maria? Panties with elastic. What size do you think? Ina, what size do you take? Stand up straight, Maria! Do you want a little handbag? No? Why not? What a strange girl you are! When Ina was your age . . . Let's see, do we have everything? I'll give you a check. Put it all together in one box. . . ."

Maria acquiesced, with a smile on her face, because she really tried to be good. She saw strange faces, hands that turned her around, scarlet fingernails. Greasy black hair, red and green combs, ladies who patted her cheeks, "*probrecita refugiada polacca.*"

Later in the taxi on the way home she quietly sobbed as Mrs. van Balekom and Ina exchanged surprised looks and signified to each other that they mustn't talk to her.

That night before she went to sleep Maria heard the clock stop. Suddenly out of the silence the ticking of the clock had come forward, plainly and emphatically, a speedy ticking, which suddenly stopped and then the quietude, immeasurable quietude. She sat up with a jerk, the ticking of the clock within her, vibrating through her whole body. But in the room there was a deathly silence. 'I heard the clock stop,' she thought, 'I, Maria, heard the clock stop. It was a tremendous happening, the greatest. I, Maria Lefkowitz, heard the clock stop.' She sat in the world, the black silence, the endless world. Maria Lefkowitz sat in the world. And then came the discovery. . . . 'I am I. I, Maria Lefkowitz, am I.' And then again the tremendous happening, 'I heard the clock stop. I heard it! I! I, Maria Lefkowitz. I am sitting here. And outside is the world, endless, and I am I.' And the astonishment, the wondering about the wonder, "I."

And then from the silence, the fear like an increasing, deafening noise, like a wave as high as a tower, that engulfed her, like tentacles . . . a deafening, crushing, choking fear. The waiting, waiting until it should grasp her. It enlarged and grew and grabbed for her. . . .

She struggled to get out of bed, kicking savagely to get rid of the sheets wound around her legs. She reached the door, looked desperately for the handle, found her way blindly through the hall to the living room.

There under the soft light of some shaded lamps they sat together, the Consul and his wife with the guests around the bridge table, Ina under a lamp with her needlework, Zus at the table with her books and newspapers.

The restful, homelike atmosphere struck Maria like a blow in the face. She stood blinking for a few moments. Then she threw herself into the room towards where Zus sat, sobbing loudly.

At the bridge table they sat rigid with the cards in their hands, Ina frozen with fright and Zus white as a sheet.

"Good heavens!" said Mrs. van Balekom.

"Poor lamb, certainly had a bad dream," said one of the guests.

Zus took hold of Maria and led her away. The Consul wiped his bald pate with a handkerchief. "*Il fait chaud,*" he said. He went to open the doors to the garden. The heavy, sweet odor of the flowers flowed into the room. Above the hills on the other side of the valley the sky was lit up by the moon. The cedar trees stood out, ink-black and motionless as sentries before the house. Maria's shrieking had stopped. They heard Zus' voice, calm and friendly, at the window of her bedroom. "Look what a beautiful night.—Do you smell the hyssop?—So many stars, eh? Do you know their names?—Quiet, isn't it?"

The Consul came back to the bridge table. "I shall have to write to Lisbon again," he muttered. "Whose bid?"

14

THE NEXT MORNING Maria came to breakfast with a mixed feeling of shame and importance. The doorknob of the dining room felt round and large in her hand. Should she come in and sit down as usual? And would she be able to be casual about it? Wouldn't she be bashful? She shouldn't show anything,—or should she rather act in a peculiar way—sit down with downcast eyes, not be able to eat, so that they would all notice and take pity on her? But the Arab servant came with the tea tray and held the door open for her so she had to go in.

In the room nobody paid any attention to her. There was a lively conversation going on. After a while Ina asked politely how she felt and said, "Did you hear, Maria, that Germany has declared war on Russia?" Then turned back to who was talking.

The Consul said the prayer as if he were in a hurry, Maria thought. And hardly was it over, when Zus began to talk again, mad now, pounding her fist on the table.

"When that is the way you feel about it you can no longer work in my office," said the Consul. "*Si j'aurais su . . .!*" Whereupon Zus burst out into laughter, throwing her head back—though Maria was sure that it was not really because she felt so happy.

"Oh, please, Zus, control yourself," said the Consul's wife. But Zus laughed until the tears ran down her cheeks.

Maria had to laugh too and then of course it was impossible for her to strike an interesting attitude. Attention centered on her, however, and Mrs. van Balekom said: "Maria, maybe if you will go and sit in the garden we'll come and get you when the doctor comes." That was her way of telling Maria what to do, "maybe . . ." thoughtfully and with tact.

Still Maria was frightened. "The doctor?"

"Yes, we'll bring some color back to those cheeks and the doctor will give you something for your nerves."

'Just say it,' thought Maria, 'you think that I am strange, you are afraid that I am crazy, that's why you call the doctor—'

After breakfast she looked at herself in the mirror to see herself as the doctor would see her. She decided to put on her best dress. But the Consul's wife saw her walking through the house and called her back, and she had to change again to one of her everyday dresses. Maria felt ridiculous, as if she had been caught in some intimate act. At first her thoughts in the garden were filled with hatred and spitefulness. Then she began to dream.

As she was waiting, watching for a car, her ears cocked for the noise of the motor, she was making up things in her mind about the doctor. He would at once be very friendly to her.—I had a little daughter your age, she is dead now. Will you come and call on me? —She went every day after that and finally remained to live there. She did the housekeeping and she wrote the names of the patients in a book. She was allowed to call the doctor "Father." When she got this far in her thoughts, he began to look like her father, then as an old man with a white beard and chestnut brown hair and spectacles,—a mixture of her childhood-God and the family physician in Poland.

As she heard the motor, and saw the top of the car appear, she began to read; and as she was called, she pretended that she did not hear and they had to come and fetch her.

The doctor was different from what she had imagined him to be. His manner was not friendly, it was even brusque. His appearance too was a disappointment—tall and skinny with jagged front teeth stained brown from smoking. She could not help looking at them.

"This is Maria," the Consul's wife said. "Shake hands, Maria"— even before she could do it on her own initiative.

They eyed each other, the doctor and the girl. To him she was a specimen of the kind of people that had changed his life. The arrival of the refugees had robbed him of his position. He had been king here; now he was reduced to his normal stature. The foreigners were more worldly wise than the European and American residents, who had been his patients for a decade and who obeyed him implicitly. The foreigners who came to him for help knew their own little afflictions which they generally attributed to their disturbed nervous systems. They saw through his consultations, operations-de-luxe and unnecessary treatments. They wanted only a medical statement certifying that their immediate departure from these climes was urgent. When they were really ill they consulted their own doctors, their countrymen who shared their fate, and he was only called in to secure room for them in the hospital.

Maria felt his distrust. She put a limp hand in his dry fingers and looked at his teeth.

"Does she speak French?" the doctor asked Mrs. van Balekom.

"Polish and German and Spanish and Arabic," Maria said quickly.

He smiled indulgently and spoke to her in rapid Arabic, which she could not follow.

She looked into his eyes in an inimical manner, but did not say a thing.

"Do you want to give her a check-up here, or in the bedroom?" The Consul's wife got up, her breath came quick and her cheeks were flushed.

"Let's talk a bit first," he said. "She's such a whizz at languages. How old are you, Maria?"

He plied her with the usual questions, in plain French now, without taking his eyes off her.

"Do you have bad dreams sometimes?" he asked her.

"No," said Maria.

"Do you go to sleep right away?"

She shrugged her shoulders.

"What do you do before you go to sleep?"

"Think," she said.

"So, you think." He nodded his head as if he had expected that answer.

"And what do you think about?"

"I don't know," said Maria.

"Do you think about boys?" he said.

Mrs. van Balekom clenched her hands and smiled nervously. Maria didn't move, looking at the brown pointed teeth.

"Do you want to examine her now, Doctor?" asked the Consul's wife.

"Yes; come, take your clothes off, young lady."

Helped by Mrs. van Balekom, Maria divested herself of her top clothes.

The doctor took a few instruments out of his bag. "Take off everything," he said, "it's warm enough."

"Yes, it is really getting quite hot," said the Consul's wife. "Come Maria, hold yourself straight."

Maria stood in the center of the room, huddled together in order to cover herself as much as possible. The doctor on the chair opposite her looked her up and down as he closed one eye.

"Does she eat all right?" he asked.

"Oh yes, she eats more than Ina."

He began to examine her, passed his hand along her spinal cord, applied the stethoscope and listened at her back. Maria stood motionless, her breath came in short gasps, confused thoughts raced through her head, she was paralyzed with shame and feelings of guilt. She thought about Hans, their trysts at the hill, his hands over her body. The doctor knew; yes, the doctor could see it. . . .

"Cough, please," he said, and to the Consul's wife, "Does she go to school?"

"No, we thought she had better not. We wanted to put some weight on her first and she has to get used to normal surroundings."

"Do send her to school," he said. "And let her be occupied. That's the main thing. Then such scenes as last night won't occur any more. This little girl must be taken in hand." He turned Maria around so she was facing him and applied the stethoscope to her small breasts.

"She is already well developed. Does she menstruate yet?" Maria did not know the meaning of the word but she understood what he was referring to.

"I don't know," said Mrs. van Balekom timidly, "I didn't ask her . . . she didn't . . . not since she has been here. I don't think so. She's still such a child."

"Hmm," said the doctor emphatically. "Well?" he asked Maria.

She did not answer, but looked longingly at her clothes on the chair.

'I want to go away,' she thought, 'I want to go home, Father, Mother, Lies—.'

The doctor gave her neck a friendly pat. "You can dress now," he said. "She is perfectly healthy; there is nothing the matter with her. Send her to school and let her go in for some sport—swimming, tennis."

They looked at her while she was putting on her clothes, waiting until she had left the room so that they could talk freely about her. Maria dressed herself, her fingers stiff, her movements awkward. She did it laboriously, with great difficulty. Then she fled from the room, bashfully mumbling a farewell.

Once outside in the garden she stood for a moment undecided. Then, thinking how she had exposed herself in her nakedness, she ran out of the garden moaning softly, looking first to the left and then to the right. She raced down the hill, breaking into a wild run along the busy streets in the blazing sun, onto the asphalt road, past the fish cannery towards the house on the hill. "I want to go home," she repeated mechanically. "I want to go home."

If there was a God, why did He allow such things to happen? And if he didn't have time to pay any attention to you why wasn't there somebody else to protect you?

God had to watch over the children in Poland, and over those in Germany and France. She knew those countries existed because she had travelled through them. Alongside Luba, she had looked out of the train window. So many roads, fields, woods, mountains—millions of them—she thought—and people! Along the railroad tracks were farms, a woman was going to the well, a child was carrying wood. That child was somebody too, she had thought. And while the train was running on, her thoughts busied themselves with the child: It was going to school, it had perhaps a small brother, it slept during the night in a bed.

People and children in the cities, people whom you did not know, but people just the same. God had to watch over all those people and children. While she thought of this, she envisioned the child with the wood in its arms, the people at the railroad crossing.

Was it because Allah was God here? Was that why God wasn't present here? But what of the Consul and his family? God was in the chapel the Consul had built. God really looked out for some people though Allah took care of the Arabs.

Why did God allow all these things to happen to her and not to Ina? God had not prevented the Germans from taking away her father and mother. True, He had taken pity on her and Luba. He had protected them in someone's attic. But perhaps those people to whom the attic belonged were Christians? Perhaps only the Christians were protected by God. No, that couldn't be either, because He had protected them on their way to France, and later when the bombs fell on the train, she and Luba had not been hit. Sure, God had protected them. Perhaps He had sent them Lies and Aart.

But why did He allow things to happen like this, to stand nude before the doctor? And hunger! And carrying the pails! And Luba's running away! And the desire to do *that* with Hans. It might be that God had only time to look after big things. To see that you didn't die, that you were not real bad,—on small things He couldn't find time. Of course not. There were all the people. Billions. She again saw the child with its load of wood and the people who waited along the railroad tracks.

Still He took care of Ina in small matters. Didn't she have her own room in her father's house, and girl friends she had chosen herself? And God had equipped her with "things" Maria sensed but which she couldn't express. Like Ina's self-confidence, her smug exaggeration of the importance of everything that was hers, and the belittling of anything she could not get; a certain intolerance coming from a feeling that she belonged to a superior class—certain attitudes and qualities through which she made Maria suffer and for which Maria envied Ina.

As she calmed down she slowed her pace, becoming aware of her surroundings. The asphalt road, and, halfway up the hill, the white cabin that stood shimmering with the sun reflected from its shiny windows. It was quiet on the road; from the field sounded the song of an Arab farmer and from the hill the shrill voices of the children. Berthe and Pierre were playing around the house. They would be happy to have her back "because it is always nice to welcome somebody who has been away from home." Thus she realized that it wasn't her personality which caused joy, only the occasion of a reunion. She knew that nobody liked her very much, but she never made an effort to be more kind towards the children as she didn't realize that a gesture on her part would result in a more intimate relationship. She only thought that she had to be gayer, but her forced exhilaration frightened and embarrassed the children. She knew that today she would be the center of attraction; afterwards they would keep out of her way or they would sigh because she was so difficult. She prepared herself for the following hours as for a party of which she would be the hostess. She walked slowly in order to relish at leisure her fantasies on the reunion: Maria, you! Lies, Maria is back! Lies' arms around her and the strong odor of her heavy body. The chair that was pulled up for her. How neat you look, Maria! Gee, I better put on my Sunday dress—and more jokes of the same kind from Lies. Are those your own clothes? the children would ask. Look, Pierre, Maria has shoes on. Do you have underwear too? Let's see. Don't be silly now. Maria has become a lady! Maria has become a lady . . . ! Friendly faces around her—the lean, tanned face of Lies, the round and blond of Berthe. And Pierre with the large eyes and old-man's grin, now he was losing his baby teeth.

Little Dolf bobbing up and down on her knee, the sweet smell of his neck. . . . Rainer indifferent, friendly though. And Hans: "Tell us everything, Maria."

When she had gone around the last bend in the road, she saw a man on the path that led up the hill. A man in European clothes. Aart! It was Aart! He walked with hesitating steps, looked towards the house. He stopped at the fence, opened the little gate. She saw the small figures of Berthe and Pierre standing still and then turning about without uttering a word and disappearing into the house.

Maria climbed the hill, her thoughts turned from the little world in which she was to have played the leading part, and again she took up the problem in which she had been involved before. Why do you do that, God? Oh why? It was my turn. It was me who was coming home. For me the welcome, the reception. Why, God? Why did you let Aart come home today; why not tomorrow?

She stood at the fence hidden by a cactus plant. She saw the children come out on the little terrace, then Lies who pushed them aside and flew into Aart's arms. She saw them go in, heard the outcries and the shouts. She slipped down in the grass by the lattice work, sitting so near the cactus plant that with every movement the spines pricked her back. She closed her eyes against the burning sun. In her mind's eye she saw what was being enacted in the cabin. At the same time the image of the Consul's car coming down the asphalt road, Mrs. van Balekom at the wheel. Ina next to her looking to the right and the left. It was as if she heard the clipped voice of the girl, "I can't understand her at all, the child must have run straight home."

When she afterwards really saw the car turning the corner, she got up and started walking down the hill. She saw that the car had stopped, and was slowly pulling over onto the shoulder of the road. She saw Mrs. van Balekom get out, speak with Ina, then look up to the house searchingly. Maria started to run, jumping over the green patches in the path, because even at this moment she was afraid to crush anything growing.

"But, child," said Mrs. van Balekom, her voice worried but without a trace of reproach.

Maria stood before her, her face contorted in a grin. She was breathing laboriously and shaken by dry sobs.

"But, child, what *is* the matter!" the Consul's wife repeated.

"There was nobody home," Maria gasped. "Let's go back."

After that day the attitude of the family changed towards Maria. Though the doctor had assured them that she was completely normal they mistrusted her. The Consul's wife reflected upon what had been said during the doctor's call, trying to find a key to Maria's behavior. She never got beyond the remembrance of his question, whether Maria thought of boys before she went to sleep. A strange question, that she turned over and over in her mind, until she was so familiar with it that she found it quite natural that the doctor had asked it. She considered Maria in that light, put the girl in the surroundings from which she was now certain she had "saved" her. She came to the conclusion that the question advanced by the doctor contained not a possibility but a certainty, and that Maria's thoughts before she went to sleep had been inspired by experience. Moreover through a conversation with Ina she found confirmation of what she had seen herself but had refused to believe, namely that in Maria's facial expression and her conduct at the foot of the hill her abnormality had been manifest.

"Weird," said Ina, whispering confidentially, "really weird. It gives me the creeps; I think that she ought to be put in a home. No, Mother, not in an institution, but somewhere where she can quiet down, where people know how to treat difficult children. Why don't you take her to the nuns? She could help in the hospital, she would be busy and . . ." Here Ina began to make excuses because she felt guilty under her mother's reproachful looks.

Mrs. van Balekom wanted to do her duty, though she had to suppress a slight feeling of disgust in her relations with Maria, a feeling for which she did penance upon advice of her father confessor and for which she also found relief in prayer.

Her conscience barely allowed her to speak about it to her husband. "Not that I want to get rid of her, dear—don't think that. Goodness knows, there is so little we can do anyway to help the war effort, being so isolated, nothing going on here."

"Nothing going on here, eh?" said Zus ironically.

"I'd gladly make the sacrifice," Mrs. van Balekom went on, trying to ignore Zus, "but for the child herself. . . . Did you write to the committee again?"

He assured her that the affair was being taken care of and that he would soon have an answer. The plan was, as he told her, to send Aart and Lies with the baby to the Netherlands East Indies. The children would travel with them until they had reached Lisbon, whereafter the committee would take over.

"Do Aart and Lies know about it?" she asked.

"*Pas encore,* have patience. I'll tell them when things start moving."

"Do you think they want to go?"

"They have no choice. The Netherlands Government in London has arranged to send dependent Dutch refugees in North Africa to the Indies."

"Sure . . . to the Indies," said Zus mockingly, "but they'll have to go in one hell of a hurry or the Japs will beat them to it."

This remark infuriated the Consul. For the first time the members of the family could remember, he lost his composure and went beyond the small fits of temper that usually indicated his displeasure and for which his wife and daughter feigned respect. He lost all control of himself and accused Zus of treason and defeatism, blaming her for her communistic—then correcting himself—anarchistic ideas, and finally he fired her from her job and told her to get out of his house.

That same evening Zus packed her trunks, but through the intercession of the Consul's wife they made up, although Zus did not unpack, finding consolation in having her luggage on chairs and tables in her room.

A cloud descended over the house. Mrs. van Balekom and Ina talked in whispers with sidelong glances at Zus and the Consul. The problem "Maria" was sidetracked. She was not sent to school now that other plans had been made.

Maria suffered from the changed attitude towards her. She wandered all over the big house trying to find some place where she could relax in warmth and understanding. She looked at the faces of the others, looked for a sign of recognition in their eyes, for but one sign of affection or even sympathy; she listened to the words addressed to her and tried to find in them a tone of kindness. She went to sit in different places in the house, hoping to feel more at home; sometimes she sat on the gay couch in the living room, then again in the dark wooden chair next to the fireplace in the newly finished room, or on the bench in the hallway, where the light from the high colored window hung like a ribbon in the darkness, or at the table in the dining room with the portfolio of plates on the Persian runner, or in the kitchen, where the busy servants walked in and out. She sat here and there, waiting for a solution to her loneliness. She listened docilely to the words of the Consul's wife or Ina— "Come on, Maria, do something." "Why don't you go in the garden and knit?" But she never went farther than a few steps in a given direction. Then she stood, hesitating, thought about what she contemplated doing, retraced her steps, and resumed her wanderings through the house.

15

Aart sat on the little terrace and stared out over the hazy bay until his eyelids burned from the brilliant light. Like a stubborn child that turns his head away from what he can't get, he avoided looking at the field below the hill.

Yesterday when he had looked for the family, he had gone there first and found the piece of cardboard on which Lies had written in her childish handwriting, "We are living in the little white house against the hill." He had laughed derisively at his own gullibility, his trust in Lies and the children, at his believing in them. Standing on the field a feeling of futility had overwhelmed him. His eyes wandered over the neglected vegetable beds where the brown shrivelled sprouts were visible in the tangle of weeds. Next to the closed cabin with Lies' message on the door, stood the hood of the trailer, now discolored and half fallen against the fig tree. At the hedge a spot of mouldering earth showed where the manure pile had been.

During his term in prison, though filled with hatred for his torturers, for Manus, for the Consul, he had waited calmly for his release, like a man who knows that his affairs are in good hands and closes his eyes in peace. He had weighed his distrust of Hans against his trust in Lies. He had always known that her admiration for him, for his strength, his adventurous character and his indifference towards society had been the actuating motives for her fidelity and devotion.

Now he knew that he had lost her. He had lost her because she was awakened; she had recognized true strength and independence in Hans.

This morning after sunrise he had seen Hans in the doorway, a finger upon his lips because Berthe and Pierre wanted to shout the news of Aart's homecoming to him. Aart had feigned sleep in order to master a feeling of shame and humiliation that then were still incomprehensible to himself. Hans had gone away and while the children whispered together, Aart had tried to strike a balance about his position in the house, looking vainly for a way to establish his prestige.

Later, when they met at breakfast, Hans had greeted him rather self-consciously. "Hello, Aart, how are you?"

Aart, holding back the questions, "Where were you yesterday?" "Where were you last night?" did not utter a word. He acknowledged Hans' presence with only a slight wave of his hand.

"Doesn't he look well, Hans?" Lies had asked, and caressing his shorn head, said clumsily, "That stubble is becoming to him, don't you think?"

She kissed him then, realizing the foolishness of her words. In the silence that ensued even the children seemed to feel oppressed. Then Hans had pushed the table towards the center, arranged the plates, the mugs and the forks, and put the bread, the milk and the honey in the middle.

From the kitchen Lies brought a frying pan with bacon. The children sat down at the table, suddenly noisy, and hiding their embarrassment on Aart's account in loud talk. Berthe took Dolf on her knees, demonstrating with a great deal of ado that the little fellow had been entrusted to her care. "Sit nice now, *ne touche pas.* Oh, dirty boy, you've got a dirty diaper again. He always has diarrhea. *Tiens,* Berthe'll feed you."

Aart looked at the bacon. "Boy," he said, "somebody seems to have money around here."

"That's in your honor," said Lies. "Hans brought it."

"Did you know that Aart had come home?" asked Berthe, but Hans did not answer her.

"We often eat meat now," she told Aart. "We have all become fatter, except for little Dolf who has diarrhea." She blew up her cheeks. Little Dolf imitated her and milk spilled from his chin down his dirty jersey.

"Tomorrow I'm going to school," said Pierre. He smiled confidently at Hans.

"Doesn't he look funny, though?" said Berthe, pointing at Pierre. "He is losing his teeth but the new ones are already coming. Just like Dolf." She opened the baby's mouth, pushed a finger along his upper jaw. Little Dolf shoved her hand away and grasped for his mug on the table. "Do you want to feel, Aart?" Berthe suggested.

"I saw it yesterday," said Aart.

They heard footsteps on the porch. Rainer came in, bringing a strong smell of sweat with him. He looked around. "It is hot in here," he said. His eyes rested for a moment upon Aart, then on Hans.

"Aart, was it so hot in prison too, *aussi chaud qu'ici?*" Pierre asked. He had never concerned himself about Aart's fate; the children had forgotten his existence within a few weeks. Now that Aart had come home Pierre's interest had been aroused. In his imagination the prison looked like a hospital, though he realized that things were different there.

"Come on, Pierre, eat," Rainer admonished him.

But Aart said, "It was cooler than here."

"Yes," said Rainer, "such an old building, all made of stone, never any sun."

"You talk as if you had been there." Aart put a piece of bacon in his mouth, and chewed it slowly.

"In the hospital everything was stone," Pierre related, "and everything was white."

Nobody answered and Pierre continued, "They did not beat the people in the hospital. Did they beat you, Aart?"

They looked at him in astonishment, then aghast at Aart. Lies lifted her hand in a threatening gesture towards Pierre.

"Leave him alone," Aart said with a wry smile.

The meal was finished in silence. Pierre, who felt that he had done something wrong, belched loudly and burst into laughter.

"Who is coming along to the beach?" asked Berthe. "Aart, are you coming?"

"There is a pail filled with diapers in the yard," said Hans.

She stuck her tongue out at him and looked at Aart for approval but Aart did not seem to be listening. He pushed his chair against the wall and went outside, where he rolled himself a cigarette. Hans came to stand next to him. "It's too bad about the field," he said, his voice like steel, as if he were forcing himself to say this but was completely in control of himself.

"Wasn't that what you wanted?" said Aart.

"It was the only solution."

"I guess so."

They stared out towards the bay, which emerged from the morning fog.

"We did everything to get you out. *Rien à faire*. The Consul has absolutely no influence, or perhaps he did not care to . . ." Hans' voice was natural now. "Finally . . ."

"I know all about it," Aart interrupted impatiently. "The *shous* told me everything. Who's that female that got me out?"

"Somebody I know," said Hans in some embarrassment. "She works in the bar where I wash glasses. It was the only solution. She knew the officer in charge. You can't get anything done in the legal way."

"Does Lies know about it?" asked Aart.

"No."

"And Rainer?"

"Of course not."

Aart walked down the steps of the little terrace, crossed the yard and went out of the gate. He went slowly down the hill. Then half-way down he stood still, as if he had suddenly changed his mind, and came back. He brought the only chair out on the terrace and sat down on it. Lies took her crochet work out, and let herself down carefully on the steps. She looked up at Aart and laughed. "My guy, home again," she said.

Hans passed by them, waved a greeting and walked out of the gate. He carried a large empty basket.

"Hans works at the market," said Lies, without his having asked her anything. "He brings quite a little money home."

He said nothing. Below on the asphalt road stood the truck. Rainer was busy trying to get the motor going. The noise reached the hill above. "My car," thought Aart. Hans hoisted himself into the back and the truck disappeared quickly around the corner.

Lies squirmed on the steps and sighed.

"Does it bother you?" he said, indicating her swollen body.

"Pain in the back," she said. "Just like the first time."

He did not answer. He looked at Berthe, who drove Pierre in front of her to the well. Both carried pails and Berthe had little Dolf on her back. Their voices sounded clear in the wide silence of the land.

Lies followed his eyes, quickly looked up at him and bent again over her crochet work. "I make one sock a day," she said. "That's ten francs a day."

Aart kept looking at the children until they disappeared behind the hill.

"Why don't you take care of Dolf yourself?" he asked.

She kept on working. The coarse crochet hook in her hand moved quickly up and down, the ball of wool turning around in her ample lap.

"Are you ill?"

"I don't know. . . ." She did not lift her head. "I don't know what's the matter with me. Was," she quickly corrected herself. "I was so miserable, not about this," she pressed her small brown hands against her body, "but because . . . everything, the whole mess, it was all so hopeless, that bunch here, the Consul, he is so stupid. Oh, I really don't know. Perhaps it's just me. I don't know."

He stared over the bay, his legs stretched out straight in front of him, his bare feet turned outward, his hands in his pockets.

"Why didn't you want to . . . last night?" he asked. His voice sounded gruff, but she noticed his wavering, the effort it took in asking this question.

"I don't know," she said. "I don't know anything."

They both thought back at the long night, in the broiling hot cubicle. The children on their mattress, billowy forms in the moonlight, stirring restlessly at every noise.

"Where was Hans last night?" he asked.

"He's never at home nights." She began to laugh. "Sure sleeping with the women," she said. He noticed the forced joke. She was trying to amuse him. She admired Hans, he knew, and she tried to hide it from him. He looked across the water, where now the coast of Spain was slowly emerging from the haze. All respect for him was gone for good, that he knew. Where he had failed, Hans had succeeded. Hans had taken them out of their poverty. As he came home yesterday he had realized this. During the night he had become sure; in Lies' resistance he had found the confirmation of his fear. She wasn't aware of it yet but the admiration for him, for his enterprise with the trailer and the field was gone. She looked at him the way others, friends and relatives in Holland, saw him. Somebody who lacked the courage to tackle reality and the world and fled to his own desert island—the car in this instance; somebody who looked for bodily, physical resistance, because he did not dare attack the moral and the psychic. They don't understand, he thought, they don't understand, they don't understand. The pain lay like a weight in his chest. They don't understand me. . . . And then to know to whom he owed his release from jail was like a wound that would never heal, that festered under his hot skin. Gratitude and rancor struggled in him, exhausting him, because he lacked the strength to be grateful.

Berthe's head with the large Arab hat appeared on the rim of the hill, then her skinny body, clad in a pair of Hans' old trousers held up under her arms by a piece of string. She came towards the house, her knees above the nettles and the cactus, her face spotted with heat, her frizzy blond hair sticking to her temples.

"Hello," she said in a friendly manner to Aart and then turning to Lies, "The Fatimas say that I cannot use the water for the diapers. We must save it because it won't rain any more."

"Oh, the hell with them," said Lies.

"They are right," said Berthe thoughtfully. "Pretty soon there won't be any more water . . . then we'll be thirsty." She stood in front of the little terrace now, her head bent sideways, and looked at them, thinking painfully. "I'll bring the diapers down to the field. Then I'll wash them at our old well."

"No," said Aart. He cleared his throat. "No, don't do that."

Berthe turned around, "Booh," she said over her shoulder. "Nobody'll notice it."

She trotted away. A moment later they saw her walk straight across the hill with little Dolf and Pierre. They heard Dolf's whimpering, Berthe's shushing voice as they went down.

"It's so hot here," Lies mumbled. She got up with difficulty and entered the house, her hands pressed upon her back. Aart stayed, staring across the bay. Indifferently he greeted the Arabs, old friends, who were passing by and bade him welcome home.

Down below on the field Berthe was washing the diapers at the well. She had her own way of doing this—that is, with the least amount of work and with the best results. Pierre had to hold her as she, bending over the well, hoisted the heavy pail. Sitting on the ground he held her by the ankles.

"If I let go, you fall in," he said. She had heard him say this so often that she no longer paid any attention to it. After she had filled two pails, she started to rinse the dirty, threadbare pieces of cloth. Pierre made himself comfortable leaning his back against the stone wellhead.

"From now on you must help me," Berthe said suddenly.

"Why?"

"Just because."

"Who says so?"

She hesitated a moment. "Aart," she lied, "Aart has said so."

"How do you know?" he asked illogically.

"Oh, dope, he told me so himself."

They both stopped talking. He looked at her, a furrow between his eyes. The sun shone fiercely on their heads. She had put her broad-brimmed hat over little Dolf. He was sleeping in the shade of the hat, exhausted by his diarrhea, against which even the herbs of the Arab women seemed to be of no avail. Berthe wiped her perspiring forehead with the back of her hand. "Bah," she said, "*merde*." Pierre did not laugh, but continued looking at her gravely.

"Are there soldiers in the prison?" he asked.

She came to sit next to the pail on her haunches and looked at him. "Yes," she said. "With rifles."

"Do they shoot too?"

"If you help me, I'll tell you a story."

"Why do they have rifles?"

"To kill men in the prison."

"Why?"

"If you don't help me I'll tell Aart."

"Why do they shoot those men in prison?"

"Because they are bad."

"Is Aart bad?"

"Yes," she said, "he has killed Luba."

"That's not true." He got up and sat down next to her. She pushed a wet diaper in his hand. "Here, in the pail, just as I do, look." She showed how she swished the cloths through the water. But Pierre did not make any move to do as she asked.

"Do they eat in prison?" he asked.

"Of course," she said, "stupid."

"Do the soldiers wear red caps too?"

"Come on, lazybones, help me now." She gave him a sudden push, so that he fell backwards. He got up, kicked her in the back with his wooden leg, and went to sit down at some distance from her.

"Goody, goody, I am going to school in town with Hans when he brings Dolf to the doctor!"

"You can't walk that far," she said.

"I have a donkey," he boasted.

She did not answer, but started to wring out the diapers. "Shall I tell you a story?" she asked presently.

"A long story?"

"All right, but then you must ask Hans if I can come along to-morrow."

He thought about this for a moment. "Is it a true story, about soldiers?"

"Once upon a time there was a boy who wanted to be a soldier because they had killed his father with their rifles . . ." she began, in order to convince him that he would like the story. Pierre came again to sit with his back against the wall of the well. "And then . . . ?" he asked.

"Are you going to ask Hans?"

He brought his hand to his forehead and touched his lips in the greeting of the Arabs which they used as a sign of a promise.

"His mother did not want him to, because she had too many other children and was afraid that they would shoot this boy."

"Why did they want to shoot this boy?"

"Now you shut up," she said thinking very hard because at this point she did not know how to continue. She shook the wrung diapers, looking somewhat critically at the yellow spots she had been unable to get out. She emptied a pail and bending over the well she said, "Hold me!" He put his hands around her ankles. "Why did they want to shoot that boy dead?" he asked again.

She hauled up the full pail, her small face red with the effort, her lips pulled away from the white even teeth. The pail landed on the ground with a plop, a wave of water splashed over her feet. "Nice and cold," she said. She knelt down by the pail, scooped some water up with her hand and drank it; a shiver of pleasure went through her body. "Do you want some?"

"Why did they want to shoot that boy?"

"They were Germans, *des boches*," she said. She emptied the pail and piled diapers in it.

"Come on now . . . tell me?"

She came to sit beside him, crossing her legs, her hands in the pockets of the old pants.

"That was in Belgium, you see. Now that boy lived way up at the top of the house. It was a red house," she said, reflecting, "an awful big house. The Germans stood on the corners of the streets with silver helmets on their heads and the boy's father shot out of the window and then they came to get him." She fell silent again.

"And then?" asked Pierre.

"Then his mother started crying." She waited for a moment as if she were trying to call the details to mind again. "She cried with her head on the boy's shoulder and the curtains were drawn and nobody was allowed to look out."

"Why not?"

"I don't know."

"And what did the boy do then?"

Berthe dug her hands deeper in the pockets of the old trousers, her shoulders sloped forward. She rested her chin on her chest, her voice came low, words were drawled out.

"The boy ran down the stairs, a deep, dark staircase. . . ."

"And then? Go on, go on now!" Pierre shouted impatiently.

She straightened herself with a sudden jerk and sighed deeply. She looked at him, closing one eye. "That boy became a soldier, see." She talked rapidly now. "And they gave him a uniform and boots and everything and he marched and shot all the Germans and then he was called to appear before the King and he kissed him on both cheeks and the priest blessed him in church, and all the people sang and there was a procession and they ate . . . all kinds of things. . . ."

"And did they shoot that boy's father dead?"

"Yes," she said. She jumped up and began to dance around, clapping her hands against her heels. "Look!" she said. "Can you do that?" And then realizing her mistake, she shouted, "My pants are coming down, my pants are coming down, look, my pants are coming down!" After a few moments she sank down next to him breathing hard. *"Pff, il fait chaud!"*

Little Dolf, who had been awakened by the racket, started to cry and got up under his hat. Berthe and Pierre laughed at the desperate attempts the little fellow made to free himself from the enormous hat.

"Get some water for little Dolf," Berthe commanded.

"Hans says that little Dolf shouldn't have any water out of the well," said Pierre.

Berthe made a face at him, her stubbornness and her desire to be the boss struggling with her affection for little Dolf. "Then we are going home."

They made preparations to leave and they were so occupied that they did not notice that a stranger had come in through the hedge. They were startled by his voice when he spoke to them. Little Dolf began to cry and stretched his arms out towards Berthe. She lifted him up and stared at the intruder.

Un monsieur—was the way she at once sized him up. His spotless grey suit, the white linen and pointed shoes immediately put him in the category of well-dressed gentlemen, a long line going back to the landlord in Brussels, who emerged regularly in her memory as an ogre.

She took in the gentleman from top to toe as she pressed little Dolf protectively against her and went to stand closer to Pierre for her own safety. Pierre was not at ease either, though he looked attentively at the man's forehead, which, high and pale, was divided by a fiery scar.

"Do you live here?" asked the gentleman pointing to the iron cabin. Pierre nodded thoughtlessly in assent and saw regretfully that the scar had disappeared under the rim of the straw hat that the stranger had at first held in his hand.

But Berthe said, "We live in a house." There was pride in her voice and distrust in her face.

"Isn't that a house?" asked the stranger, amused.

Berthe struggled with the question. She was not yet master of the formulas of comparison and aggrandisement. "This house stinks," she said. "Bah!" And beating around her she added, "Flies. Now we have a white house . . . with a toilet. This . . . this is no house, that is . . . *rien* . . . nothing, just nothing. Pooh!"

The following questions put her in the familiar quandary. "Do you live with your father and mother?"

She shook her head in denial. "With Lies," she said hesitatingly, "and Aart."

"Who are Lies and Aart?"

"*Des Hollandais.*" She had heard that answer from Maria.

"And with Hans," added Pierre.

"So, with Hans, *hein*?"

"Yes," nodded Pierre, "he earns the money."

The stranger went to sit near them on his haunches in order to gain their confidence by his physical proximity. He stuck out a finger towards little Dolf, who, however, quickly hid his face in Berthe's neck.

"Have you been in the war?" asked Pierre, pointing at the scar under the hat, and without waiting for an answer, "Me too."

"The Nazis hacked off his leg," said Berthe and then in order to relieve her conscience of a lie, "He doesn't care."

The stranger got up, wiped his forehead with a colorful handkerchief and then wiped the inside of his hat also.

"Where do you live?" he asked.

"In a white house," said Berthe reticently.

"With Hans, *hein*?"

The children both nodded.

"And Hans earns the money, *hein*. How?"

"He works in the Souk," said Pierre. "He is terribly strong. Have you been in the war?"

"May I go home with you to drink a glass of water?" asked the stranger.

"I'll get some water for you," Berthe offered. "Here, from the well." She began to put little Dolf down, but the stranger stopped her. "Never mind." He looked up at the sky which seemed to be vibrating with the blazing heat. "There's going to be a sirocco," he said. "You better hurry home."

"Nope," said Berthe. "A sirocco!" she laughed out loud. "A sirocco!" triumphant at the ignorance of this elegant gentleman.

"You'll see that I'm right," he said laughing painfully because of the girl's scorn. "I must hurry home."

"This wind is in the west," said Pierre seriously. "The sirocco comes from the east."

The stranger looked at him, the forced smile disappeared from his face. He seemed inimical now, so that Berthe and Pierre stood closer together.

"When you see Hans, give him my regards and tell him that I have a message from his father," he said. "Don't forget that now, from his father."

The children stared after him in astonishment as he disappeared from the field through the opening in the hedge. Berthe got her composure back first. She stuck out her tongue. "What a lousy guy," she said, and then loudly, "*Monsieur Merde!*" She clapped her hand to her mouth, frightened, but Pierre took up her exclamation and as they walked home, they sang, stamping in measured unison, "*Monsieur Merde! Monsieur Merde—ta gueule, ta gueule!*"

Aart and Lies had gone out. Berthe and Pierre had the day to themselves. They played at being father and mother. Pierre played his part with conviction, though Berthe first had to bribe him with the promise that in the afternoon she would be a German while they played the war game. They romped with little Dolf, letting him stand and walk too much, but they gave him a change of diapers when he cried for it, and they shared their bread with him.

They did not talk about the stranger and when Hans came home they did not think about it, because Hans brought new clothes for Pierre, who was to go to school—a pair of trousers and a sweater, a pair of shoes of which one was put away, nobody knew what for, and a copy book and pencils. He had bought these things with the money the children had received from the ladies on the beach and which they had contributed with alacrity.

During the night, lying on the mattress, Berthe whispered, "Pierre, listen! *Monsieur Merde, il fait comme ça!*" At the sound that she pressed out of her small body, they held their laughter until they almost choked, so that nobody would hear them

16

IN AFTER YEARS Pierre did not remember anything that had happened in school the first day he went there. Everything passed him by in a whirlwind of new experience. What did stay in his mind, however, clear as a projection on a picture screen, was his meeting with Luba during recess. There had been a moment when all the children rushed outside through the narrow entrance doors of the school and he, carried along in the wave of pushing children's bodies, found himself in the playground face to face with Luba. Yes, the image stayed, rooted in his memory. He remembered in the midst of the freed horde of children, who were running around, rowdy, shrieking, shouting, trying in some way to get rid of their surplus energy, three small figures stood motionless under the blindingly white sun. He and Luba and Berthe—for in his memory Berthe was present also. In reality he was alone with Luba. She looked at him coldly. She saw in him the personification of Manus' lying to her. Pierre, in his excitement and confusion, tried in vain to file Luba among the pictures of the day. He answered her glance with an almost unconscious expression in his eyes, and on his mouth a friendly though tremulous smile.

Luba spoke up first. *"Qu'est ce que tu fais ici?"* as if he did not have the right to belie Manus' words by his presence.

Pierre had no answer for this. But then he came to his senses. Luba, he knew it was Luba and he asked: "Where is Berthe?" because they had always, the three of them, been together.

"Come along," she said and led him to a place in the shade. They did not speak. Pierre was too much taken with the children playing around him; Luba was struggling with the questions she could not formulate—the why and wherefore, and America.

Only when the bell sounded for the resumption of classes she asked, "Are you back again?" at which Pierre nodded his head in the affirmative. Later at home Pierre was too tired to tell anything at all. He was asleep even before he had eaten his supper.

The next day Luba had a series of questions ready. Pierre told tall tales about the new house, the toilet, the good food and the money that Hans earned. She also asked things, too, to which he did not know the answers: Where Maria was, and who did the cooking? Luba did not mention America.

That afternoon she climbed up behind him on the donkey and rode with him to the small house on the hill.

Nobody knew why she had come back. As she did not tell what had happened to her and did not answer the questions they put to her, expecting her silence and excusing this in advance, no one was the wiser. She had become a thoughtful little woman. She lived in a world of her own, as if she had cut all ties. Always, she was alone on her island. From it she handed out her opinions, contributed to the conversation, joined in quarrels or fun—but she never left her island.

The children showed her a certain measure of respect, perhaps because of her attitude, or perhaps because they were in awe of her experience about which they knew not a thing.

Pierre allowed her to sit in front of him on the donkey when they were going to school and going home.

A few days after her return he waited patiently for her as she stood talking with an Arab at the back of the school building. When she hoisted herself in front of him on the donkey's back he did not ask any questions and did not tell anybody what he had seen either. His silence was remarkable because asking questions had become a habit with him. Of course he was interested in the real Arab who waited for Luba at the school, but something prevented him from mentioning it.

"That's that," she said. She clicked her tongue and they rode away. Pierre looked around and saw the Arab standing on the road, following them with his eyes. But Luba did not turn around once and after a few moments she started to speak about school.

They were in different sections. The school, run by two French ladies, separated the children according to sex. In the left wing of the low, friendly building were the girls, to the right the boys. Luba and Pierre were both in the lowest grade. Luba, who had already had a few weeks' instruction, got some attention, while Pierre, now the school year was drawing towards its end, was more or less left to himself. He had only been taken in because of the insistence of Hans, and undoubtedly, too, because the kind ladies did not want to refuse the crippled little fellow. Moreover, they would not accept tuition for him, declaring that they could not teach him anything now, anyway, and that in any case he would have to repeat the grade again. But they had not counted on Pierre's energy. Against the professional indifference to him he reacted aggressively. The young teacher discovered that Pierre had set his mind to learning to read and would not be satisfied until he had been shown all the letters of the alphabet.

"What kind is that?" asked Pierre, "Is that an *A*?" knowing very well that it was a different letter. In this way he also fooled his housemates. Even Aart gave in grumbling and drew, with stiff fingers, letters in Pierre's copybook.

The alphabet was a source of quarrels between Pierre and Luba because Pierre was sure of his business sooner than she was. They argued endlessly about the identity of a letter. Berthe, though she had only vague memories of the alphabet and jealously pretended that school and learning were matters of complete indifference to her, mixed casually in their disputes. Sauntering by them, or even from where she sat and it was impossible for her to see which letter was the cause of the dispute, she would calmly remark: "It is a *P*," or disdainfully, "Of course that's a *W*, stupid," thereby making the confusion even greater.

Little Dolf had been kept for a few days in the hospital for observation. Berthe not only felt neglected because she did not go to school, but also lonely. She gave evidence of this in a healthy manner, by a would-be indifference, but also by fits of temper and pranks. One evening she invited the girls from the village into the yard, where she amused herself noisily and urged the Arab children on to tease Pierre and Luba. Once she chased the donkey away so that Pierre had to go out and catch the animal and was late for school. She saw him stumbling around on the hill, red with excitement, almost in tears and yelling for Luba, who had started to walk to school, to wait for him. Then Berthe hid herself. She only came out of hiding at night, silent and feeling guilty, though she knew that none among the grown-ups had noticed her bad behavior.

After a few days Aart fetched little Dolf from the hospital. The doctor gave him strict instructions for feeding and taking care of the baby. Berthe undertook the nursing with the utmost zeal. Thus she found her balance again, because as a nurse she thought she was as important as the scholars.

She also chose the wiser course, admitted that she could not read, and participated in the study of the alphabet. So they sat all three on the steps in front of the house whispering as if they were sharing a secret. Late at night by the light of the oil lamp that held them in a warm yellow circle, they read haltingly out of the little book, a booklet with pictures, around which their lives now centered. Now and then their voices sounded loud, tearing through the silence that lay upon the land. A dog in the village would start barking, other dogs in the distance answered with long drawn-out howls.

"Be quiet," Lies admonished from the small terrace. "You're waking everybody."

Then the children would bend down again over the book, whispering. They looked like conspirators. They felt important Now they learned what other children had been taught; they had their share in the knowledge of all people.

The teacher was young and friendly, born in Syria and a Frenchman heart and soul. His task was an impossible one, but he was not in the least daunted by the difficulties. He stood in front of the class like a judge who, though he knew with what party his sympathies lay, observed strict neutrality. The class was made up of two groups: the French, native children, undistinguished, though each of differing character, with the natures of French colonials, bourgeois and autocratic; and the children of the refugees from the continent of almost every nationality and age, and with the wise and tired stamp, the earmark of emigration; a difficult, intelligent group.

Monsieur Cesatie exercised a magnetism upon Pierre which if it did not excel his eagerness to read at least equalled it. He looked lovingly at the small, lively figure, clad in plus fours and a velvet jacket. He liked the way he spoke, polite and precise, the words slipping from under his somewhat prominent upper teeth like Christmas presents, wrapped and tied tastefully. He was just as articulate with his hands, moving them in elegant but still manly gestures. And whatever happened, his eyes, round and black as prunes, always had a friendly gleam in them.

Pierre was fascinated by his bonhomie which always attracts children. He experienced a pleasant sensation as if somebody were scratching his back before he went to sleep. He listened to all the conversations between the teacher and the children—a play of give and take, which he followed with his eyes, with his whole being. Monsieur Cesatie cheerfully encouraged the French children and calmed down the refugees who were always ready with an answer, and who thrust up their hands and moved them back and forth to draw his attention. He chatted with those who were shy or reasoned with others who spoke haughtily before their turn.

". . . *Eh bien, François,* think hard now. Come on! Come on! *Parbleu,* boy, you act as if you didn't know. Yes, yes Palli, I see your hand very well, but François knows the answer too. No? *Tiens, qu'est ce que c'est que ça.* Quiet, Heinz, it's François' turn! Patience, patience, Joseph! *Allons, François, mon petit. Non?* Who knows the answer? Gerard? Charles? Well, then Palli may give the answer!" Monsieur Cesatie did not allow his disappointment to show and continued with the lesson, directing the easiest questions to the French children in spite of himself.

When a picture was to be discussed, a specimen of the colorless, formless, talentless drawings that hang proudly from every school wall all over the world, Pierre was allowed to participate and he did not fail to let himself be heard.

"*Allons Pierre, qu'est ce qu'on dit, hein?* Now it's your turn. What do you see in the picture?" Monsieur rubbed his hands with satisfaction and came down to sit on Pierre's bench. Pierre, happy, flattered, his heart in his throat, looked up at him.

"Look at the picture, my boy!" And to the class, "*Silence!*" Monsieur Cesatie took the stick, pointed things out, turned his head about in the manner of a little mechanical toy.

"A house," started Pierre ". . . a gentleman, a garden, a cat. . . ."

"Stop, stop, not so fast! What's the gentleman doing? Where is he going? Come on, you know. Use your eyes!"

"He is leaving because the Boches want to shoot him dead."

The whole class burst into laughter, and Pierre, who had meant it seriously and felt he must justify himself, rattled off in a shrill voice above the racket: "He must run away, the Germans are around the corner with silver helmets, and he has just fired on them from the window."

". . . *Silence, silence!*" Monsieur Cesatie rapped with his stick on the bench. "No, *mais non*, he is going to his office, my boy. You see, he is carrying a briefcase under his arm."

"That's not true," said Pierre. "He has to flee." He rubbed the stump of his leg under the bench, it was suddenly burning; tears stood in his eyes, he felt a lump in his throat.

"Not this gentleman, *mon petit*. This is a monsieur. He is going to his office. Look, his wife and children are standing at the gate and they are waving after him. *Voilà*, the dog and the cat are looking after him too. Isn't that nice? He'll return in the evening after office hours. Then they'll be waiting for him." The teacher spoke cheerfully, convincingly. The children were quiet now, some because they felt Pierre's sadness, others with the cruelty of children who anticipate an impending blow.

"That's not so," Pierre's voice trembled. "He must flee and he is not coming back, but they don't know about it." He stretched out his hands, pointed at the lady and the children, the dog and the cat. "They don't know it yet."

"He's lying!" came a voice from the back of the class.

"He isn't, *c'est comme il dit*," said a small boy who was not generally talkative. He looked out of his dark eyes and nodded seriously, "It is as he says, *er hat ganz recht!*"

"The Nazis have no silver helmets!" shouted another. "Nobody has silver helmets, *Dummkopf!*"

A boy stood up on his bench shooting an imaginary machine gun: "à—à—à—à—à. . . ."

Monsieur Cesatie mopped his brow, hid behind his bright white handkerchief.

"This picture was painted before Pierre was born," said a know-it-all. "Then nobody needed to flee. That was before the war, when there was no war."

"That is true," assented Monsieur Cesatie. And then gaily: "Did I tell you that I saw a caravan yesterday?"

"Me too!"

"Where?"

"Real camels?"

Monsieur Cesatie talked energetically about the caravan.

On the playground life was somewhat complicated for Pierre. He could not take part in the wild games and at the beginning of recess he wisely allowed his little friends to give free play to their newly acquired freedom. He waited, leaning against the wall, and their jumping and prancing around fascinated him without rousing his envy. Then a boy would come and put an arm around his shoulder and together they would walk away. There was always some important activity or some point to discuss. They would go to see whether Luba had tethered the donkey securely. Or they would argue whether Monsieur Cesatie was stronger than Monsieur Beaumont, as no doubt he was. Or who could spit the farthest. Then a game would start that needed much preparation. Who was on whose side. What would be the zone of safety. Was the trench in front or behind the line. Pierre was generally a sentry, a gunner, or a general, always someone who did not have to run. The bell for the resumption of classes always sounded too soon, just after extensive preparations for the game had started. They continued to play until the girls had gone in, then they let everything go and crowded through the door. They sweated and their voices were hoarse and shrill. Playing with boys was a novel experience, and Pierre ignored Luba on the playground.

But Luba had no use for him now. She was the oldest in her class. The girls vied for her favors, though a small group of little Frenchwomen, with pale and elderly little faces like last year's apples, were unfriendly to her. For no reason of course. Luba's indifferent, preoccupied attitude aroused in others the desire to ingratiate themselves with her. They approached her with the set opportunism of children—I like Arab dresses better than ordinary dresses—I wish I could ride to school on a donkey—I think Luba is a beautiful name. They put their arms around her waist, stepped on each other's toes, pushed and crowded until they hung like a cluster from her arms and nobody could move a step. It seemed, too, that at home they spoke highly of her. Mothers approached her after school was over. She was asked to parties. Some children brought her their favorite toys. Luba did not reciprocate. It mattered little to her, except that now and then it would give her a feeling of power, being the boss when games were played. It never lasted long, it soon bored her.

The decision to go back to the family had come to her without much thinking. When Manus waited for her at school and asked her why she had gone back, she did not answer. She was probably just as astonished as he was. Manus had followed her with his eyes when she rode away, not sure of his feelings. Had his pride been hurt, was he sorry or was he glad that he was delivered from the burden? Anyhow he was relieved that everything had passed without difficulties, startled at his lucky break, feeling as if he had escaped unhurt after he had passed a falling wall. He shook his head and grinned secretly, even many weeks after.

Luba seemed not to think about him any longer. She was contented. In the morning when it was still cool they rode along the asphalt road to school. The donkey was a friend, though he did not always obey. They scratched his scurvy hide and Luba invented names for him. She lay along his neck, her arms around it and talked to him. His "answers" she conveyed to Pierre, who could never hear enough of it.

She called the donkey Joan of Arc. The lady teacher had told a story about that person, but Luba had not paid any attention at the time though she had remembered the name and the sound of it had a funny significance for her. "Kif-kif Bourricot" was another appellation and "Vieux Débrouillard," "Petite Suzanne," and "Papa Zut." To every one of these names a story was attached, the variations were endless, Luba's notions unaccountable.

"What does Papa Zut say today?" Pierre would ask.

Luba would bend forward and listen gravely. "He says that last night they cut open his belly and filled it with gold pieces." Papa Zut was generally one way or another mixed up in financial affairs.

"I can hear them shaking around."

Luba pointed at the road behind them, a mirror in the sunlight. "He is losing them now. We should give him some of little Dolf's medicine."

Then they burst out laughing.

In school Luba did not laugh much.

In the afternoons on the way home they were tired. The donkey sometimes refused to budge on account of the heavy burden. Then Luba had to walk. She would stay behind and sing little ditties that she made up herself.

The long holiday came to them as a surprise. Nobody had definitely told them about it and apparently they had not listened when it had been talked of. And Pierre slapped a boy who announced that he was glad that he would not have to come back the next day. "You mustn't say that." He stamped his foot with anger. "You mustn't say that!" The children who stood around them scattered in astonishment—the victim was too surprised to hit back, some began to laugh. Then they all laughed, and the boy who had been slapped ran away, in funny jumps.

After nine months of going to school the other children longed for their freedom. It was unbearably hot in the schoolrooms, and dark, for the blinds had been drawn. The bathing season was in full swing and the children wanted to go to the beach and play in the sea. But to Pierre the vacation was an anticlimax. The interruption of a meal on which he had just started.

Monsieur Cesatie became a stranger. Suddenly, his cheerfulness seemed no longer for the children but because of his own plans. Pierre followed him through the classroom but the teacher was too busy with the last schoolday routine to notice Pierre's dejection. At saying good-bye, however, he seemed to feel the little boy's unhappiness in the cold, lifeless handshake. He grasped at the first means of consolation his eyes fell upon, an apple that he had brought for his own supper. Pierre had never seen one like it, large, and fragrant as a whole orchard. He went outside where Luba was skipping rope, skilfully jumping up and down between and over a set of ropes deftly manipulated by two girls. Luba was completely absorbed in the game but still aware of the spectators. She was like a princess in the midst of the ladies of the court. When she saw Pierre, she stopped skipping immediately and joined him, indifferently stepping over the ropes with a slight gesture of dismissal to the girls. She looked at the apple in the hollow of his joined hands and then at his face beneath the shabby sun hat.

Without uttering a word they rode home. Luba allowed Pierre to sit in front, her arms around his waist so he would not fall. He needed both hands to hold his apple.

17

WHEN THEY CAME HOME they found Maria with Aart on the porch. She had run away for the second time but nobody knew about it yet. Aart thought that she had come on a visit. Little Dolf was sleeping in a soapbox covered with gauze. The children found that there was a strange atmosphere around the house. The door stood wide open and they saw the white figures of Arab women moving in the room. They remained standing at the bottom of the few steps. "Lies is sick," Aart said. "You can't go in."

"Hi," said Luba to Maria, and then suddenly louder and with great warmth. "Hello, Maria!"

Maria tried to fight her tears back, she could not speak, her lips formed a greeting but no sound came out. Luba was suddenly very busy with the sunflowers alongside the house. Aart looked at the little sisters and shook his head in astonishment.

"For how long haven't you seen each other?" he asked. Luba came to stand next to Pierre again and she looked thoughtfully at Aart.

"We're having a vacation," said Pierre. He thought after all that it was pretty important. "Two months' vacation. Goody!"

"Are you coming to live here again?" Luba asked Maria.

Maria nodded her head in assent with a sidelong glance at Aart. In the house loud Arab voices resounded. Haisha came outside wiping her hands on her dress. Behind her tripped Berthe, empty pails suspended from her hands. She jumped down the steps and ran in the direction of the well. Her gait, her attitude indicated how important she felt and how she wanted to impress the others. They looked after her.

"Is Lies very sick?" asked Luba. Haisha spoke to Aart and he went inside.

"Is Lies very sick?" repeated Pierre, and then to Maria, "Did you see my apple?" He showed her the fruit in his hands. "The teacher gave it to me. Don't you go to school?"

"What school do you go to?" Maria came over and stood at the edge of the little terrace.

Pierre pointed in the direction of the city, and Luba said, "We go to the French school."

They heard Lies sigh, a long-drawn-out sigh, then the voices of Aart and the women.

"What is Lies doing?" asked Pierre.

"She is sick," said Maria. She did not know what was the matter with Lies but she suspected that it had something to do with her pregnancy though she did not understand what it could be. The noises from the house gave her a sick feeling, as if she were a witness to forbidden things she should know nothing about. They made her afraid. Perhaps it would be better to return to the Consul's house. If she went now, nobody need know that she had run away; they had all gone to Tetuan and would not be back before midnight. But she stayed, she wanted to know what was happening to Lies.

"Aren't we going to eat?" asked Pierre. He repeated his question when Aart came back to the terrace. Aart did not listen to him. He rubbed his face, his eyes shut in thought. Berthe approached over the hill, her body bent, her chin resting on her chest; water spilled over the rim of the pails. Aart met her and took the pails from her. "You know where the hospital is, don't you?" And without waiting for her to answer, "Run like hell to the hospital and ask for the doctor. Say that a European woman has had a miscarriage, *une fausse couche*. Can you remember that? *Fausse couche*. And tell him to come immediately. Say it's a European woman. Say that she's your mother!"

"My mother," said Berthe hesitant and then resolutely, "oh, yes, *je comprends*." She smiled at him, winked her eye good-naturedly. "*Ma mère, eh? Alors, toi, tu es mon père*. Hello papa!"

"Come on, girl, hurry, Goddamit!" Aart swore, confused by

Berthe's joke. She was frightened at his outburst and she became solemn again, showing an expression of importance and being grown-up. *"Ma mère faisait une fausse couche,"* she repeated stressing every word and gravely nodding her head. She turned round, walked a few steps, and shouted. "Dolf must have his vegetables at six o'clock." Then after another few steps, "I shall go to the market and fetch Hans . . . !" She ran down the path, holding her curly blond hair together with both hands.

". . . Fetch Hans. . . ." Aart set down the pails. He remained standing there until Berthe had disappeared around the curve in the road.

". . . Fetch Hans. . . . Fetch Hans. . . ." Hans, Hans, Hans, a plaguing refrain, that he kept on hearing. The complete lack of confidence in him manifested itself in the children in this manner. And with Lies? A desperate, powerful sadness clutched at his throat. He had reached a point where he had to come to a decision. If Lies gets by with her life . . . his thoughts stopped for a moment at her crazy reckless deed . . . the impulse of the moment or a well considered plan? What did it matter whether she had followed impulse or plan, the motive for the action was the same. . . . If Lies survived, he must act. Get away from here, Lies and little Dolf and he. He would have to regain her confidence, re-establish their family entity. After that he would be able to make new plans, another trailer, or maybe a primitive existence among the East Indian people. He had vague plans. Yes, he wanted to go to the Indies. As soon as Lies was better, if she did get well, he thought, he would go to the Consul. The Indies! . . . Yes. . . . Aart brought the pails inside.

The children stayed outside all night, which they enjoyed thoroughly. It was a game, like "house," or "Christmas," or "the voyage around the world" which they often played.

Months ago they had frequently slept outside either by chance or habit. Tonight it was necessity and therefore fun. They stayed in the yard, as far away as possible from the house, in a corner near the fence though they had never chosen this spot before.

Pierre had been the first to install himself there, immediately after the sun had gone down when he had returned from the village where he had gone to buy bread. "Come, Luba, come and sit down here. Berthe! Maria! Come here!" Embarrassed because he sat all alone there, lost in the midst of the stubble, he called the others together. And when they did not at once respond to his invitation he got up and began to gather wood and inflammable refuse for a fire. A bait. They approached and looked critically at the result of his efforts. "What are you doing? Oh, a fire. Pierre is going to make a fire!" And then at once participating in the game, "Yes, let's have a fire!" As if at an agreed-upon signal they scattered in different directions to look for more wood and more refuse. They instructed each other to ask for matches in the house, until Luba finally decided to do it. They all stood below the little terrace and Luba called in a muffled voice, "Haisha, Haisha, may we have some matches?" Inside it was quiet now, frighteningly quiet. The door stood ajar. Near the flickering light of the coal oil lamp they could see Haisha sitting on the floor and a section of the mattress where Lies' legs were continually in motion. They could not see Hemo, but it was she who came outside with the matches. She peered out over the road to see whether Aart was coming, or the headlights of the car, because Aart had gone himself for the doctor after Berthe had come back without having accomplished her mission. The hospital doctor was out and she had not been able to find Hans.

"He's not coming," said Pierre. "I'll watch out," he comforted her. Hemo laughed; she always laughed at him and he liked that.

Berthe fell asleep near the fire, exhausted after her hurried trip.

Maria stared into the flames, also tired and still having a sense of guilt and impending disaster. It was too late to go back; she was afraid of the dark. Now she could only wait until they came to fetch her and what she would tell them, she did not know. 'I won't go back,' she thought, 'I hate them all.' She called to mind the figures of the Consul, his wife and Ina. They looked repulsive and nasty to her. 'I hate them all. Zus too, sure, Zus too. I won't go back.' But behind her she knew was Lies with her sickness, for which she had just as big an aversion and was afraid of and yet was curious about too.

Luba and Pierre softly sang a little song that they had been taught in school. "*C'est bon pour moi, c'est bon pour toi, c'est bon pour tout le monde. . . . Bon—bon. . . .*" "Come on, Maria," Luba ordered, and then more friendly, "Sing with us, won't you?" Then commanding again: "You sing: "*Bon . . . bon . . .* and then you clap your hands."

Maria was embarrassed when she played that sort of game; she soon felt ridiculous. "*Bon . . . bon,*" she murmured almost inaudibly. Luba changed the ditty, greatly to the amusement of Pierre, "*C'est bon pour moi, c'est bon pour toi, c'est bon pour Kif-kif Bourricot . . .* hee-haw, hee-haw. . . ." But Maria did not want to sing the refrain with them. She began to talk with great animation to distract them, though she did not know how to tell anything that had really happened. She could not speak about her loneliness in the Consul's house and outside of that no experience had penetrated her consciousness; she only remembered what she had gone through emotionally. She thus told of a party that she had attended in her imagination. Luba and Pierre were listening, their faces turned expectantly upon her above the smouldering fire. Berthe fought stubbornly against her fatigue but was continually falling asleep, her head bent over her lap.

All the while various women from the village came to look at Lies, white figures against the blue evening, walking noiselessly across the yard.

Maria told about the big party in the nouse of the Consul, though she had been sent to bed after the arrival of the guests. First in the window seat of her room, from which she could see a corner of the drawing room and the terrace, and later in bed with her ear against the wall, she had taken part in the *soirée*, imagining that she was the center of attraction, dressed in a low-cut gown of flowered silk with wide sleeves and a flower in her hair. She saw how the smart gentlemen stood around her, glasses in hand and all simultaneously offering her a light for her cigarette, as in a certain advertisement in the magazines. When after a few hours musical entertainment had been presented, she imagined that she was the lady who stood leaning against the grand piano with a lace handkerchief carelessly dangling from her hand. Though she did not know the songs, she sang some melody, so excited by her imaginings that she thought she sang the right tunes, and Ina, who came in because of her singing and who told her angrily to go to sleep, did not disturb her dream. She had been completely happy.

She told the children about this party as if she had really been there. She described the guests, the elegant dark suits and the colorful uniforms of the gentlemen, the ladies' dresses. The drinks that were served by the servants and the beautifully decorated dishes with the pastries and sandwiches. She repeated conversations and gave an account of the clever answers she had given the gentlemen, all of whom occupied important positions. She told about the success of her singing and the request of the Pasha that she give his daughters singing lessons.

"Did he come on horseback?" Pierre asked. He was bored but was waiting patiently for the real story, which, so he thought, was still to follow.

"No, of course not; in a large car."

"And then . . . ?" asked Pierre. "What happened then?"

Maria suddenly found she did not know how to continue and Pierre, relieved that the boring narrative was finished, stretched his hand out towards Luba. "Bite my finger?"

From the house came a shriek. "That's Lies," said Pierre seriously. Maria trembled with horror. Berthe woke up. "What are you doing?" she asked sleepily. Pierre stuck his hand out towards her, "Bite my finger, will you?"

"Why?"

"Just because," said Pierre. "Why is Lies shouting?" he then asked.

"She's in pain," said Berthe dreamily. She let herself fall backwards, drew up her knees and stretched out her legs with a jerk. "That's what Lies does 'cause of the pain."

"Why?"

"Why—wny—why—" Luba imitated him, "you're always asking why."

"Who can blow his breath longer than I can?" Pierre asked. He pursed his lips and sucked in the air.

"I'm hungry," Berthe complained. She was again lying down with her knees drawn up.

"Me too," said Pierre.

"Why don't you eat your apple?" Berthe asked. She sat up. "Yes, your apple, give me a piece of your apple? Oh, I know what. We'll roast it in the ashes. Give it to me. *Allons*, Pierre!"

He looked at her in utter astonishment. "My apple? It's not to eat." He grabbed for the fruit, which he had hidden in his clothes. "It is not for eating."

"Of course it is."

"It's my apple."

"Stingy."

Pierre looked with pleading eyes at Luba. "Not for eating, eh Luba?"

"I'm hungry," said Berthe. "I haven't had anything to eat. Nothing all afternoon." She looked straight at Pierre. In the moonlight her little face was very pale, her eyes seemed dark. "I didn't have anything to eat, nothing at all, not all day."

Pierre held the apple protectively against himself. He looked helplessly at Luba, then at Berthe, then at Maria, who did not seem to be aware of the conversation. "I got that apple as a present, it's not for eating."

With a lightning-like movement Luba snatched the fruit from Pierre, set her tiny, white teeth in it and took a bite out of it. She returned the apple to Pierre, looked at him unmoved and did not speak.

From the house came a loud wail, the plaintive, powerless voice of Lies, and then consoling voices and little Dolf's crying.

Pierre looked at his ruined treasure with utter misery.

"Now it's my turn," said Berthe.

Docilely Pierre handed her the apple.

Towards ten o'clock Hemo was standing watch alone. The lights of the village had been extinguished. The fire was now completely out, the children had fallen asleep, Luba and Pierre leaning against each other, Maria and Berthe stretched out on the warm earth.

They were suddenly awakened by the arrival of Aart and the doctor. The doctor was a young man. Busily chatting, he followed Aart along the uneven path and then disappeared with him into the house. The door was closed.

"Lies has a *fausse couche*," said Berthe dreamily.

Pierre sat up. "Luba," he said in the shrill voice of a child, still half asleep, "Luba, what shall we do tomorrow? There is no school."

"We'll go and watch the fishermen." Luba shoved away from him and put her head in Berthe's lap. Pierre undid the little wooden leg with slow movements of his fingers, rolled over on his side and fell asleep again. Aart came out of the house with the pails. He walked by the children on his way to the well but kept his head turned away. When he came back he didn't look either.

Maria followed him with her eyes. She saw his tall figure silhouetted against the light of the moon. They are not coming to get me, she thought. What shall I do when they come for me? I won't go with them. If Lies dies, she thought suddenly, then I am it. "It." It, meant the eldest of the girls, a vague promise for a future, in which she would be the boss. Somebody of importance because of the many responsibilities: little Dolf, cooking, the house, Berthe, Luba. An important person, along with Hans.

She got up quietly and climbed over the fence.

"What are you doing?" whispered Luba.

"Shh, go to sleep."

She waited, crouching in the grass until she was sure that Luba was again asleep, then she walked around the fence until she was near the house. She looked for a sheltered spot where the grass was tallest and again lay down. She was fully awake now, because she wanted to know whether they would come to get her. When about half an hour later she heard the car and saw the Consul himself climbing the path, she remained motionless. She hardly dared to breathe. She saw the light of the torch he held in his hand moving over the yard, heard his labored breathing, when he stood, hesitating for a moment at the gate. She heard his conversation with Aart, followed the beam of his torchlight over the sleeping children and listened intently to their sleepy answers to his questions. "I don't know," said Berthe. And, "She's gone away; she went that way," from Luba. The beam of light slid over the hill, went from left to right. The Consul grumbled. Aart answered. Their voices became louder and then suddenly Aart wheeled round, walked in the direction of the house and closed the door behind him with a bang. The Consul stood irresolutely in the yard. Again the beam of light broke through the darkness. Maria pressed herself against the ground. She heard the Consul swear softly and scold, "*Pantoufle . . . idiot . . . j'en ai marre . . . sacré nom de Dieu . . . ça suffit . . .* now I'll fix him." She had to laugh at his powerless fury. The short fat silhouette in the moonlit night moved over the yard, stood for a moment near the sleeping children. Like a fat monkey, she thought, a dirty swearing monkey. She felt herself the winner because she had heard him swear, thinking at the same time of his folded hands and castdown eyes before the meals. Goody, she thought, goody, goody, I heard him swear.

After the noise of the car had died away, she rejoined the children and immediately fell asleep. Rainer's coming home did not disturb her. Neither did the doctor's departure.

They awoke and did not know where they were, but there was Hans looking down upon them and they heard his scolding voice, in which sounded astonishment, friendliness and pity, ". . . What the hell is going on now? Something new again. Why are you sleeping outside? Look at you! You're soaking wet. Good way to catch pneumonia. . . . Come, get inside!"

Pierre laughed triumphantly, because Hans did not know why they were outside and they were in the right.

"We can't go inside," said Luba, her eyes blinking in the sunlight. "Lies is sick."

"Well, damn it," Hans swore as he looked at the house. "And what's Maria doing here."

But Maria pretended to be asleep.

Berthe sat up straight and stretched. "Lies has a . . ." she thought that she still knew the word but her memory failed her. "Lies *a fait une fausse couche*," Luba came in helpfully.

But Berthe kicked her, she wanted to tell Hans. "Naw," she said, "Lies is sick. This is what she did, look." She let herself fall backward with drawn-up knees, and rolled against Maria. The children began to laugh, but Berthe, unperturbed, gave a demonstration of Lies' movements as she had seen them the evening before.

Blood rose to Hans' face. "Cut it out," he said curtly.

Maria now pretended to be waking. She stretched and stretched, moaned, stuck her thumb in her mouth as if she were a baby, at the same time peering at Hans from beneath her eyelids.

Pierre reached for his wooden leg and fastened the straps. "May I go with you to the village?" he said.

"How did you get here, Maria?" asked Hans. She suddenly sat up and said, "Oh . . . hello, Hans."

"How did you get here?" he repeated.

"Where is my apple?" asked Pierre. He searched inside his blouse, looked around on the ground. "Where is my apple?"

Luba and Berthe looked at each other for a moment. Berthe burst into laughter. Luba remained silent.

"Where is my apple?" Pierre asked again, but over his face came the shadow of remembrance.

"Here," said Berthe, slapping her belly. It was meant as a joke. Nobody laughed, however. She prepared to defend herself. "You ate some of it too," she said. Her round, blue eyes looked at him with an angry expression. "And Luba too."

"But it was your fault," Pierre moaned, recognizing his irreparable loss. For the first time in his life he experienced the bitter regret of a loss which he could blame on no one except himself.

For Berthe, however, the affair was finished. She was occupied with catching a flea, which she remembered had bothered her the day before too.

Hans stood irresolutely between them.

"Did Lies have a miscarriage?" he asked Maria.

She shrugged her shoulders, her eyes slid over his face, his hair, his sturdy body in the blue overalls.

The door of the house squeaked and Aart stepped outside, a pail in his hand. He stretched and then shielding his eyes from the sunlight came down the steps. Hans saw how tired he was. But even if he had been awake, all night—and that must have been the case—his tiredness was still not only caused by that. Aart was finished, Hans thought with pity.

Aart beckoned to Berthe. He ignored Hans.

"I'm hungry," said Berthe complainingly. She instinctively took advantage of the enmity between Aart and Hans, which at the moment surcharged the atmosphere. "Let Luba go and get the water, I am hungry. I got him," she then said happily, forgetting her little maneuver as she caught the flea. She pushed a finger on which was a black speck, the crushed flea, under Pierre's nose. She got up and walked towards Aart, who handed her the pail. She disappeared over the hill, humming.

"What's happened to Lies?" Hans asked. He took a few steps in the direction of Aart, but kept his distance.

Aart tightened his belt. He did not answer.

'My enemy,' thought Hans. 'I am the scapegoat, he loads me with the guilt for his bad luck.' Had he only just discovered this now? Had he never known it before? He had not been so conscious of it, never so directly; that he knew. It was as if he stood outside himself and saw Aart, and himself as an onlooker. Two men. No excuse any longer because he was younger, or that on account of his youth other conditions, other considerations counted. He was a man. From now on men would be his friends or his enemies, because he was one of them. And then there was the realization that he really was grown up, and astonishment that this realization should come to him now, on this cool, sunny morning here, in the unkempt yard opposite Aart, who was his enemy. Why here and not in the market, for instance, where he acted independently, on his own, and schemed in order to keep his head and shoulders above the whirlpool of competition and deceit? Or in the bar, where he did the work of a man and led the life of a man, and participated in the night life, a raw wound pulsating with malignant fevers? Where he was always on guard, especially during the last few weeks, in spite of the late hours which made his spirit dull and unresponsive. Why here and not in Marga's room where now he had the upper hand in the game between lover and companion. Why should this realization come now and not during his conversations with Jilali, if they still could be called conversations, since the Arab evaded him more and more, not only when he talked to him, but also as a pupil. His thoughts centered on Jilali. Something was going on and Marga had warned him to be careful, though she could only call in her feminine intuition and intelligence as a reason for her warning.

Aart was still standing beneath the porch.

"What's the matter with Lies?" Hans asked again. "Why did the children have to sleep outside?"

Rainer's head projected above the balustrade of the terrace. He had spent the night there.

"There's no room for the children inside," said Aart. "That should be clear, I think." He moistened his lips—speaking seemed to cause him the greatest difficulty.

Hans walked towards him. They now stood facing each other. "That's no way to do, to let the children lie out of doors all night. You could have seen to it that they slept somewhere under a roof in the village. Things have changed here now, see, since you . . . lately. The children are being taken care of, see. I take care of them now and much better than you ever did."

Aart looked at him. His face was drained of all expression, no sign of hatred, of enmity, nothing but exhaustion.

Coward, thought Hans. If you were a man, you would hit me in the face.

"They can sleep inside tonight," said Aart. "Lies is dead."

18

Now THEY HAD to wait for the boat to Lisbon. Once a month the antiquated vessel was loaded with lucky refugees who until the moment of their departure did not dare believe that it was true and kept a watchful eye on the shore from which disaster might yet come. People had indeed been hauled off the boat, mostly on the instigation of the ship owner himself, for a bribe. His name was Vermylde, a Belgian who did a thriving trade in human misery and yet kept his reputation as a humanitarian because he was the only one who would take people to the other side, or to Portugal. He tipped the scales one way or the other. Once the refugees had run their martyrs' course through the consulates concerned, they were delivered into the hands of Vermylde. Not only did he rule over the shipping to Lisbon, but as agent of the big companies he sold the steamship tickets at his disposal for America or South America according to his whim. His methods, however, were not in the least a matter of whim; his system had been carefully built through experience. It conformed to a split hair to the system of orderly complication and corrupt order that had been established by various authorities. It used the criminal short-sightedness of the diplomats, the stupid indifference of the government employees, and the universally prevalent prejudice. In the labyrinth of Vermylde's system the sharp and cunning ones found a way out, while the gentle, the awkward and the simple of spirit wandered along the crooked paths for months and sometimes for a year until they collapsed. Those who tried to follow their own paths were crushed against the fences or were strangled in the jungle outside.

The Consul stood at the entrance to the labyrinth but did not dare advance another step, because, as he called it, only the official way was available to him.

He had by almost superhuman efforts within the limitation of his capacities, will power and perseverance, procured the papers for Aart and the children. Almost superhuman efforts . . . . this description of his exertions pleased him; it had stuck in his mind, this expression, which he had probably picked up from the war bulletins. This reiterated itself for instance after a telephone conversation with Lisbon, when he finished the difficult composition of complicated telegrams, or after calls made on diplomatic tiptoe. Almost superhuman efforts . . . he thought contentedly when he settled himself in the garden to enjoy the coolness of nightfall. Now he was to terminate his transactions with Vermylde, but after three weeks he still did not know whether the man had consented or refused to take Aart and the children, though a date had been set for the possible departure. Possible departure! "Three adults and four children, is that right? I'll do my best. On the boat of the seventeenth of August is still room, but . . ." The Consul stood at the entrance to the labyrinth. In his hand he held many documents, confirming telegrams of a Jewish aid society in America, from the Dutch embassy in Lisbon, from the Quakers, from the American State Department in Washington, a letter giving the consent of the Portuguese consul, one from the authorities in Lisbon, even a very promising epistle from the Spanish administrator in Tetuan concerning a safe conduct. The Consul stood at the entrance of the labyrinth and peered to the right and the left for a guide. Personally the Consul liked Vermylde, who had always behaved correctly towards him, even during the civil war in Spain when there were many here who seemed to be in favor of the reds and other bandits. But the Consul had been warned against him, and it was indeed true that the man did not come straight out with his intentions.

"Go and talk to him yourself," he had counselled Aart. And he inveighed against Zus. "Just talk. The man has never been caught doing anything dishonest. If he really were so corrupt would the American consul and the Portuguese and the police . . ." The Consul could not bring himself to hate, but Zus' attitude, her derisive laughter, sometimes made him almost forget his Christian duty to love his neighbor. And that, with his high blood pressure. . . .

On the quay the lucky ones, the chosen ones, were waiting—next door to Vermylde's office on the sidewalk. of a French café. The signal of the departure might come at any moment now, in an hour, in the morning, towards evening, tomorrow, the day after, next week. Nothing to shorten time but talk. And they were tired of talking. A hungry man talks about bread, the lonely about the past, the robbed about riches, the prisoner about freedom; the immigrant talks about bread, the past, riches, freedom. The conversations at the quay went round and round like people on a merry-go-round at the fair. After days of waiting a whistle was sounded and the merry-go-round was halted: "For God's sake, stop, talk about something else, will you?" Then the people would be silent except for now and then a word about the weather, a boat sailing out, the puffs of smoke over Gibraltar, a passing Arab, a dog, a battered donkey. Children played among the little tables at some wonderful improvisation or just tag, or hide-and-seek. Later on they quieted down, listless or whining. "Why don't we go now? Aren't we ever going?" "Are we going to sleep again in the hotel tonight?" They had dark rings under their eyes, they were tired of waiting. The fathers took turns in asking questions at the office. The timid stood at the counter and were easily brushed off by an employee; the brazen made a scene. Vermylde could seldom be found. Sometimes he appeared for a few minutes, but nobody could get hold of him—he slipped through their fingers, shook them off with a movement of his narrow shoulders, a frown of his low brow. "*Bien sûr, bien sûr*, patience, you'll be leaving in an hour. . . ."

When the signal was given—never by Vermylde but by an employee—a wild scramble began among the travellers. They ran to the boat, dragging their luggage and their children along; they crowded before the gate of the customs house and pushed each other towards the decrepit ship as if every minute of delay might be fatal.

In Vermylde's office the negotiations started afresh for the next shipment, checks and banknotes changed hands, intermediaries went in and out.

At the counter people stood waiting for their turn.

"But my visa has expired."

"I am sorry, Monsieur, Vermylde is in Ceuta. I don't know when he is coming back. No, he can't be reached. *Je regrette beaucoup.*" The people walked out of the office. Mild people felt an almost irrepressible urge to drop the whole affair; or, crossing the boulevard under the palm trees, and passing by the people on the beach, to go straight into the sea; to swim along with the bathers, but to continue until their arms and legs were exhausted and they drifted out with the tide.

The strong stood for a moment in front of the office, putting quick thoughts and new plans in order: What to do first? . . . Yes! . . . and then starting again from the beginning, in a different way, they hastily climbed the steep street which to them was a symbol of their fighting strength. It was good for them, the strain of climbing, the sweat running down their temples and backs, the pounding of their hearts. Distraction: the preparations, the talk, the threats, the deals they made.

The children followed the preparations for the departure with the greatest interest. They felt important and they liked to contribute their penny's worth of thought. Of course with the exception of Maria, none of them had a clear picture of what really was to happen. They sat together and talked in whispers.

"Vermylde is a meanie."

"Shh . . ."

"Hans said so himself."

"That isn't true, the Consul is a meanie."

"That isn't true," interrupted Maria, whose remembrance of the van Balekom family had become rosy with distance, "that isn't true. He was at the funeral, and he cried."

"Naw."

"I saw it myself, his eyes were filled with tears." And being ashamed because she had talked in such an offhand way about the quiet emotion of the Consul, "Go and wash your face, stinker, you never wash yourself."

The victim slunk away in the direction of the well, but that did not satisfy Maria, "And you too, and you, get going." The children obeyed her. She had taken things into her own hands at the right moment. After they had come home from the funeral she had borrowed food from the villagers on her own initiative and had cooked the supper. When the children handed her their plates: "Maria, can I have some more?" ". . . Me too, Maria?" and with the distribution of the food, she had felt herself grow even bodily; she felt stinging pains in her small breasts and cramps in the calves of her legs. She had taken Lies' place, but she improved on Lies. She took better care of them all, and was more motherly. She fixed and fussed and the children obeyed her, except when Hans was in the neighborhood. Hans was the boss. Maria had recognized that.

They listened to the conversations between Aart, Rainer and Hans and discussed what they had heard, giving their own meanings to it.

"Vermylde is dangerous," said Pierre, behind his hand, "he has a rifle and he fires it and the Consul is afraid of it."

"Who says he has a rifle?" Luba asked.

"He has a rifle."

"Really," Berthe nodded with conviction.

But Luba remained matter of fact. "He is dangerous in another way. With money."

That they did not understand at all; neither did Luba, Pierre was furiously biting his nails, a habit he had acquired during the last few weeks. "Hans is not afraid of him anyway."

"I saw him," said Pierre one Sunday afternoon when they were sitting on the steps in front of the house.

"Who?"

"Vermylde. He is about that tall and he has this kind of eyes," he half closed his eyes. "There is a scar on his, on his . . . on his forehead. Like this . . ." He made a motion as if he were cutting across his forehead with a knife.

Berthe looked at him attentively, her mouth half open with the effort of her thinking. "That was somebody else. That was another man." She got up from the steps and walked towards Hans, who was busy fixing a tire with Rainer. "Hans, there was a man," she pointed to the field below, "a *monsieur*," she corrected herself quickly, "and . . . and . . . greetings from your father."

"*What?*"

"That's what he said. Pierre, come here. Listen. Didn't that gentleman talk about greetings from his father, that time in the field?"

Pierre looked very confused.

"What's that, Berthe, what are you talking about?" Hans caught her by the arm and gently shook her. "What's that? Who? Who was it?"

She looked helplessly at Pierre; now she did not herself know what she was talking about. For a few seconds the clouds had opened up and a stretch of blue sky was visible, but then, Hans' face suddenly so red, so strange and fearful in his anxiety, had paralyzed her mind.

Rainer got up from his crouching position and looked from Hans to the children.

"What's she talking about?" Hans asked him.

He shrugged his shoulders. "Kids' talk."

But Hans would not let them go. "What was it, what happened? Think hard. Who said greetings from my father?"

Maria and Luba had joined them. Hans knelt down next to Berthe. "Come on now, Berthe, what did you just tell me?"

"They are always inventing stories," said Maria. "You mustn't pay any attention to it."

"That's not true." Pierre defended his trustworthiness and that of Berthe. Nothing seemed worse to him than not to be believed, even when he knew he was lying. When it was a question of the truth, it shook his confidence in the grown-ups.

"Just before you said that Vermylde has a rifle," Luba affirmed. "Just a little while ago," she pointed behind her to the steps where they had been sitting.

Rainer laughed and bent over the tire again.

"He *has* a rifle," said Pierre.

"Pierre has seen it himself," said Berthe.

"I didn't," said Pierre blushing and looking sideways at Hans. "Somebody said so."

Rainer laughed. "I'd drop it."

The children slunk away. Berthe was sniffling. She rubbed her eyes and was almost in tears. But a few moments later they had forgotten all about it. They were playing "boat to America," straddling the balustrade of the little terrace. Little Dolf was a passenger who had almost drowned, but had been saved in time by Pierre.

Hans bent over his repair work, heard their excited voices and jubilant shouts. Sweat dripped in his eyes. "God, it's hot," he said.

"Can you imagine what it must be like in Marrakech?"

"Everybody is asleep all afternoon in Marrakech, Achmed says. . . ." Words . . . words, and the tire is in his hands. "There! A little bit more, hold it a minute . . ." In the region of his stomach he felt a pressure that made breathing difficult. In his mind fluttered thoughts with a single meaning—scram . . . scram . . . before it is too late . . . scram. . . .

"The rest you can fix by yourself," he said. "Tonight we'll put it on the wheel. I'll go over to Vermylde once more."

"Aart was there just yesterday."

"The more pressure you put on that fellow the better. *Ce salaud.*"

"Hans, it is Sunday!" Rainer called after him.

"I know where to find him."

He went to Marga, however, as he always did when waves of

fear beat together over his head and threatened to tear him away. The road seemed endless, and in order to control his impatience, he thought only of the road. He thought of the memories that had gathered around each hole in the grey asphalt, each laurel tree, the incinerator in the distance, the fish cannery, the low dune, over which one could look out upon the sea. Thoughts, images, phantasies, resolutions, conjectures, souvenirs, all those had accompanied him on this road, day in, day out; sometimes his eye had fallen upon a landmark and the thought had been interrupted, or the mind had suddenly dropped that train of thought as some object on the road had caught his attention.

At Marga's he could not at first speak confidentially. She had callers, girl friends in the same business who were whiling away their time in talk. They spoke of subjects that irritated him, as they would have equally irked any young man with the intolerance of his age. About men, dresses, other women and their work. What one had said and the other had answered, and so forth and so on. And when it was time for them to leave for work Marga had to leave too, so that Hans could only take her aside for a moment as they were walking along the boulevard. She did not call Berthe's story "kid's talk," but she did not attach much significance to it either. "*Une gosse, elle est stupide*, she does not know what she's talking about, or what she heard. Still it would be better for you to leave as soon as possible. You're nervous, which is not surprising. Maybe something is up. How are things getting along?"

"All papers are in order, the passage to Lisbon is not sure. Vermylde has given half-promises but we have nothing in black and white . . . oh, perhaps I'm just imagining," he concluded, feeling ashamed. Here between the promenaders—for to Spaniards on Sunday the boulevard was their *rambla*—he wanted his worries to be but figments of his imagination. But she grasped his hand firmly between her fingers. "No, you're sensitive, you're not hysterical. If you have such suspicions, there must be a reason for it. A boy with your past has horse sense."

"We have no money to bribe Vermylde with. The Consul refuses to have anything to do with it. Only through channels . . ." He imitated the words of the Consul, the poor Dutch, the faltering French. She laughed. She pressed his hand, before she let go of it. "*Tu t'inquiètes beaucoup, hein, alors,* I'll lend you a hand." She made a movement as if she were rolling up her sleeves to go to work.

"How? How will you go about it?"

"Oh, you just wait. Come on now, stop worrying. Look around. Isn't it perfect?"

The colorful parade did not interest him. He could not, laugh wholeheartedly at her amusing observations, her witty comments on the people who exhibited their bright finery, their smiles, and their bodies to each other, as they roasted in the sun—a mosaic of colors in which the blue-black of the heads was dominant, carefully groomed hair, a shining helmet on the men, a gracefully undulating hood set off with combs on the women; clothes as myriad hued as his grandmother's patchwork quilt, many flowers introducing lighter tones—white, pink, lilac. Happy people laughed and chatted, turning towards each other and then away again, in circles and rows, groups and pairs, walking back and forth on the boulevard, the *rambla* of the Spaniards. On Sundays all this was theirs.

The date for the departure had finally been fixed. Vermylde himself had visited the Consul and afterwards had confirmed his visit and his promise in writing.

"What did I tell you . . . !"

The Consul under the illusion that his position, his name and his gentle pressure had worked the miracle, enjoyed his victory. Zus, moved by his naïve satisfaction and pride did not have the heart to disillusion him. Aart could find no explanation for the unexpected. Hans alone knew who had wrought the miracle. He had watched Marga at the bar, first at the corner of the counter bending confidentially towards Mohammed el Kebir, and some nights later, boisterous, as if she had been drinking, with an Arab and Vermylde.

After their short conversation on the *rambla*, she refused to say anything more about her efforts to Hans.

They did very little talking these days, awaiting their parting silently, as is always the case when preparations for a separation have been made, everything has already been said and nothing remains but the waiting. People before the separation, even somewhat impatient to get on with it, because the affair is closed and there is no place for the past in a new beginning.

The last days before the departure were nerve-racking. Everybody knew that the boat never left on the fixed date, whatever the secret reason might be. For Aart and the children it was the more complicated because they had to be ready to leave at any moment of the day, and after they had vainly waited on the quay they had to go home at night in order to sleep. Rainer's rattling vehicle was a help. It had already been bought and paid for by Achmed but he allowed them to use it. Before daybreak they drove to the city and after sundown home again.

The children made a joke about it. Every morning it was: "Bye bye, house. Bye . . . bye. Never see you again . . ." And then all together in a husky voice, "Until tonight, house!" It was irresistibly funny, even Aart grinned; and as the continued waiting made them more and more nervous they laughed louder, until tears stood in their eyes. And then on the quay, from which they could see the little house, a small white cubicle in the midst of the green, they shouted: "We are not going yet, house. Well, till tonight then. We're coming home soon, house. Go ahead and cook the dinner. We'll be seeing you!" The others who waited had become familiar with the routine and though they kept at a distance from the shabby, neglected little troup and forbade their clean, carefully dressed children to play with *those* children, they laughed heartily at it. However, they accepted Aart in their group. He sat among them with little Dolf on his lap. They sympathized with him and had some respect for him, for the news of Lies' death had spread throughout the city.

Hans and Rainer remained at their work and phoned every hour to Vermylde's office.

The children played on the quay, the customhouse men and the police tolerating them. For days Pierre played sentry, and nobody could understand how he knew so many variations of that job. But then nobody knew how many sentries might have halted him during his brief existence. The occasions when they did had no doubt impressed his memory. He opened and closed the wide heavy gate so many times that the Arabian police employees got fed up with it. Sometimes Pierre was a loud Nazi, who let his hands slide over Berthe's and Luba's dresses, accompanying the performance with: "*Jawohl, Fräulein, jawohl, jawohl!*" Or he made them play British soldiers who knew the German watchword and shot the German sentry. He changed their parts time and again to the great worry of Berthe, who got completely mixed up. Sentry, soldier, policeman, citizen, officer—Pierre ruled all. He liked it best when the Arab children played with them—the sort of children that can be found on the quays of every harbor city all over the world, playing and begging, happy and unrestrained. Pierre, his blond hair damp with sweat, his face splotched with red, took the lead. He could only move around slowly and he tried to compensate by assuming a loud voice and profuse gestures. When they got so excited that they bumped into him, he would sit off to the side.

Maria soon got bored and joined those who waited on the café terrace. At first she kept herself at a distance, played the part of the discreet young girl who has been well brought up but is now in unfortunate circumstances. Later on she performed small services— fetched a glass of water for somebody, took a child to the toilet, wound a skein of wool. Her helpfulness came from a need for affection. And these people represented the milieu in which she had been born and in which she had spent the first twelve years of her life. She enjoyed the conversations between Polish women; the sound of her own language made her feel warm inside and induced a glow that overcame her nervous tension so that she was happy to the point of wanting to cry. Those were exciting days. She felt happier than any of the others. And then Hans, who came to bring them food at noon, would walk up and down with her, and though the sun shone down upon her with its colorless heat her world seemed clad in gold.

Hans was walking home, his daily trip home, which he resolved to enjoy even more today than he had ever done, because this was goodbye. In a few hours they would leave. He was bringing the children a substantial breakfast. In the middle of yesterday afternoon people had already been loaded onto the boat—and "loaded" was certainly the right word, he thought bitterly. Unexpectedly, after all this waiting, Vermylde had given the signal for departure. Within half an hour they would leave. "Come on, come on . . . hurry up . . ."

Berthe had come to fetch him and Rainer, sobbing nervously because she was afraid that they might miss the boat. But hours went by, the people sat huddled together on the deck still waiting, without protection from the murderously hot sun, while on the quay Vermylde's employees walked back and forth. But still the signal for departure was not given. Finally Vermylde himself had driven onto the quay in his car and chased the people off the ship, without excuses, without telling them the reason for this new delay. "Tomorrow at nine o'clock you leave. It may be later, but whoever is not there, won't go. There'll be no waiting."

"I'll have something to say about that scoundrel when I get to Lisbon," said somebody.

"And how about the people who will still want to go? Do you want to rob them of their last chance?"

"Such hyenas as Vermylde go free," said a third. Tears of fury and disillusion stood in his eyes.

"They ought to murder him," said an old Pole. Everybody knew that his Portuguese visa expired that very day, that all his money was gone.

"Try to go along on a fishing smack," he was told, though everyboay knew that it was impossible. But he shook his head.

"I'm fed up," he said, "*zostaw mnie w spokoju*. Leave me alone." He walked away from them, alone, like one banished, and nobody could find the heart to offer him consolation.

At the customhouse they had to have their papers stamped. And as they waited in line they tried to find an outlet for their wrought-up feelings in scolding and cursing the employees, who were completely innocent of any blame for the delay.

Hans knew now what had saddened him so much. Not the nagging and scolding of the refugees, but the complete stoney indifference of the customhouse men. They didn't even listen to the words directed at them because those who spoke did not exist as individuals for them. They were cattle, ready for shipment. They probably thought that it would have been more appropriate if they had applied the stamp to their skin—instead of to their papers.

I am one of them, thought Hans, a head of cattle. He could still taste the humiliation that rose like gall in his mouth.

I am one of them, the stamp is on my skin. On the skin of thousands, of millions.

And, he asked himself, could one expect of all those so marked that they should be like others; that they should forget the stamp on their skins? Does a child forget the beatings it has received in its youth? Can a child that has been mistreated grow up into a well-balanced, happy human being? Did they expect a normal world, after this war had been fought to a finish . . . ? Had anything good ever been born from hatred? And didn't they know that one half of humanity hated the other half? And how was it that he knew and others did not? This was the last war. . . . He laughed bitterly. I am seventeen years old, he thought, how is it that I know and those older than myself do not?

In the stillness of the morning he heard the sound of a car. A large limousine was approaching. Refugees, he thought, on the way to Tetuan for safe conducts, a last effort to escape from the lion's den.

Sometimes they would stop and take him for a part of the way. If these asked him, he would refuse. This morning he would rather walk. When he heard the brakes being applied to the wheels he turned around with an excuse already on his lips.

That very moment, even before the men had jumped out of the car and surrounded him, he knew that this was the end. He felt no fear, no shock—rather a deep quietude was in him. His passionate reflections were swept away like clouds before the wind.

They pushed him into the car and onto the back seat—his face in the shadow of the closed curtain, Johnson was waiting.

So, that's how it is, Hans thought, such things really did happen. He was completely objective in his thinking. He silently formulated his observations in commonplace—trite journalistic terms: the long arm of the Gestapo . . . the dragnet of espionage. . . . And it seemed to him that he had heard before what Johnson was saying now. "How happy your father will be when you're back in Germany." He looked the man straight in the eye and noticed the expression of satisfaction and pride written all over his face. Clever job, he thought. He thought about his father, about Marga, about the children who would wait for him in vain.

The car flew down the road, over the little bridge, past the fish cannery, along the hill. He could not see the house; the side curtains of the car were closed.

"Bye-bye, house," he thought. "Never see you again. . . ." He smiled at the little joke he had made, the joke of the children.

THE END